THE DELPHI DECEPTION

BOOK II OF THE DELPHI TRILOGY

By

CHRIS EVERHEART

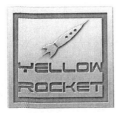

Yellow Rocket Media LLC

yellowrocketmedia.com

The Delphi Deception
Book II of the Delphi Trilogy
copyright 2013 by Chris Everheart

ISBN-13: 978-0-9859125-4-3

ISBN-10: 0985912545

Young adult fiction, secret societies, suspense, conspiracy.

Design by Everheart Media

Dedication

To Sam —for accepting me, loving me,
and teaching me how to be a kid.

Acknowledgements

Every time I finish a book I get to look back from this milestone and see how much other people have given of themselves to support me and my work. As an author, I'm lucky enough to be able to put in writing for the whole world how grateful I am to these people.

Pat Everheart deserves the biggest thank you for living with me and putting up with my artistic temperament. She also contributes enormously to my work on a daily basis. I'm grateful for you, Darlin' One.

Mike Huffman, my close friend and business partner, for his constant and patient support of my work. You deserve a huge amount of credit for bringing this book to readers.

My generous friends who host me when I'm traveling: Missy, Keaton, and Brodie Huffman, and Lisa Wilde. I always feel at home with you.

Pam Johnson lent her expert eye and challenged what was on the page to make this book the best it can be, all while sparing my feelings—a balancing act she does very well.

Hannahlily Smith for her dedication to young readers and for sharing my books with them.

To librarians and teachers everywhere for doing the hard work. I owe you a lot.

Amanda Wellens for reading the manuscript and for giving expert advice.

Meghan Lederer for great feedback on a very rough manuscript.

Scott Warren contributes to my work every day by playing many roles: sounding board, reader, critic, philosopher, seeker. Can't wait to read your book, man.

Kitty Juul for her readership, feedback, and enthusiasm. It's great to have friends like you.

Kris and Joan Juul for sharing their love of reading and for encouraging me.

Every writer needs a guy like Gary R. Bush in their circle, offering continual friendship and honest feedback. Thanks, pal.

To Pat Dennis for the kindness and for the mentorship. You've been right—about everything!

Cheers to the BAM barista—the sober writer's Moe.

Natalie Viars for reading and loving my stories. When your now is precious, your future is always bright.

Pat Frovarp and Gary Shulze, owners of Once Upon a Crime bookstore in Minneapolis. Because of you, this writer always has a home.

Elaine Krackau and the team at PR By the Book for their dedication to my work and for getting the word out.

Joe Costello for his backstage efforts. The man behind the curtain deserves attention once in a while.

Thanks to my friends who support my work and tell everyone they know about my books: Christine, Jeremy, Aidan, Olivia, and Tyler Wollersheim; Kristin Erickson; Gwen Ruff; Diana Huffman; Julie Wolfe; Shelli Boman Regnier; Paul, Lisa, Reese, Riley, and Rose Wilcox; Laura Wolf; Yunnuen González; Tammi, Ron, Chase, and Haley Gipp; Jo Ellen Verna; Cheryl Graves; Cindy Boepple; Marilyn Victor; Michael Dahl. There are many more—if I missed you, let me know and I'll write you in when I see you.

To Heather Burch for the kind words and encouragement.

To Steven James for being an example and for including me.

Finally, my heart still aches at the passing this year of best-selling author Vince Flynn (1966-2013), a real gentleman, kind and generous, and a hero to me. Thanks for the example and the encouragement. I promise to make it count.

CHAPTER 1

My head is pounding, my right knee aches, and my armpits burn. The rubber pads of the crutches peel away the skin under my arms as I step-swing, step-swing as fast as I can away from the hospital. They don't know I've escaped and the longer it takes them to figure it out, the more time I'll have to make a plan—a plan that will keep me alive long enough to save Ashley.

Downtown Arcanville is buzzing. I didn't think about the time. 7:30 a.m., rush hour. Bodies, cars, trucks, and buses crowd the streets—people going to work, shops opening their doors, kids on their way to school. In the fray, grown-ups glance at my crutches and sweaty forehead. Teenagers notice my blue velour tracksuit like it's a fashion statement. I look a little out of place. But if they knew my story, they wouldn't be so casual.

The stunt I pulled in the hospital yesterday was crazy. I left the recovery ward, snuck down to the psych ward on these crutches, and tried pulling Ashley out of her bed to safety. No plan, no destination, just *somewhere else*.

It only took the staff ten seconds to find me, drag me out of there, and put Ashley back into a chemical trance with an injection. Then they moved me to a room in another ward where the nurses could keep a closer eye on me. It didn't work for long. I slipped out this morning during their shift change and ran for my life.

I've put a mile behind me already. How much farther to go—another mile? Two? God, I don't know if I can make it. I want to move faster, but my bruised and exhausted body is rebelling, threatening to completely give up and leave me sitting helpless on a street corner. That's if the police don't catch up with me first.

I don't think anyone at the hospital figured out who I really am. The plastic band they put on my wrist said I'm Zachary White, the name on my passport, the one I've hidden behind like a shield for the past ten years. As soon as I got out the door I tore that thing off and threw in the garbage. The name seems like a joke now that I'm back in Arcanville, now that I'm learning the truth about my family and my past.

How can I be so sure that my identity is still a secret? Because if the staff had identified me, the Committee that secretly runs this town would have started their gears of destruction grinding. Black-clad men would have come and finished what Screed, their cold-eyed security director, tried to do two nights ago with the bumper of his speeding car—separate me from Ashley and permanently eliminate me as a threat to their plans.

I keep checking behind me for a squad car, a badge in the crowd, the barrel of a gun aimed between my shoulder blades. The Committee's black-suited soldiers could storm out of the campus straight ahead and haul me to their dungeon or wherever they take kids who won't behave themselves. But there's no attack, no chase. The torture of *nothing* seems worse.

Instead, it's just an average morning for the fifteen thousand people of Arcanville. They have no idea that just thirty-six hours ago I led Ashley into their Committee's headquarters—the monolithic library at the center of the ancient college campus.

The Committee must be keeping the break-in quiet. If these people had any inkling that I got inside, that I learned about the League of Delphi—their worldwide secret society—the horrors they've committed and how they continue to exploit girls like Ashley with their twisted Pythia Program, they wouldn't let me live. They'll do anything to keep their secrets. They've killed before, and they'll do it again.

CHAPTER 2

I crutch down the sidewalk on Fourth Street with my eyes lowered, trying to shrink into the crowd. When I reach the corner at College Boulevard, I freeze and lift my gaze. Across the street, the long brick wall—six feet high, capped with yellow limestone and foot-high black iron spikes—looms in my eyes like the Great Wall of China. Only, this great wall surrounds Arcanum College.

I shudder at the thought of entering through its tall, red stone arch again. Just a few days ago I stood under that gate marveling at how many souls—including my parents—have passed through it in the more than three hundred years it's been here. Now all I can think of is how impossible it is to escape its grip once you've gone in.

A crowd of young pedestrians on their way to campus starts gathering at the street corner. Having so many people this close makes my skin tighten and my senses sharpen, even if all they're doing is waiting to cross the street.

I glance far down the boulevard toward the corner at River Street, where I stood on top of the wall straddling the iron spikes the night before last. My damaged right knee was screaming at me to stop, but my terror prodded me to keep running from the campus security guards.

I chose to listen to the terror and jumped over, limping for the bridge around the corner. But before I could cross the river Screed caught up with me and ran me down with his big, speeding Lincoln. I can still see the bottom of his black car flying over me and crashing through the bridge railing. He came out of the wreck in a coma. As awful as it is to say, I hope he stays that way, because he's the only person who can identify me as the intruder who got away.

Ashley wasn't so lucky. When she went home to grab some clothes and money to run away with me, her sister Katie called the authorities. Ashley ended up back in the place she most feared—the psych ward.

A bump to my shoulder jars me back into the now as a girl slides past me. Her straight brown hair shines in the morning sun like Ashley's. But it's not Ashley. It's a college student with a book bag slung over her shoulder. The crowd around me steps into the street. The WALK sign is lit and I'm the only one standing still.

Not one single part of me wants to go into the campus again, but I'm short on time, feeling more pain every second, nearly exhausted, and it's the fastest way to get to the help I need. My choice is a simple one—go forward or doom Ashley to be the League of Delphi's prisoner forever. I force my body to move and tip forward on my crutches.

CHAPTER 3

I cross the street and pass under the huge red granite gate that arches over the original campus entrance. "Arcanum College" is carved into the blocks overhead with "Est. 1706" chiseled into the keystone.

I try to be quick, swinging my body—bad leg first—down to the walkway, but I'm blocking the stream of students rushing to their classes. They flow past me like river water around a rock and move on ahead. Some glance sideways at my grandpa tracksuit—velvety fabric the color of the sky with elastic bands at the wrists and ankles. The tennis shoes are out of style and too small for my feet. I'm not blending in very well.

I had to steal these clothes from the old man sharing my hospital room. He was unconscious and I found the track suit and shoes in his closet. I'm not proud about ripping off an old man, but I needed something to wear for my raid on Ashley's room.

My jeans and hooded sweatshirt never caught up with me, probably cut to ribbons by the Emergency Room nurses when the ambulance brought me in. I don't care about a pile of shredded rags that used to be my clothes. I'm more concerned about my wallet, cell phone, and the flash drive that were in the pockets. I need that stuff back, but I didn't exactly have time to go searching the hospital on my way out the door this morning.

I'm regretting yesterday and my half-assed rescue attempt. Even if I'd been able to get Ashley unstrapped from the bed and out of the psych ward, I still would have been a teenager in an old man's clothes, fleeing on crutches out a hospital exit, and trying to drag a zombified girl in a hospital gown along with me. We never would have made it to the parking lot.

Maybe I should have planned better. But a visit from the man I knew only as Crazy Larry short-circuited any logic I had left. He proved that he was much more than the local bum I'd assumed him to be. He filled in the blanks in what I had learned about the Committee and the League and their plans for Ashley, and I freaked. I had to do something. But I failed and only dug a deeper hole for both of us.

After they pulled me from Ashley's room I surrendered, expecting to be punished for the stunt, and waited for the security guards from campus to come get me. But no one mentioned locking me up or kicking me out. No scowling men showed up. They didn't strip me and put me in a straight jacket. They left me in these clothes, showed me to my new bed, and went back to their routine of checking on me every couple of hours. I tried to sleep between fits of rage and worry and visions of escape.

Now, I'm hoping this ridiculous outfit plays better with the younger crowd on campus, that it's more a curiosity than an alarm. If I'm lucky these college kids will think they're seeing a new style they haven't caught onto yet, instead of wondering what this half-crippled weirdo on crutches is doing, hanging around their school in charity clothes.

The problem is that this college and the town surrounding it is the most homogenous place I've ever seen. Skin color has nothing to do with it. People of every race and ethnicity live and go to school here, which should mean various clothing styles and music, a wide variety of interests and causes, maybe even some cultural tension. But Arcanville and the campus have none of that. Aside from the occasional accent of a foreign student, everyone here is practically the same, a sign that the League of Delphi's tentacles stretch around the globe and they don't tolerate uniqueness.

Despite a few unwelcome looks, I'm grateful for the crush of bodies. I need all the cover I can get. The reason is just ahead of me at the center of campus—the beast, the huge library that the students aren't allowed to use. The Committee's *"center of weirdness"* is what Ashley called it.

The sight of the building turns me to ice. Even a block away I can feel a glacial chill rolling off it like a black mountain. Sitting atop its own little hill, the three-story, burnt-brown brick walls are molded into round turrets at the corners with a toothed crown running all along the top. A two-story glass office annex has been built onto the front, but it doesn't make the place look any less forbidding.

It was the first building Jan Van Arcan built on the campus after he settled here in 1702 and founded the college. It took me a while to figure out its purpose. Why would Van Arcan build a library at the middle of campus and never allow anyone to enter it? Then, when Ashley and I saw an old history book with a picture of it before the glass front was added, I recognized its medieval design. The high, blank walls, the bulging corners, the enormous front doors—it never was a library, no matter what they call it. It's a *fortress*, the first New World outpost of the ancient and secret League of Delphi.

Outwardly, it's just a building. But it has its own gravity that draws me to it. I couldn't *not* go inside when I had the chance. But now our little invasion is costing Ashley and me everything. And I can't take it back. I can only try to save both of us.

The sidewalk outside the library is empty except for two guards in black fatigues who pace at each end of the block, staring people down and silently warding off anyone who would even think about coming close. It's the only outward sign that something has gone wrong. But people are unfazed by it, don't seem to notice.

The thought of being seen by the guards pushes my stomach into my throat. Screed might be the only one who knows my exact identity, but there are a lot of possibilities that could still get me recognized. I stalked the campus for days looking for a way into the monolith, and even though I was careful, they might have security camera pictures of me. Or maybe one of the guards chasing me the other night got a good enough look to recognize my face. And there are these crutches. They might know that their intruder was hurt in the chase.

Maybe it's just my old paranoia creeping back in. Or maybe my worry is smart. I'm not sure anymore. Since

I came back to Arcanville, I've noticed that this horrid town has a way of making what's completely insane somehow completely possible.

I dodge to my left onto a narrow lane and crutch down the sidewalk. A safe distance from the back corner of the library, I peek between trees and see the black baseball cap of a guard stalking the notched parapet along the roof. The barrel of a rifle pokes menacingly above his shoulder. There was no guard up there before two nights ago. Our invasion and Screed's catastrophe have really put them on edge. They don't know how someone got in or out, but they're determined not to let it happen again.

CHAPTER 4

I pass a wrinkled, centuries-old classroom building with its red bricks and yellow stone trim. As the library disappears from view, my dread loosens a notch. Somehow I thought that going inside the other night would demystify the place, but what I learned in there only tortures my mind more. And Ashley getting caught compounds it. I feel better when I can't see that giant tomb of a building, but I doubt it will ever be completely gone from my mind.

I peg forward on the crutches, feeling a rubbery weakness in my body. As much as the dark energy of this campus drains me, though, this symptom is not from exposure to the library. I'm over three hours from my last pain pill, and the ache is sapping my strength. I haven't had real sleep in three days. The doctor said I'm lucky to have only a mild concussion, but my head feels like it's full of water. I belong in a hospital bed, recuperating from Screed's hit-and-crash, not racing across town on stilts.

The crowd of students thins as I pass out of the campus center. I feel some relief when I see the rear exit, a narrow, six-foot gap in the brick wall with a section of heavy iron gate hanging to each side. It's not decorative. This campus was built for security in the seventeen hundreds, before the land was settled and the politics stable. The League of Delphi established it as the first chapter in a vast New World of resources and opportunity that would become the United States.

Of course, they didn't know that then—or did they? Based on what I've found out about the League, they may have *known* what would happen on this continent, that a great nation would one day be founded and grow here and that an outpost would ensure they could get even more wealthy and powerful. Everything I've seen around here in the last few days makes that nutty idea possible.

I shudder and speed up to get out of this living graveyard. But an unwelcome sight appears just outside the gate—the front end of a black car rolls slowly into view. My heart thumps with one thought—*"Screed!"*

He's supposed to be in a coma, pulled out of the wreckage of his black Lincoln barely alive. Did he suddenly wake up and start hunting me again? Is he so mean that even near-death won't keep him down?

The white door and gold badge decal of an Arcanville police car follow the black fender into the gap. I duck behind a tree and try to catch my breath. Not Screed. I should feel relieved. But the Committee runs this town, Screed was in charge of their security, and the police answered to him.

The nurses have probably found my bed empty and reported it. Someone may have told the police about a boy crutching this way from the direction of the hospital.

It's all bad news for me. Once they catch me, they'll make sure to hold onto me, tie me down and shoot me full of something that will keep me in my hospital bed. They'll have Ashely and me where they want us—under control with our minds blown. I don't know if they'll be even that gentle with me, but I'm not willing to find out.

That's why I have to get through that gate and to the other side of the Old Village. I need to reach Crazy Larry. He's the only one who knows the truth and can help me. I thought he was just a weirdo, the lone bum in a wealthy town. But when he came to the hospital yesterday he didn't stop at telling me the League's secrets, he told me he's my uncle—my father's brother, who I never even knew about.

He said the Committee put him in the Pythia Program when he was my age and used a version of the Pneuma stuff—that *poison* they've been injecting Ashley with—on him. Named for the woman who sat in the Temple of Apollo at Delphi, Greece, spinning prophecy in ancient times, the Pythia program has the gruesome task of preparing gifted young girls for the role of oracle, delivering divine insights about now and predictions about the future. But every so often, the League tries a new Pneuma compound on boys, hoping to get the same bizarre results they've been getting from girls for 3,000 years. According to Larry, it hasn't worked yet. Instead of giving him prophetic visions of the future, it only made him violent and crazy.

As soon as he was able, he ran away to heal his mind. Then, after years in hiding, he made his way back to Arcanville to reconnect with his hometown. We share that. I was hidden away by my mother—safe—and came back here a few weeks ago, hoping to learn who I am. Now that I know what's really going on in this town, coming back seems stupid.

But I'm hoping it's more than a reconnection that motivates Larry. I'm hoping he wants to settle a score with the Committee and will help me burn them down. But Larry isn't a fighter, and I'm not sure he's right in the head. Would a *sane* person who knew the truth come back here?

CHAPTER 5

The squad car stops in the frame of the gate. I bundle my crutches in front of me to keep a glint off the shiny aluminum from drawing attention. Leaning into the trunk of the tree, I check behind me to see if any security guys are coming to meet the cop. If they're teaming up to search for me, they'll want to cover the few campus exits from the inside and the outside. This rear gate into the Old Village is the smallest. One cop with a gun could stop and hold anyone being flushed out by the guards.

The clock in my head ticks like a hammer strike, louder and louder. Best scenario for me right now would be that the hospital has reported me missing, and they think they're only looking for a boy who's crazy in love and ran away after failing to break his bipolar girlfriend out of the psych ward.

But when the Committee and their chairwoman, Maryellen Bradford, realize that the boy they found the other night, unconscious on the sidewalk next to Screed's wreck, was the same one who tried to spring Ashley yesterday, they'll know that Screed hitting me with his car was no accident. They'll know I'm the one Screed and his men were scouring the campus for in the dark of night. As soon as they put that two-and-two equation together, the whole town will be swarming with Committee security and police.

I look to the gate again, trying to peer into the squad car's window. All I see is the profile of a buzz-cut cop in the driver's seat.

I know one cop in this town—Sergeant Billings, who responded to my 911 call the night a kid named Connor, drunk and high, wiped out in Bobbie's Coffee Shop. Billings was also at the bridge the night Maryellen Bradford's son, Sutton, jumped into the river. It was that kid's suicide just a couple of weeks ago and this town's complete non-reaction to it that got me thinking there was some creepy stuff happening here. I remembered Sutton, a happy and nice kid, from elementary school before I was moved away. But lately he had been a top student who tumbled to the bottom. And according to his notebooks I've read, he was asking way too many questions about the Committee and their dealings.

Billings' account of that night only made me more curious. He'd been on patrol and never got a call about the emergency. He had just happened to be cruising by the bridge when he saw Sutton's dad and Screed already there, supposedly trying to stop the teen from jumping off the railing. The veteran police sergeant had been seconds too late to save the kid. He seemed truly sorry about it, but that's all he would say. He wouldn't answer any more of my questions, acted suspicious of me—or maybe *afraid* of the Committee.

But I learned something else that evening. When I made the 911 call that got Sergeant Billings and an ambulance to Bobbie's to help Connor, the call didn't go

16

to some emergency operator, it went straight to Screed. So, even if Mr. Bradford had called 911 for help saving his son's life, he hadn't reached the police. The cold-eyed security director had answered the call himself, had kept it a secret, had gone to the bridge, and had done what Larry says he'd done—talked Sutton *into* jumping.

These are the people who want to catch me. If they'll kill kids who ask too many questions, they'll do anything to stop me. Like Larry told me, *"I knew they were going to kill me one way or another—psychologically, physically, spiritually."*

After ten years of tests, mind-crushing experiments, and preparation for the League's exploitation, all Ashley wants is to be left alone so she can live her life. I know from personal experience—and what my mother did for me—that only happens when you're away from this place.

Take her away, take her away, my brain keeps chanting.

Yes, yes, is my only response.

I stare at the squad car, silently urging the cop to leave and clear my path, when I hear a stern voice behind me.

"Hey."

I turn my head. A man in black fatigues and cap stands a few feet away, one hand hovering by the pistol on his hip.

CHAPTER 6

I flinch when I see the security guard. My heart triples its beat as I stare dumbly at him, anticipating his next move.

He's coiled like an Olympic discus thrower, standing flat on his feet, his knees slightly bent, and one foot shifted forward. His shoulders tilt and his right hand hangs behind the weapon strapped to his belt. The bill of his black cap shades razor-sharp eyes. Poised to quick-draw, he'll put two bullets into anyone who makes a wrong move. He's on edge. I know it's because of me, but I hope he hasn't figured that out yet.

"What are you doing?" he asks, looking me up and down.

As my heart climbs into my throat, I get a better look at him. Unlike most of the grizzled guards around the library, he's only a couple of years older than me. I try to produce an answer, an explanation for hiding behind a tree, but my brain is like a snow globe, swirling with random thoughts I can't catch hold of.

The guard's eyes narrow and he lifts his left hand toward the radio handset clipped to his shoulder—calling for backup!

"Pardon, monsieur," I say, surprised to hear French come out of my mouth. It's completely unintentional, my terrified brain defaulting to the language I've spoken for the past ten years at my boarding school in France.

The guard's radio hand freezes and he tilts his head in confusion. He doesn't understand what I've said and his eyes flash self-doubt. Lacking the hard confidence of the older guards, he's easy to read.

I see an opening. Needing to keep his one hand off the radio and the other off his gun, I decide to go with it and scramble my brain for the next French words I can think of.

"Écureuil!" I say, meaning *Squirrel!* But I don't know why and I don't know what to say next.

The guard grimaces. He's staring at me, and because he doesn't react in any other way—like pulling his gun or tackling me—I realize that he *doesn't* know who I am. He's not searching for me. He's just come upon something suspicious.

Possessing nothing but the crutches hidden behind me, the only weapon I have to fight him with is my brain. Opening his doubt wider, I put a finger to my lips. "Shhh …" I say. *"L'écureuil Roux d'Américain."* I point my finger past the tree.

His eyes shift to follow and his left hand drops away from his radio.

Next, in the most ridiculous French accent I can muster, I say, "Amerhican Rhed Squirrhel. Verhy rarhe." I use the accent like a fake limp—a suggestion of harmlessness. Plus, if he thinks I can't speak English, maybe he'll leave me alone.

19

His shoulders relax. As I jabber, he scans my weird velour tracksuit and pauses on my out-of-style shoes and sockless ankles. "Where are your books?" he asks.

I hesitate. College campus, no books—*suspicious*. If he's not satisfied with my answers, this will turn ugly fast. *Stay cool. Stay cool.*

He must take my pause as a symptom of our language barrier, because, to my relief, he lifts his right hand away from his pistol and hooks his thumb over his shoulder to pantomime a backpack strap. "Books ..." he says.

He's going down a mental checklist, trying to put together an explanation—and he's asking for my help doing it. He's the one out of place now, a young man on a rich college campus, confronted with a language he's never spoken or possibly ever heard firsthand.

"Pardon?" I ask.

He shifts out of his shooter stance and I know I have him. He presses his hands together in a prayer position and hinges them open. "Books," he enunciates helpfully. "Where are your *books*?"

"Ah, livre!" I tip my head at the old brick building next to us. "In ze clazrhoom," I say, giving him more accent.

He's getting frustrated. "ID?" he asks.

I stare at him blankly.

He fidgets then makes a square in front of his chest with his thumbs and forefingers. "Identification ..."

I gesture again to the building, suggesting that my ID is with my backpack sitting in a classroom. I don't even know if it is a classroom building. For all I know it's an office building. Could be a gymnasium. I just hope he doesn't know either. "In ... boohk bahg ..." I say in broken English and shrug an apology.

He doesn't know what to do. He's probably not supposed to hassle the students, but the guards are reeling from the break-in of their highest-security building, and he has stumbled on something legitimately wrong — an oddly dressed kid on campus with no backpack, no books, and no ID lurking behind a tree.

I need this encounter to end before that cop outside spots something weird or another guard shows up and corrects every mistake this young guy is making. I point to the building and say, "Biolozhee." Then in broken English with bad grammar and mime gestures, I describe how I saw this rare squirrel from a classroom window, came downstairs, and snuck up behind this tree to watch it. That's when he found me. Now, be very quiet so as not to scare this treasured tree rat away.

The young guard listens intently as I finish my explanation. I need him to hear me and believe me because I can't play this charade much longer. I'm starting to sweat from the pain in my knee and the hammering clock in my head.

I stop talking and lock eyes with him, beaming innocence and *French-ness*. He stares at me for a long, excruciating moment then takes one more peek around the tree trunk to make his bothering me seem legitimate, nods, and turns away.

As he leaves, I slump against my crutches, glad he didn't spot them and have one more thing to be suspicious about. I catch my breath but feel more frantic than ever. This was supposed to be the easier route, but now coming this way seems like the worst idea. I need to get out of here.

When I turn around and look outside the gate, the squad car is gone from the curb. After one more glance back to make sure the guard's gone too, I grab my crutches and make for the gate, hoping that cop is blocks away by now.

CHAPTER 7

I can't get through the Old Village fast enough. This bunch of tiny brick buildings was the original Arcanville, growing up next to campus in the first couple-hundred years after the college's founding. Now it's five blocks of shops and curious eyes. I'm one phone call away from the police dropping a net on me, so I don't want to give any of these people time to decide that I'm out of place.

On the other side of the village, I duck into the old neighborhood where mostly Arcanum College staff and faculty live. These houses are designed on the theme that the whole town has borrowed from the college—red bricks and limestone trim—and they show the dim weathering of many decades. The low brick walls with iron-spike tops bordering each yard are a mocking reminder that no matter where I go in this town, the Committee and the League surround me.

I reach a street corner that blows a dark wind of dread on me. The three-story mansion I'm looking at is as ominous as the library. It's the only other structure in town built with those dark brown bricks burnt to near black in the builders' kilns. Also like the library, it's perched on a low hill to make sure it overwhelms any nearby structure. Ashley and I learned in the local history books that this was Jan Van Arcan's house, originally the center of a farm that fed the early residents before they had a town.

So this house and the black building they call a library were the first permanent structures here. And even after the library was completed, the college, which was *"dedicated to the education of youth in the ways of the prophecy,"* did not open to students until 1706—three years later. The Old Village sprouted and grew as people came to join the mission.

I can just imagine the bearded Van Arcan looming in a window among the upper corners and coves of the house, scheming to plant the League of Delphi's agenda on a naked land and let it radiate outward from their library-fortress.

I shudder and realize that I've stopped moving, which could be deadly right now. Van Arcan's buildings have that affect on me. I defrost myself and swing forward on the crutches. As the ache pulses more widely out of my knee, I regret ditching the leg brace before I left the hospital. I didn't want that giant splint drawing more attention to me. But the doctors put it on for a reason, and I'm starting to understand why.

I press on. Just a couple of blocks over, at a street bordering the river, I find the woods and the narrow path I've been aiming for. I'm almost there—or at least a temporary "there." If I can make it to Larry's cottage at the back of these woods, I'm one step closer to saving Ashley, and myself, from Delphi's stranglehold.

CHAPTER 8

A few bits of paint flake off the frame of the screen door when I knock. The trim on this old cottage was once white, I'm sure, but now it's a dirty gray from years of wind and weather. The place is quiet.

A big house stands a hundred yards toward the street, a residence abandoned for I don't know how long. It's not visible through the dense woods that keep Larry's privacy, and no one else comes back here. That's why I felt a sense of relief as soon as I ducked into the woods.

Since my crutches thrashed every branch on my way down the path, I have to assume that Larry could hear me coming. Is he not answering my knock because he's away or because he doesn't want to talk to me?

I knock again more firmly to let him know I'm serious about seeing the whites of his eyes—whether he wants to see me or not.

Before I hear so much as the beat of a footstep inside, the inner door pops open, startling me. I rock back on my crutches as Larry's face floats into view on the other side of the screen. He looks so much like my father that for just a second, I believe it's him. But when Larry pushes open the screen door, the daylight shows all the differences from what I remember of Dad.

Larry's features are not as fine as my father's. The eyes are the same shape and color, but his brow is heavier and uneven. Larry has a slightly crooked nose too. I can also tell that under the beard his jaw line is a bit blocky. There's a shallow and crooked cleft near the tip of his chin, under the whiskers. And while my father's hair was dark and warm, Larry's is dusty, with strands of gray.

In his own words, Larry "dropped out" after the Committee's Pneuma experiments on him and went traveling around the world. That was right after I was born. He said he held me when I was just a few hours old, which was a big deal because my father—his older brother—didn't trust him. If his childhood was anything like Ashley's, the preparation for the Pythia program would have made him nutty long before the Pneuma compound pushed him into violent psychosis. No one would have wanted him around.

So I never knew this uncle existed, don't remember seeing a single picture of him. The *Chronicles of Delphi* that Ashley and I found shelved in the library mention him in my family's history, but not by the name Larry or anything like it. The *Chronicles* also say Larry is dead, which he told me was the status my father—then chairman of the Committee—had entered to keep the League from pursuing him as an escapee. It probably saved his life.

Some of Larry's features are familiar, and there's a sense that I should know this man. But I really just met him a few days ago.

"What do you want?" Larry asks. It's his standard greeting—never "Hello" or "How are you?" I've gotten used to it. It's not confrontational. He only asks what he wants to know.

"I ..." Words fail me. I have no answer to such a simple question. Clear thoughts are harder to create as the ache in my knee eats up more and more of my brainpower. I don't *know* what I want. I escaped the hospital and came here for help freeing Ashley. But exactly what that entails, I'm not sure.

Unlike most people who've seen me this morning, Larry isn't puzzled by my appearance. He saw me yesterday in this same tracksuit. I found him sitting in the family lounge down the hall from my room and confronted him. I should have been grateful—the only family I have left, standing watch on me the morning after Screed tried to kill me—but instead I was pissed off, thinking that he had tricked me into invading the library. I accused him of using me to find out what's going on in there so he wouldn't have to risk it.

But with practiced patience Larry described exactly what Ashley and I saw inside. He *had* taken the risk, he had been inside. When I came along, dying to know what was in there, he gave me a way in, through the abandoned steam tunnels under the campus.

As I stood in the lounge, spitting accusations at him, he gently explained that it was for my own good, that I wouldn't have believed him if he'd just *told* me what the Committee and the League are up to, that I needed to see it for myself. He was right.

27

Now Larry stands in his doorway waiting for me to say something. In his well-worn khaki pants and faded blue pullover sweater he's a little ragged, but clean and calm. He radiates the patience of the ages, and seems like he could stand here forever while I unscramble my brains.

In that few minutes we had together yesterday, Larry told me the dark recent history of my family in Arcanville—everything I needed to know. He described how Maryellen Bradford, with Screed's help, intimidated my father into resigning as head of the Committee so she could take over. Not long after, Dad left for a business trip to Europe and never arrived. His plane crashing into the Atlantic Ocean was the *official* story. But like Larry before me, I saw my father's status listed as "Absentis"—missing—in *The Chronicles of Delphi*. And like Larry, I don't know if Dad is still alive or where he could be.

In Larry's opinion, my mother was smart for taking me away and leaving me alone in France, not mentally ill and paranoid like I thought. She had married in from outside the League and couldn't stand the town or the society. She knew they would ruin her and indoctrinate me. Getting me out of Arcanville after my father went missing and hiding me away at the Rochemont Boarding School was courageous, not cowardly.

Larry stops scanning me, his eyes freezing at my knee. "Where's your leg brace, Champ?" he asks, using my father's nickname for me. He saw me yesterday trying to steer on the crutches with my leg buckled stiffly into the splint.

I want to explain that I took it off and left it at the hospital, but I can't seem to form the words. Now that I'm at my destination, any adrenaline that was fueling my run has evaporated, and the pain is overshadowing even my ability to speak.

He sees the helplessness in my face and pushes the screen door open wider. Grunting against the agony, I push through and peg into the cottage for the first time. It's surprisingly neat. The outside is so worn out that I don't expect the airy and bright interior. The large windows let in dappled sunlight on three sides of the tiny house. The living room connects to a small dining room and a narrow galley kitchen. There's a short hallway to the left with two doors, which I assume are a bathroom and a bedroom. Everything about Larry on the outside is tattered and worn, but his internal life is very neat and orderly. Getting to know him is a series of surprises.

He gestures to a heavy, old wood-framed chair with thick cushions. I lower myself into it with a groan. Even the act of sitting hurts. It takes most of my strength to lift my right leg and rest it on the ottoman in front of me. Now that I'm seated, I realize how exhausted I am from a morning that's already too long.

Larry stands over me. "A lot of pain?" he asks.

I can only nod pitifully and wish I were back at the hospital where the pain pills are.

He looks from my face to my leg, contemplating. "I have something for it ... if you're willing."

The statement raises a mix of curiosity and dread in me. Yes, I want something for the pain, but am I *willing*?

How bad can his *"something"* be? "Willing to what?" I groan.

Larry frowns. "It's not what you'd call *traditional* medicine. Something I've picked up in my travels."

It must be some kind of New Age remedy he discovered when he lived in India—a giant, clear pill crammed with fibery brown stuff made from the dried and ground up liver of an Asian bear.

He sees the doubt in my face, probably sees the wishes of clean white hospital pills dancing in my eyes. "It's safe," he says convincingly. "I use it every day. But it's not pills or injections."

He uses it? He may not be the sanest person in this town, but he's at least one of the few willing to deal in the truth. Good enough. I nod, causing the water in my head to slosh miserably. His hokey Indian remedy's gotta be better than feeling like this, even if it kills me.

CHAPTER 9

As Larry steps over to the kitchen and opens a lower cabinet, I lay my pounding head back against the chair, scanning the room lazily.

On the old, narrow couch to the right of my chair are two small metal boxes stacked on top of a tattered booklet, all printed with foreign lettering—same as the script on the newspapers I've seen Larry carrying and reading. I couldn't place the language before, with its rounded and hooked letters and straight lines connecting them. Based on what Larry told me about his absence from Arcanville and his travels, I now think it's an Indian language, probably Hindi.

The silvery boxes are barely larger than the one my cell phone came in—which reminds me again of the personal stuff I left at the hospital. My already painful head fills with regret and worry. I left traces of myself there. My ID is in my wallet. The flash drive that I carried into the library has the network bot that I planted through Screed's computer and a file I stole off his desktop. I've been pretty careful about scrubbing my cell phone every couple of days, but maybe they could still get something off it or find records of Ashley texting me.

When Larry closes the cabinet and turns toward the dining table, he's holding a huge enameled bowl—an old-fashioned washbasin, white with blue flecks. My stomach sinks as I think of old-school doctors bleeding sick patients half to death, usually the half that the disease hadn't already killed. Over the basin is draped a dirty looking brown cloth covering a pile of something.

I glance around the little house, feeling nervous, exhausted, and helpless all at the same time. I don't know what he's about to give me for this horrific pain, but I'm already sorry I agreed to it.

"Is this an *Indian* cure," I ask, hoping Larry can't tell how scared I'm getting.

"African," he says flatly.

I wait but he doesn't explain further. "I thought you've been living in India." I want to keep him talking, try to get some clue about this *not-what-you'd-call-traditional* procedure.

I can still run away from here. I could sneak back to the hospital, go to the emergency room and pretend I'm someone else. I could get some pain medication and a leg brace without a hassle. But that's just desperation talking. I can't go back there—not for my pills, not for my belongings.

"I said I spent a lot of time in India," Larry says calmly—his only mode. "Traveled all over."

To make room for the basin on the table he has to slide a cardboard carton the size of a microwave oven out of the way. The carton is new but beaten up, like it was shipped a long distance—and the now-familiar squiggly lettering on the side tells me it was. He picks up a spiral notebook and I get a glimpse of the open page covered with intersecting pencil lines and numbers. He drops it into the box.

Larry clunks the bowl down on the table and my brain ticks one second closer to this mysterious healing ritual. He lifts the brown cloth and starts taking out wax paper packets that look like they're full of herbs—some of the fibery brown stuff for the giant pill?

"So, what happened in Africa that made you need this cure every day?" I'm sure I'll be able to detect any sinister edge to his answer and predict if he's about to torture me.

Larry corrects me gently. "It's a *remedy*, not a cure. Africa is where I found it. I was injured a couple of years earlier trekking over the Himalayas."

"Himalayas?" I knew twin brothers at Rochemont who climbed Everest with their father before their senior year. They did a presentation to the whole school—pictures of them slogging up insanely steep slopes, wearing high-tech climbing gear and oxygen masks, pops of bright colors against the white mountain and crystal blue sky. "Did you climb Everest?" I ask Larry.

He shakes his head. "We were coming back into Nepal and got caught in a rockslide. Half of us—the lucky ones—were buried by the rocks. Killed."

My chest tightens over my breath. "Jeez, what happened to the *un*lucky ones?"

Larry goes still as a statue and I instantly feel the air around us thicken. He only moves to lift his eyes and gaze out the window as if he can see the very mountainside off in the distance. A shadow crosses his face, the same shadow I saw yesterday as he described to me the awful visions he'd gotten from the Pneuma injections.

I regret asking, wish I could take the question back. But I can't.

"It was a narrow path along the mountainside," he says slowly, "halfway up a two thousand-foot gorge."

That's all he really needs to say. I could fill in the rest of the picture myself. But he goes on.

"I heard a rumble, like thunder, and looked up to the sky—the weather in the mountains turns foul without notice. When I saw the clear blue, though, I thought *avalanche*. That high up, the snowpack can flake off and run down slope like a tsunami. But this was summer. The snow is usually melting that time of year, not sliding. When the first stone fell in our path it was like the first drop of rain in an epic storm. We all shared the exact same thought at that moment—doom."

Usually, Larry's entire body is serene, his breathing deep and measured. But now his chest pumps shallow breaths. He's left his body behind to go stand on that mountain again, in the looming disaster. I don't like the look in his eyes.

CHAPTER 10

Larry stares into a world that only he can see. He's talking, telling a story, but it's like *he's* the audience, not me. I feel alone even though his body is standing right there at the table, just a few feet from me.

"It felt like the mountain was coming alive, trying to throw us off. I thought about *running*." He grins wryly at the word. "But there was nowhere to run. We just stood there as the stones started raining down—a trickle at first. Within seconds it was a shower. The mountain started to thunder. Then it hit. A huge boulder from probably five hundred feet above pounded down and took Tenzing out ..."

"Tenzing?" I ask, wondering if that's a thing or a person.

"My guide. His red jacket was wiped from the picture in front of me—gone. He didn't even have time to scream. Another boulder smashed into my hip like a truck and swept me to the edge. I was a goner, fertilizer for the grass at the bottom of the ravine. I went over the edge, but on instinct I hooked the corner of a footstone with my fingertips ..."

Larry turns his face to me, a gale of wonder and terror in his eyes.

"It wasn't a loose rock. It turned out to be part of *the mountain*. This sliver of a handhold was the mountain itself, reaching out to me when I needed it. All around me was this hailstorm of dust and ice and rocks and boulders, smashing my face and arms. But I held on. It's like the mountain *knew* that I had to make it out of there, that I had to get back to my ..."

Something in Larry's story wakes him up. His eyes clear, the storm cloud passing. He blinks at me, coming out of his dream, his vision of the past. It's no more or less real than the images of horror the Pneuma compound induced in his mind as a teenager. He lives the terror and the wonder all over again in the moment.

I shudder and he turns away. I guess the African witch doctor didn't teach a good bedside manner.

Larry is quiet for a minute. He carefully spreads out the brown cloth on the table in front of him. His hands tremble as he begins pinching herbs from various packets, sprinkling them liberally around the towel. He takes a flat yellow paper from the basin and unfolds it. I can see the dried leaves inside, arranged like slices of salami on a cold cuts tray. He peels off a dozen or so and lays them on the cloth in the same tight, overlapping pattern, his hands calming with the ritual.

I recognize the preparations now and try to think of the word for it ... a *compress*—not so mysterious after all. My sigh of relief breaks Larry's silence and invites him to finish his story.

"All that was left was me, two porters, and a junior guide, all injured to some degree, most of our supplies and food gone. I was the worst off. Couldn't walk, could barely move my arms. I thought I was permanently paralyzed. I was so close ..." He pins me with his eyes. "I could see the other side. It would've been easy to just let go, to just *die*."

My breath catches in my throat as I stare back into Larry's infinite universe of pain.

He shakes his head bitterly. "But I wouldn't. My life— my mission—is too important to just let go."

He takes a deep breath, giving me permission to breathe too.

"Took them two weeks to get me to Katmandu." His voice is clear now. He's out of the nightmare. "Three weeks there before they could move me again." He folds the cloth into a neat bandage about six inches wide and a foot-and-a-half long and sets it back in the bowl. "Finally got me back to India and a decent doctor ..."

Before turning to me, he bends and reaches back into the bottom cabinet and comes up with a half-full bottle of clear liquor in his left hand as he carries the basin in his right. He keeps chatting on his way back into the living room.

"But the damage was done. My right hip was fractured in two places, my femur in three ... tibia, ankle, even my toes were broken."

Those injuries account for the swinging gait I noticed as he walked away from our first encounter in the alley behind Bobbie's Coffee Shop.

Larry shakes his head, continuing the injury inventory. "Ribs, shoulder ..." He raises the liquor bottle to his mouth as if he's about to take a drink—and I can't blame him—but instead he traces his thumb along the crooked cleft in his chin. I understand the gesture—his face was also banged up by the rockslide. And why wouldn't it be? No part of him—outside or inside—would be spared in a cataclysm like that.

I look at my right leg and the swollen knee underneath the sweatpants. We definitely have more in common than DNA. If our society doesn't cripple us mentally, our adventures will cripple us physically.

"But you don't have a bad limp," I say.

He gestures to me with the basin and liquor bottle. "Exactly."

He sits down on the couch and puts the basin on the ottoman next to my extended leg. "If I skip a day, my leg hurts," he explains. "If I skip three days, I start limping again. A week, and I can barely walk."

"Is this ... remedy ... traditional in Africa?" I ask, wishing for more reassurance, but he provides none.

"Not really. I learned it from a witch doctor in Cameroon. He was a sort of specialist." He unscrews the cap on the bottle and dumps an ample amount into the basin, soaking the brown cloth.

The sharp stench hits my nostrils and burns my eyes, twisting my face and tickling angrily at my throat and stomach.

"Pure grain alcohol," Larry explains.

Holding back the impulse to puke, I squeeze a few

words through my clenched teeth and try to keep my throat from turning inside out. "Is it medicinal?"

Larry smirks. "For some people, yes. It kills others. It's basically *moonshine*." He wraps the soaked compress around my knee. The cloth is ribboned with brown stains from constant use. It looks filthy, like it would smell of rotten meat if not for the alcohol and herbs wafting from it.

"How exactly will it fix my knee?" I can hear the accusation in my voice. Chemistry wasn't my strongest subject, so I'm having a hard time believing it.

"I told you I learned it from a witch doctor." In one smooth motion he dips a hand into his pocket, whips out a silver cigarette lighter, flips it open with a metallic clink, and sparks it. "It's magic."

He raises his eyebrows and—before I can stop him— touches the burning lighter to the wrap on my knee. The whole thing bursts into flames.

CHAPTER 11

If my knee weren't crippled I'd jump up and run around screaming, throwing flames off my leg onto every combustible thing in the place. In two minutes this dry old cottage would be a raging bonfire.

But I can't get up. All I can do is yell, "WHOA! What the ..." I jerk as if I'm going to leap off the chair, but Larry puts a hand on my shoulder.

"It's all right," he says calmly. Urgent is not in his vocabulary. He's just set me on fire and he's telling me to be *mellow*? A scene flashes through my mind of a grass-skirted shaman in the West African jungle lighting Larry's whole right leg on fire from hip to little toe.

"But it's ..." I'm about to say *"on fire!"* but stop myself—that's obvious. And Larry won't listen anyway. He believes he has everything under control. He watches in fascination, that far off cloud in his eyes.

As the towel over my knee burns and the fumes fill the room in a fog of incense, I try to concentrate on a vision of the African "doctor," but the "witch" keeps stepping in front of him.

I want to check out of the terror, run my mind far off where I won't be afraid, but the sudden surge of heat on my knee snaps me right back into the room. Somehow I didn't expect it, but now it's the only relevant detail in this bizarre scene.

Larry gazes into the flames like a cowboy at a campfire, completely placid and unconcerned.

The heat instantly shoots up to a searing temperature and my skin feels like it's about to peel clean off. I reach to slap out the flames when Larry waves a hand across the conflagration and it dies down. *Magic? Witch?* His hand stops in front of my chest, not a magic gesture that controls fire, but a warning to do nothing because the alcohol is burning itself out.

Within seconds, the flames dwindle and leave the bandage steaming over my knee. I'm panting from the scare. Larry is his usual indifferent self, no more riled or calm than before he set me on fire.

The bandage should be charred from the flames, but it's not. "How …"

Larry already has the answer. "It's treated with an African tree sap that insulates the cotton fibers. The alcohol breaks down the dried herbs like a solvent and activates their medicines. When it burns, the steam is driven into your skin and the emollients go directly to the cells. This is basically an old poultice recipe that's set on fire instead of soaked with vinegar and left on the skin for hours. The heat you feel is the steam, not the flame."

The steam rolling off the bandage is thick and acrid — smellier than the unburned moonshine. I feel lightheaded and I can't tell if it's from the fear or the fumes.

"The witch doctor fixed you," I say breathily. My

voice is a mile off as my mind drifts away from my body.

Larry nods, his eyes on the cloud billowing up from the bandage.

I sink deeper into the chair, forgetting about my painful knee as I drift into another world. As I watch the steam rise to the ceiling a name bubbles to the surface of my mind. I know I shouldn't say it, but I can't stop myself. "Timothy," I mumble. It's Larry's real name. I'm standing inside the forbidden library, holding my family's heavy volume of *The Chronicles of Delphi*, reading with astonishment the name of the uncle I never knew I had. "Timothy ..." I breathe again.

My heavy eyes drift back to Larry. He's glowering at me. I've never seen so much emotion in his face. He's ... angry? Afraid? Confused? I can't tell through the haze swirling around inside and outside my head.

"Timothy is dead," Larry-Timothy says through a smoky tunnel. How can I hear him so clearly even though he's so far away? "He was a good boy. Would have been a good man." Larry-Timothy speaks of himself in the third person, making his very presence somehow tragic. "He didn't deserve what happened to him. But he's not here anymore."

I know what he means. When Mom took me away and changed my name, I tried for a long time to stay who I was, tried not to become someone else. But eventually you realize that there's no room for the old you in a new, fake life. You give up and just become whatever the situation wants you to be.

Ashley drifts into my mind, strapped to a bed in the

psych ward, getting turned into someone—some *thing*—that she doesn't want to be. I twitch, trying to wake up my body and reconnect my brain to it. I need to get Ashley out of there before they erase every last part of her from those beautiful, molten-brown eyes. Larry-Timothy puts a hand on my shoulder and presses me back into the chair. "Easy, Champ," he says soothingly. "Take it easy."

My father called me "Champ." Larry reminded me of it ... when did we talk about all that—yesterday, last week, *a thousand years ago*?

It's exactly the same gesture, exactly the same *words* my father said to me when I was six and got knocked to the mat in karate class. My shoulder hurt so badly I thought my arm would fall off. Dad pressed a healing hand on the sore spot. *"Easy, Champ,"* he said. *"Take it easy."*

It's my last thought before everything goes black.

CHAPTER **12**

My eyes open and the darkness disintegrates. I have no reference point for where I am because I don't know where I've *been*. I look around the room, trying to remember the scene. A figure sits at the table a few feet away. Larry. I'm in his cabin. It all comes back to me.

He's perched on the edge of the chair, leaning over a spiral notebook—the one I saw him drop in the carton earlier. With a pencil gripped in his knobby fingers, he flips between pages, tracing lines and calculating numbers. It dominates his attention and I get the feeling that his mind is standing somewhere else right now—like earlier when he projected out of here and onto that mountainside.

I draw a sharp breath like a corpse breathing for the first time in a millennium. There was no dream, no sense even of being asleep. There was sudden blackness and now there's light again. I press a thumb and forefinger into my eyes, trying to rub out the darkness.

When I look up, Larry is staring me at me as if trying to decide if I'm actually waking up or just stirring. We lock eyes and he folds the notebook closed, dropping it back into the big carton on the table.

44

"How are you feeling?" His tone is as flat and earnest as when he asks, *"What do you want?"*

I stretch my arms and neck. "Good, I guess. How long have I been out?"

Larry comes over to examine me. "About three hours."

A wave of guilt hits me. I had intended to get help and go back to break Ashley out of the psych ward. Now here I am, sleeping? For three hours? This is just ... betrayal!

I start to get up but Larry puts the familiar hand on my shoulder and sits down on the couch next to my chair.

"Easy," he says, and I remember my father and Larry-Timothy and all the other names I should never speak. I said his real name. I hope he doesn't punish me for it. I won't say it again—out loud *or* in my head. Just thinking the name Timothy violates some rule ingrained deep in my mind.

Larry lifts the wrap from my knee, and I brace myself for the redness, melon-sized swelling, and sharp agony of torn ligaments. But I see none of that. The towel is peeled off to reveal only a knee, nothing unusual or stricken about it.

Astonished, I stare at Larry.

He looks me in the eyes with all his expectations fulfilled. "Give it a try," he says.

I move my leg gingerly, afraid to break his pain-relieving witch doctor spell. But it works, without ache or limitation. I bend my knee, relieved. "That's amazing!" I smile like I just saw the best magic trick ever.

Larry folds up the once white bandage, puts it back

in the blue-flecked basin, and stands up without a word. He takes it all to the kitchen and starts water running in the sink.

While his back is turned to me, I say, "That stuff knocked me out."

He nods. "It does that the first few times. The fumes are strong and easily overwhelm you. But you get used to it."

I can feel the benefits. Aside from my pang of guilt and concern for Ashley, I'm feeling rested and energetic.

Larry works carefully at the sink, unfolding the cloth and dumping the herbs and leaves. He wets it and scrubs out the remnants then uses it to wipe the basin clean. I think of a Catholic priest after communion at mass, when they wipe the remaining wine-turned-blood out of the cup so thoughtfully and reverently that the simple task takes on monumental meaning. Larry's done this maybe thousands of times since his experience in Africa.

"What took you from India to Africa?" I ask.

"Missionary work," he says automatically, so fast that it sounds like the practiced punchline to a common joke. But he doesn't laugh.

"What other tricks did you learn?" I ask sarcastically.

Larry still doesn't turn around. "It's not a *trick*, Champ. These remedies, like the sutras of India, and the marital arts of East Asia, are *technologies* developed over thousands of years. They can be learned and implemented if you have respect for them."

A lump rises into my throat. Without even raising his voice, Larry has smacked me down.

He finishes his washing and turns from the sink, his eyes showing a touch of sadness. "If you treat them as tricks you miss the entire point, you dishonor the spirit of those who gave their lives to develop them."

The theme hits a little closer to home, too. "Like the Pneuma?" I ask. "The Pythia and the Oracle? They're thousands of years old."

Larry nods. "Yes, like that. And does it seem like a *trick* to you?"

No, it doesn't.

He pats a towel over his hands as he steps over to the couch. "Just because something has mystical features doesn't mean it's not real," he says, sitting down. "Healing, meditation, prophecy ... they each have components that are unexplainable by our logical minds. We tend to call phenomena like that magic or tricks or *evil*."

Larry's missing my point. And I need to get to the reason I came here. "But what the League does with the Pneuma compounds and the girls ..."

He shrugs. "In my mind that's abuse of power and knowledge, not evil in the power or knowledge itself."

It sounds like he's making excuses for the enemy. "You don't think the Committee and the League should be stopped?" I ask. "You don't want them to pay for what they did to you? Maybe that's your real mission here, why you came back." If I can get Larry to use his resentment against the Committee plus what he knows about them to help me, I can save Ashley.

He reads it in my face and he's not taking the bait.

"That's why *you* came back, Champ. I told you why I came back."

Yes, he explained it to me yesterday at the hospital. But I don't believe him—or I don't *want to* believe him. "Because you were *lonely*? Because you wanted to be around something familiar again?"

As my anger rises, Larry watches me like a zoo exhibit, wearing his calm like condescension. He has sniffed out my manipulation and is keeping his distance from it.

But I won't shut up, and I only get more angry. "What they're doing to Ashley—what they did to you—is *wrong*. They need to be stopped. You're blowing your chance to get revenge for what they did."

I see the slightest pinch of discomfort in his face at the mention of *revenge*, but I can't tell if it's sympathy or annoyance.

When he speaks, his words are measured and gentle but somehow fake. "If you go wandering the world looking for revenge, Champ, you'll live in a world of trouble."

With that little lesson over, he turns to the immediate issue. "When you showed up on my doorstep again this morning, I asked you what you wanted. You were in so much pain you couldn't even think." He nods at my healed knee. "Well, I removed the block. Now tell me what you really want or be on your way."

So here it is. This isn't a safe haven. He let me in so he could get me out. I'm not welcome here and he's stripping away all the formalities, all my games. But I have no other options.

I choose my words carefully because I doubt I'll get another chance to say them. "I ... need ... help," I say.

His eyes tell me he appreciates that I'm being deliberate.

"I want to get Ashley out of the hospital, away from Delphi, before they turn her into a ..." I stop myself from saying *"freak."* Larry's an unfortunate product of the Pythia Program and he probably wouldn't like the label. "... into a *cripple.*"

He's listening.

Encouraged, I continue. "I was thinking, maybe there's a tunnel under the hospital. We can find it and get her out through there."

When Larry gave me instructions for getting into the library from the underground passage he'd discovered, he explained why the tunnels are there. In the mid-nineteenth century a steam plant was being built to pipe steam power—the highest technology of the time—to the entire town, starting with the college. Something happened—maybe sabotage—that stopped the grand project and left the network of tunnels to be forgotten. I'm hoping there are more passages than he's found so far.

But he's shaking his head before I even finish. "The tunnels don't extend beyond campus. That's as far as the engineers got before they abandoned the project."

"Are you *sure?*" I plead. "I mean, what if there are some unexplored parts ..."

"I told you, I've been all over down there. It's a dead end."

I'm burning with frustration now. "There has to be *something* I can do. I have to find a way. Will you help me?"

Satisfied to finally hear the reason I came here, Larry stares at me a long time. But I can tell he's not considering his verdict, only how to word his answer. He decides to make it direct.

"No," he says.

CHAPTER 13

I feel like Larry just slapped me in the face. Besides Ashley, he's the only other person in this town who will acknowledge the truth—and he's *family*. But he's refusing to do a thing to help me.

My anger tears loose from the thin ropes that were holding it back. My words come out in hot disgust. "You'll do missionary work to help strangers in Africa, but you won't help me—your own *nephew*—here in your hometown? What kind of man are you?"

Larry snaps upright in his seat, an angry scowl furrowing his face. "The kind that doesn't want his head chopped off!"

His fury pushes me back into my chair. The violence the Pneuma induced in him so many years ago is not gone, it's just below the surface.

"How do you think I've survived here the last two years, Champ?" He tugs at his ragged shirt. "They don't notice a homeless bum. Everyone looks right past me. I've been sneaking around avoiding eye contact with Maryellen Bradford, Screed, and anyone else I used to know around here. And it's worked so far."

That's true. I could learn a few lessons in stealth from him.

"You come back here and raise hell for a couple of weeks and it gives you the right to tell me I'm doing it wrong? Do you know what they'll do to me if they find out I've come back here, if they find out I'm *alive*?"

I can only guess, but Larry has specifics.

"They'll *execute* me. They'll take me out somewhere in the twenty miles of virgin forest surrounding this town and put a *bullet* in my head. And then they'll smile when they write 'Mortuus' in the *Chronicle* next to my name." He points a finger at me like a dagger. "When I told you how to get into the library I was doing way more for you than I ever intended. So don't tell me I'm not doing enough."

Now I'm feeling defensive. "But they're going to destroy her mind with that poison, and I can't let that happen."

"And then what? Are you going to run around to every chapter in the world, saving teenage girls from the League?"

"I don't know!" I snap. "Right now, I care about Ashley—only Ashley. The others ..." I stop that thought. I can't worry about anyone else right now. I pull my eyes away, searching for a way to make it work. "I won't let them get away with this," I growl.

Now that he's shown me what a tough spot I'm in, Larry settles down, becomes gentle again. He leans back and smiles sadly.

"What?" I ask suspiciously.

He takes a long pause. "You're just like your father," he finally says. "Smart, idealistic ..."

I guess it's a compliment, but it doesn't help me. "I don't know if I'm all that idealistic." I feel the fire of rage lighting in my gut. "I came back here for revenge. I can see that now."

Larry nods. "You want Maryellen Bradford and Screed to account for what they've done."

I stare hungrily into space, an image of those two clouding my eyes.

"You want the League—the whole world of chapters and their rich members—to pay."

The fire burns up my throat and into my head as he talks.

"You want to burn it out from the inside and leave the society a dried husk, not even a footnote to history because three thousand years of secrecy has made them nonexistent."

The words come so easily to him and they strike me at my core. Larry has a way of clarifying things for me, of putting my feelings into form. If I have my way, not a single one of these people—in Arcanville and beyond—will be left with a life when I'm done.

"That's why I won't help you," he says.

"What?" I can't believe it. How can he say exactly what I'm thinking and not feel the same, still refuse to help?

"You can't have it both ways," he says.

The swell of rage caves in, dropping into my stomach.

"What do you mean?"

"You might have come back here to avenge your mom and dad, but your priorities have changed. You've taken on ... *obligations*." He laces the last word with significance.

"Ashley," I mutter.

He nods thoughtfully. "You have to decide, Champ. Satisfy your rage against the Committee and the League ... or help *her*."

My stomach goes cold. I hadn't even considered it as one or the other. I've been assuming I could do both.

"The question you have to ask yourself," Larry says, "is which is more important?"

CHAPTER 14

I feel like a fool, a failure. The idealism Larry says I inherited from my father is a liability now. It blinded me first to my true aim in returning to Arcanville then to the impossibility of succeeding once I started to care about Ashley.

She was helping me find the truth I was so hungry for. I was so used to being alone that I couldn't have planned on falling in love with her. I learned my mission and blew it all at the same time. Now *she* is the mission.

"Ashley," I say. "I have to save Ashley."

"Well, you overshot the mark here, Champ," Larry says. "You brought too much heat on you, too much attention."

As I realize how turned around I've gotten, a gaping pit of desperation opens inside me. "What should I do? The police are looking for me. I saw them outside campus."

"The police are the least of your problems," he says. "Now that the Committee knows someone was inside the library and Screed has been taken out, they're going to be ferocious."

And they have another ferocious asset. "Katie's on their side," I tell Larry. "She knows who I am, recognized me from grade school. She came to my room yesterday. I saw the Committee's ranking list of kids in Maryellen Bradford's office. She tried to get me to tell her who's above her."

"Did you?"

"No, but she said that if I don't, she'll tell the Committee who I really am. I haven't seen her since." I shake my head in frustration. Katie was using me from the first time she flashed her laser-blue eyes at me. "She's the one who called the Committee on Ashley," I say through gritted teeth, "and got her sent back to the hospital."

Larry tilts his head curiously. "She told you that?" If he knows anything about Katie—which he might—he'd be surprised to hear that she admitted to anything.

"She didn't have to. I figured it out. She hates Ashley and she'll do anything to score points with the Committee and claw to the top of the list."

Larry watches me, contemplating, then says, "The Committee runs this town, Champ. It's inescapable. And now that there's been a major security breach, the League will get involved too."

The idea of the League coming in to protect their interests adds another layer of complication and fear. "What'll they do?"

He reads my eyes. "To Ashley? You're lucky there. As a Pythia candidate she's too valuable to harm."

He's trying to tell me she's *safe* with these people?

"I'm not going to leave her," I insist.

"I'm not saying you should. But there's another option, a better one."

"So you'll help?"

Larry sighs heavily. "I'll give you some *information* that will help."

I lean forward.

"I know how they work," he says. "They don't turn up the dosages all at once. They have to step it up in stages. And with the girls, the real damage isn't done until they get to the convent in Greece."

It gives me a little hope. "When is that?"

Larry contemplates it, seeming to run through a calendar in his mind. "I'd guess eight to ten weeks at the earliest. But ..."

"But what?" I expect more bad news from him, but he surprises me.

"Ashley's a fighter. She'll resist the chemicals on instinct. So the prep period will probably be longer. She'll buy you another eight weeks or so."

I calculate. "That's four months, total. What about the Committee and the League? They'll come after me."

"They don't know who you are yet. They haven't connected the new boy working at the coffee shop with the boy who went missing ten years ago. Screed knows, but he probably won't wake up to tell anyone. Your try rescuing Ashley would be a giveaway if anyone in the Committee was paying attention, but they're too busy fortifying the library to really investigate the break-in. It won't last long, but right now they're rudderless without Screed."

"The guy did a number on himself. And he told the head security guard my physical description outside the library that night."

"Screed's condition buys you a little time." A sense of eagerness edges into Larry's voice. I take it as interest in helping me. "You have the advantage right now. You can slip away and regroup, make a plan to intercept Ashley when they move her. That would be the best time, when they're out of their element and vulnerable." He pauses and shakes his head gravely. "But if you hang around here and keep up this craziness, they'll know soon enough who's behind it. Then ... "

I nod. "Ashley will be gone for good."

Larry pauses a few seconds to let me think.

I can see everything he's saying mapped out in front of me. I've blown it, but I can get it back. If I'm careful I can really do something. Larry doesn't know about the bot I planted on the mainframe computer. It should find me a doorway into their network within a few weeks. Once it's activated, I can access it from anywhere and I'll be able to find out when they'll move Ashley. I can save her and plan a proper payback for the entire League.

"Do you have enough money to travel with and get by?" Larry asks.

I think of the emergency bag I hid by the railroad tracks on my way into town a few weeks ago. I was smart enough not to carry it around with me or keep it at my apartment. It has a few thousand dollars in cash, fake IDs, and credit cards. "Yes," I say, "I'm OK there."

Larry stands up. "Then don't hang around here, Champ."

I push myself out of the chair, determined to save Ashley and strengthened by the will to do it right this time. I reach for my crutches.

"You won't need those," he says.

I set my right foot down and carefully put pressure on it as I stand up. No pain, no stiffness. And my head feels clear, not full of water. I straighten myself and give Larry a grateful look.

"Told you," he says.

"Won't I need more treatments—every day, like you?"

He shakes his head. "Your injuries weren't that bad. You should be fine."

I go to the door and open it, Larry following closely. Outside, I step off the stoop and turn around. "Hey, listen, Larry ..." I want to apologize, say thanks, and ask for advice all at once.

"Not a word," Larry says magnanimously as he fills the doorway. "Just get someplace safe and get in touch with me." He hands me a scrap of notebook paper with an email address on it. "I don't have a phone," he says. "I check my email at the public library. I'll keep an eye on Ashley for you. When we find out the Committee's schedule for moving her, we'll make a plan."

"'We?'" I repeat the all-important word. "So you'll help?"

"I'll do all I can."

I stand in the shaggy underbrush of the yard and look up into the doorway at Larry. My uncle. Family. Is this what it means? I guess it's the best we can do.

"So long, Champ," Larry says and closes the door.

I turn toward the path and run.

CHAPTER 15

I run down side streets and alleys, avoiding campus and the crowded streets of downtown. I don't want to be seen. I ditched my crutches, but the weird blue tracksuit is enough to get me noticed. If Larry's right, I have only a little time to get out of town before the Committee turns up the heat and really starts investigating. For all I know, Katie has blabbed and they're already onto me. With every minute that ticks by, I'm one step closer to being caught.

I'm winded when I get to my neighborhood but there's still no twinge in my knee, absolutely zero evidence that I was nearly crippled just a few hours ago. A block from my apartment I duck into an alley, skirting hedges and garages to the end. Before I step onto the sidewalk, I take a careful survey of the corner, looking for any person or car out of place.

I don't see anything so I step onto the sidewalk and cross the street, walking quickly toward Mike's house and my rooms above his garage. I scan the street as I walk. No black cars parked and waiting. No hooded eyes peering out of windows. Everything is normal—which is even more worrisome. The Committee's agents could be hiding, their radios chattering with reports of every step I take. But no one jumps out of a shadowy front door. No one throws a net over me as I step and scan nervously along the sidewalk.

At Mike's house, I duck into the driveway. When I got back to Arcanville I rented the apartment from him with cash and a handshake. I pay my rent and he stays out of my business. In fact, I've barely seen him since I moved in. It's a perfect arrangement.

I go around the back of the house to the garage and the wooden stairs leading up to my place. My bike is not in its usual place under the steps. I left it at the coffee shop the other night. I kick myself mentally. It's my only vehicle for getting around town quickly and now it's locked in the back room at work, where I don't dare show my face after skipping the past two mornings.

Bobbie is probably wondering where I am. She put her trust in me, hired me without knowing me when I came back to town. She needs help at the shop because her nephew, Eddie, can't stay sober enough to be there when he's scheduled to work.

Bobbie owns the coffee shop here but she lives in Woodbridge, Arcanville's nearest neighbor twenty miles away. Other than Larry, she's the only adult I've met here who acknowledges that this town is weird, making me like her a little bit more. But she has no idea what I've learned, how deep and wide it runs.

A few days ago she saw that something was wrong with me and tried to get me to talk about it. But as things have gotten darker and more confusing, I've withdrawn, leaning only on Ashley. I feel bad now for letting Bobbie down. I need to get my bike back without having to look her in the eyes.

I was working at the coffee shop two nights ago when Ashley came in and said her babysitting gig was canceled and she wasn't expected home. It was the right time to raid the library. But is there ever a right time to learn what we learned inside?

The thousands of *Chronicle of Delphi* books with the 3,000-year history of every Arcanville family; the revelation in one that my father is missing not dead; the inner sanctum of the Committee chambers; the cruel ranking list in Maryellen Bradford's office with her own son, Sutton, dead by suicide, completely removed, and Ashley, damaged by the Committee's practices, at the bottom. I could have let it all go, forgotten about it and run away to spend the rest of my life on a desert island somewhere, far from any of this rotten human influence.

But what I couldn't ignore was the file I found on Screed's computer. I should have just planted the bot on the mainframe and left. But once I opened the letter from the League's Board of Prophecy, everything changed.

Katie and the kids at school and the whole town treat Ashley like she's insane, damaged and dangerous. I was suspicious of her too at first. But the letter proves that she's not crazy, that the Committee has been testing and experimenting on her since she was five years old. The nervous breakdowns, the trips to the psych ward, her strange and horrible visions were all caused by the various Pneuma compounds they've shot her up with over the years. Her aptitude for prophecy makes her *special*, the Board says, and Arcanville should be proud to offer her as a sacrifice.

Now Mrs. Bradford's pharmaceutical company has created the ultimate Pneuma compound, one that will generate usable prophecy faster and more efficiently than any ever known. They'll squeeze Ashley even harder, until she's empty, and do the same to every other girl in the Pythia Program.

I didn't tell Ashley. When she was lucid I couldn't, didn't know how. She deserves to know what's happening to her, but since they've gotten her back in the hospital and medicated, there's no use trying. She can't understand anything on this side of reality. Now my only option is to run, leave her behind until I can come back and free her.

But the letter mentioned one other factor that makes my new plan even more risky for Ashley. While I'm waiting for the perfect moment to rescue her, the advanced Pneuma compound the Committee is using on her is so powerful that it could permanently burn her mind out—or kill her in the process.

CHAPTER **16**

I plod up the stairs as if I'm carrying Ashley on my back, suddenly feeling heavy and tired from the storm raging inside me. The pain in my soul is worse than any Screed's speeding car could put in my body.

When I reach the landing at the top, I find the thin paper gum wrapper I closed in the doorjamb two days ago when I last left my apartment. It's my primitive burglar detector. I had begun to think it was a stupid, paranoid habit—until it worked.

A few days ago I came home and found the gum wrapper missing. I thought Screed, having figured out I was the one snooping around the Committee's business and researching the secret history of the League, came here to snoop. But it turned out to be Katie, looking for clues to what I was up to with Ashley and hoping to learn who was above her on the ranking list.

Today, all's clear so far. But I pat the pockets of my ridiculous tracksuit and realize that I don't have my key. It was in my pants pocket when Screed ran me down. Now it's lost in the hospital with my other belongings. And the windows on this side of the apartment are locked too.

I glance down at the house for any sign of Mike. Nothing. I don't want to break the door—the noise will attract attention. But I have to get in and get some clean clothes.

I have one option. This apartment was obviously added on top, years after the garage was built. A skirt of the old garage roof rings the exterior like a shirt collar. The shingled strip is maybe a foot wide—enough, I hope, for a foothold.

I throw my legs over the railing and step onto the narrow ledge. My toes point up awkwardly on the steep angle. I'm forced to press my body against the siding for balance and realize immediately that this is a bad idea. One degree of lean backward, one slip of a toe, and I'll fall. But I have to get inside.

I inch along the roofline to the corner of the second floor and grab it, grateful for a handle, and pull myself around. I'm at the rear of the apartment and halfway to the kitchen window. I usually leave it open because the apartment gets hot in the daytime, and I don't like walking into an oven when I come home.

On this side, the band of shingles follows its forty-five-degree pitch upward, forcing me to lie down and shuffle on my belly. One knee and elbow hang over the edge as I pull myself up the slope. If anyone sees me up here like this they'll scream for sure. Then it hits me—*did* I leave the window open? The days are cooler lately and the apartment has been cold when I get home at night. If I closed it before I left two days ago, it'll be really hard to open it from this angle. I'll be reaching down diagonally and trying to lift it. If it's locked, I'm completely screwed.

And it's worse—if I can't open the window, I don't know if I can get back to the landing. Shuffling backward and getting myself upright with one leg and one arm hanging off the ledge seems impossible. That leaves only one escape route. I look straight down and see the shrubs and lawn twenty feet below. I'm struck with a crystal clear picture of what'll happen to me—to my legs and arms, to my spine and head—if I fall or try to jump down from here. My heart snaps and my mind launches out of my body into a terrible cloud of vertigo. I'm falling, falling!

"Shut up!" I growl at my brain. "Shut up and do this!"

Hearing a voice—even my own—pulls my mind out of the terrifying tailspin. I take a deep breath and force my heart to slow down. I take another and reel my mind back to my body. One more breath reconnects my brain with my eyes, hands, and feet, and focuses me again.

I'm to the side of the window now and I reach out, praying for good news. I extend my arm as far as I can without tipping off the ledge. I fold my hand around the window frame, feeling … nothing. It's open!

I sigh with relief and shimmy farther up the slope. But I'm running out of room as the strip of old roof pitches up to the peak and connects with the newer roof of my apartment. A couple more feet and I won't be able to squeeze into the narrowing gap. I've got to get off this ledge.

I lower my right leg to the opening and tip my body over the edge while gripping the shingles with both hands. Pushing out thoughts of all the deadly mistakes I can make right now, I find the bottom edge of the windowsill with one foot then the other. I grab hold of the electrical access pipe next to the window with my right hand, reach down to the window with my left for support, and slowly bend my knees until I'm squatting on the sill. I struggle to keep myself upright, because leaning backward means losing my weakening grip and tipping headfirst to the ground.

Once I'm low enough, I straighten one leg then the other and I'm half sitting in my kitchen, half hanging in the air outside. I pull on the edge of the counter with my heels, dragging myself until I'm lying in the opening, and slide the rest of my body inside.

I roll off the counter and lean against it, panting and staring at the empty air outside the window. If I had given even a moment's thought to the stuff I've done in the last week—including this—I never would have done any of it. I'm grateful that my stupidity hasn't gotten me killed yet. I survived the last few minutes but I'm suddenly struck by the idea that my life of danger will never be over. I put it out of my mind. It's all too much to contemplate.

I wipe the film of sweat off my forehead and turn to look around the apartment. I have to decide what to take, how much I can carry on my back at a dead run, ahead of … whoever.

Before I can move, there's a knock at the door.

CHAPTER 17

I freeze, hoping it's a phantom noise—a squirrel on the roof or Mike banging around in the garage below. But the knock sounds again. Not the roof, not the garage.

Someone's at the door. A shadow is cast against the curtains covering the door's small window. The police? The Committee's security guys?

I crouch down next to the kitchen counter and scan the apartment, looking for a weapon. The most dangerous thing in this place is a flimsy kitchen knife. With as much danger as I've brought on myself, I never thought to buy even a baseball bat for self-defense?

The knocking gives me one hope, though. If they're not breaking the door down, maybe they're polite enough to go away when no one answers.

I scoot over to the little dining table and hear simultaneous shuffling out on the landing. I hope they're turning to go away but the shadow stretches to look into the window next to the landing. They won't see anything through the drawn curtains, but I stop anyway, showing no trace of movement.

The table in front of me is littered with stuff—all of it incriminating. My laptop computer sits next to a

69

pile of papers with my Delphi research and computer programming notes. There's a stack of notebooks that Ashley and I stole out of Sutton's parked car in a midnight prowl at his parents' house. I can't let anyone get hold of these things. When Katie was here she must have dismissed all of it, but if the Committee's investigators see this, they'll put it all together and realize how much I know, exactly how dangerous I really am to them.

When I glance to the door again, the shadow is gone. The blood rushing in my ears is loud enough to drown out any sound. They must have given up and gone back down the stairs.

I stand up and tiptoe to the bathroom, grabbing some clothes off the "clean" pile on the way. I get out of the old man's tracksuit and think about a shower but change my mind. The noise of the plumbing could attract unwanted attention, plus I can't stay here a moment longer than absolutely necessary. Within a minute I'm dressed in jeans and a hoodie and back in the main room.

As I reach for another handful of clean clothes to stuff in my backpack, I catch the shadow at the door again and my stomach twists. They're not giving up!

The knock comes again, louder this time.

I duck and wait for the rapping to stop but it's insistent. I picture a platoon of guys in bulky black SWAT gear and helmets lining the steps like a troop of army ants poised to bust in. I want to shrink into a ball and save myself.

But when the shadow speaks, the voice shoots a gush of hot lava up my throat. It's a voice I never wanted to hear again and somehow believed I'd never have to.

"Zach, open the door!"

I'm paralyzed with rage.

"I know you're in there! Open up! It's Katie."

CHAPTER 18

I rush to the door as Katie's rapping turns to pounding. I unsnap the deadbolt and rip the door open, silencing the knock and sending her falling forward through the doorway. I grab a button on her jean jacket and yank her the rest of the way in.

"Whoa!" she shouts, spinning on her feet.

I glance outside—no one on the landing or in the driveway. I close the door and turn around to find her standing by the couch, glaring at me.

"Idiot!" she protests. "What is wrong with you?"

I stare back at the beautiful, detestable face that was looming over my hospital bed yesterday when I woke up, announcing that Ashley got caught stealing money and her passport from their parents' safe.

"You …" I growl. I step forward, feeling the carnivorous predator take over my senses.

"Oh, knock it off," Katie sneers, the same smug tone in her voice as when she informed me that I put Ashley back in the psych ward by involving her in my crazy plan. "You're not going to hurt anybody."

The words stun me. I want to kill her with my bare

hands, snuff out her miserable, meddling life. But she's right—I'm not going to do it, because there's been enough destruction in this town, all in the name of Delphi. I can fight and cause more useless damage or I can do as Larry suggests—run and regroup, create a *useful* plan.

I'm holding on to some of the rage, though. It'll keep me on edge around Katie and prevent me lapsing into anything that feels like trust. Tall, with curly brown hair and bright blue eyes, she uses her looks and charm to lure boys in. But she's not who she pretends to be. I doubt there's one of us yet who hasn't regretted getting close to her.

I shake my head and turn away, grab my backpack and stuff my laptop into it. "Just get out of here." I try to sound threatening but my worry for Ashley oozes out through my voice.

"She's *fine*, Zach," Katie says tiredly.

I turn to the table and slide Sutton's notebooks into my pack. When Katie snooped in here a few days ago I'm sure she saw them. I'd left them out because I was reading and rereading them, trying to decode every sketch and symbol, every incomplete sentence. Even if his name and initials weren't on them, she would have recognized them a hundred feet away, his trademark artwork scratched and inked into the covers—trees and skulls, nature and death.

She and Sutton were close before he died. I think she pushed him to an edge he couldn't live on—demanding that he keep up his grades and achievements while discounting the disturbing things he was learning about the Committee, the League, and the Pythia Program. She

73

knew it was all too much for him. She was trying to push him out of the top spot on the ranking list, where she thought he didn't deserve to be. And it worked. The first line in that notebook of his I found at Bobbie's Coffee Shop—the one that got me into this whole mess was: *"Katie hates me ..."*

Finding these notebooks here must have been a clue that Ashley and I were on the same trail that Sutton had been. Even though she doesn't believe most of the bad stuff, she couldn't stand that we were investigating it.

I shake my head. "You didn't see Ashley in that bed ..." I shudder at the image of the dim hospital room, Ashley spaced out and hollow, begging for me to unstrap her and get her out of that psycho hellhole.

"You can't help her," Katie says. "She's always been crazy ..."

I pivot and cut her off with a growl. "She is not ... *crazy!* It's the Committee, the League, the ..."

Katie waves a hand. "I'm not going to have that argument again, Zach." Like the rest of the kids in this town, Katie's just trying to do what the Committee tells them to do—claw their way to the top of the ranking list so they can reach the inner circle quicker as adults. More achievement, more status, more money. Don't worry about the people you step on getting there or who you have to leave behind—even your own sister.

Katie wants to go way beyond that and become the first woman president of the League of Delphi. Even if she knew that the League survives and thrives by chewing up and spitting out young women like Ashley, I somehow doubt she'd do anything different. In her eyes Ashley would go from a freak to a casualty, collateral damage to be written off.

I bring my backpack over to my clean clothes pile and cram in some shirts, underwear, and socks. I find a clean-enough pair of pants and stuff them in.

"Then what do you want?" I ask, wishing for this conversation to be over, wishing I had one secret nuclear weapon I could bring out to shut her up and finally make her go away.

But *she* has the A-bomb. "You know *damn well* what I want."

Yes, I remember the demands she made yesterday — tell her what I saw inside or she'll expose me, get the entire League of Delphi security force after me, five hundred Mr. Screeds tracking me to the ends of the earth. Time for her to be disappointed.

"Well, you're on your own," I say. "Because I'm leaving." I go into the bathroom, grab my deodorant and a bottle of soap. When I step out, zipping the toiletries into the front pocket of my pack, I freeze.

Katie stands in front of me like a statue, staring me down and holding her cell phone in front of my face. "You're not going anywhere."

CHAPTER 19

If Katie were pointing a gun at me, it couldn't be more threatening. I expect an evil grin to sprout on her face, but she's all business, cold as a marble column. "One call to Mrs. Bradford," she says, "and you'll be in the dungeon of that library spitting your teeth out."

I doubt she knows about the underground passages below the campus, but maybe there are rumors of some dungeon jail in the basement. I'd bet there's actually one in there. And after what I did to the guards, I'm sure they'd love a chance to get me back in the library and play tennis on my face.

I want to say something like, *"You wouldn't ..."* or *"If you do, I'll ..."* but I have nothing to threaten her with. She's holding all the cards. With the push of one button on her cell phone, the little bit of time I have will instantly evaporate.

"I told you yesterday that I'm not done with you," she growls. "Did you think I was joking?"

Joking does not seem to be something Katie's capable of. But I'm not going to say so right now.

"I want to know what you saw in there," she says. "Who's on the list above me?"

I close my eyes for a moment, contemplating what to say. I could just give her the names—Bryan, the boy she's trying to date and Misha, her current best friend—and leave her to her business of taking them each down a couple of pegs so she can climb on top, like she did to Sutton. But before I leave town, I need something too.

I give a resigned nod. "I'll tell you," I say.

Now a grin of victory creases her lips and she lowers the cell phone. She thinks her worries are over.

"*After* you help me get my stuff from the hospital," I say.

Her brow furrows. "What *stuff*?"

"My ..." I stop myself from telling her the details "... personal belongings. What they took off me in the ER the other night, from my pockets. I need my stuff."

I can see the calculations running in Katie's eyes. She's thinking of all the ways this could be a scam. "No," she says, pointing the phone at me again. "This is the deal— you're going to tell me what I want to know then I'll give you a twelve-hour head start before I call Mrs. Bradford and tell her all about you, including your real name. Won't she find that interesting?"

She told me yesterday that she and everyone from second grade thought I was dead after I disappeared. I came back, protected by their years of forgetting, but I was stupid enough to go to a movie with her, thinking I could have a date with the girl I used to have crush on and stay anonymous. The whole time, I was actually helping Katie piece together a puzzle in her mind and she found confirmation in our grade school yearbook.

My real identity is my most closely guarded secret. I compromised it and she's using it against me.

But I'm firm on this. "If you want to know what I know, I need my stuff." I'm sure it's all in some random drawer at the hospital. My wallet is not such a big deal—they'll put my name together with the library intruder soon enough. But that flash drive has the original copy of the computer bot I got from Anton, my best friend and favorite hacker who still lives in France. I need that to stay secret if I'm going to keep what little advantage it gives me against the Committee. It also has the League's letter I swiped from Screed's PC. Because it basically explains the whole Pythia Program, they'll freak if they find out I have it and it may make things even worse for Ashley.

Katie takes an angry step forward. "You're not getting this, dummy. It's not a negotiation. You need the twelve hours to get ahead of the Committee because if they catch you, they'll turn you into hamburger. So tell me what you saw in the library or I push a button and end your miserable life."

"Go ahead," I say coolly. "And right before Mrs. Bradford—or whichever Mr. Screed they bring in next—kills me, I'll tell them the break-in was your idea. I'll tell them that you told me how to get in and forced me to report what's inside, even though you're not supposed to know."

"I don't know how to get in there. And I still don't know what's inside."

"They don't know that. And before I die, I'll also make sure to tell Mrs. Bradford that you pressured Sutton, her only son, into killing himself so you could get one more notch up the list."

"That's a lie!" Katie snaps.

I shrug. "I don't find you very convincing. And I doubt Mrs. Bradford will either. She's smart enough to see through your nice-girl act. Besides, you were Sutton's girlfriend. You were close enough to get into his head. I'm sure that's something Mrs. Bradford will appreciate."

Katie is shaking with rage now. Her plan is crumbling. "You …"

I raise my hands to show that I really mean no harm. "All I want is my stuff. As soon as I get it, I'll be out of town and out of your life."

She looks from my face to the backpack in my hand to my face again, recalculating.

"Am I wrong in thinking that you can help me get into the hospital?" I ask.

"What do you mean?" Katie shoots back, but she knows what I'm talking about.

"When I woke up yesterday, the nurses and the doctor were pretty comfortable having you around."

Her shoulders slump in defeat, as if I'm using some vital secret that she accidentally gave away. "I volunteer there two days a week after school." When she sees the grin of irony on my face she snaps, "It's a résumé-builder for college."

"So you have a …"

"Yes, I have a key card. And, yes, I know my way around." She shakes her head in disgust, like her charity to sick people has become some kind of strategic weakness. "But, so help me, Zach, if you pull anything …"

"I get my things, I tell you what you want to know, and I leave town," I assure her. "That's it. No tricks." I don't say she'll never see me again, because when I come back for Ashley later our paths might cross.

She drops her hand and the threatening cell phone. "Fine," she sighs. "Grab your …" she glances around my messy apartment "… *disgusting crap* and let's go. I want this over with and you out of …"

The sound that cuts her off is abrupt and distinct, coming from the driveway at the bottom of the stairs. A car door slams.

CHAPTER 20

I shoot an accusing glare at Katie.

"I didn't call anyone," she blurts. The look of panic on her face is convincing enough. If she gets caught in here with me, she'll have way too much explaining to do.

But I'm not entirely sunk. If it's the police and they don't know the whole truth of my identity yet, they may just take me back to the hospital. I'll be even closer to my flash drive.

"Don't move," I tell him. "Don't say a word."

She nods, frozen in place. If she's scared to talk and the police take me away, I might even get out of town without having to tell her a thing about the library.

I thread my arms through my backpack straps, step lightly over to the window and peek through the crack in the curtains. At first I'm relieved because I don't see a police car. Then I realize that what I am seeing is worse — much worse.

My heart jumps at the sight of a black sedan parked in the driveway. A man in black fatigues and cap — the young campus guard who let me go this morning — disappears around the corner toward Mike's front door.

81

Another guard, older with stubbly black hair over tired eyes and a worry-etched face, stands by the driver's door. He turns his face up to my window.

I pull back when I recognize him.

"Who is it?" Katie whispers.

The man standing in the driveway is the head security guard from the library. When Ashley and I came out of the manhole surrounded by bushes right across the street from the library, he was standing on the opposite sidewalk, directing the search. Screed pulled out of the garage and gave him my description, yelled at him because someone had gotten in, and told him to find me. At that point they didn't know that Ashley was involved. But when she got home to grab money and her passport, Katie figured it out and called them. This might be the man who took Ashley prisoner. "It's the Committee."

"Oh no," Katie gasps. "I have to get out of here."

She steps toward the door but I block her with an arm. "Stop. Screed's guy is down there watching the door."

Katie glances frantically around. "Well, what are we going to do? There's only one way out of here." She looks from the door to me, and her face changes in a flash from terror to cunning. She takes a step back.

I know instantly what she's thinking and I point a threatening finger at her. "Do not scream," I growl.

Her eyes tell me she's seriously considering it. It would be easy to convince anyone that I'm holding her prisoner here.

I think fast and decide to offer a bit of information to

keep her quiet. "There are two people above you on the rankings in the library. If you get those guards up here and tell them I kidnapped you, you won't find out who your competition is until it's too late. Do you want that?"

She clamps her mouth shut. It's close enough to an answer.

I reach over and turn the lock, willing the bolt to be silent, but I cringe at the faint metallic snap. I peek through the curtains again. The guard below is distracted as the young one steps around the corner with Mike, my landlord, who has a ring of keys in his hand.

"You have five seconds, Zach," Katie whispers. "Get us out of here or I'll scream."

CHAPTER 21

The low murmur of Mike's voice sends a jolt of panic up my body. I can't hear what he's saying but I can tell by his tone that he's complaining to the head security guard.

The guard says something back as the first foot hits the bottom step.

The creak of wood unfreezes me and I reach for Katie's arm. She tries to resist, sneering a warning at me. I make a threatening face back and pull her toward the kitchen.

More complaining by Mike outside, another response from the head guard—this one demanding as the voices progress up the stairs.

When Katie and I reach the kitchen counter and the window, I tip my head toward it and whisper, "Go."

She leans over the counter and looks down. She rears back, aghast, and shakes her head.

I glance to the door and the approaching footsteps, put my mouth next to her ear. "Not down, *up*."

She pulls away and stares into my eyes.

The voices on the stairs grow louder.

"There's a pipe next to the window," I explain quietly. "Grab it and pull yourself up to the roof."

I didn't know Katie was afraid of anything besides underachievement.

"You first," she breathes.

"No." I push her toward the window. "Do you want to get caught in here alone?"

She glances to the door. She can't deny it. We have mere seconds before the Committee is on top of us.

"Go!" I hiss. "Just don't look down."

She turns and lifts her butt onto the counter. Lying back, she reaches for the edges of the open window, pulls her upper body through it, and stops.

The men near the door.

This is no time to hesitate. I lean over the counter. "Do you see the pipe?" My voice is barely above the volume of a thought now.

She looks to the side of the window and nods.

Footsteps outside.

"Then *grab it*," I growl.

She does and starts pulling her body upward as the footfalls reach the landing.

"You guys can't just come in here like this, Mr. Dante," Mike complains.

I look at the door and see the three shadows through the curtains. Dante must be the head guard.

Katie is planting her feet on the windowsill. We need more time. I take a quick inventory of the apartment. I can block the door, but not with furniture or anything that will tell them I've been here.

I see a possibility! I crouch and shuffle silently to the door.

Mr. Dante's voice is so close now, the grim groan of a man who's eternally exhausted. "This is official Committee business," he explains to Mike.

I stand up, carefully keeping my body to the side of the door, and reach up to the molding near the top of the frame. Sometimes the door sticks when I try to open it. The trim is broken and works its way over, snagging on the door's edge. I asked Mike to look at it a couple of times but—no surprise—he never fixed it.

"The *Committee*," Mike grumbles. "That's the answer for everything around here."

As he gripes to Dante, I push on the piece of molding, working it inward with the heel of my hand. There's a light grinding sound as it slides over the edge of the door but the men are too distracted by each other to hear it.

Dante shoots back at Mike, this time with a dark threat. "You intend to block me from doing Committee business? You'd better *think* about that …"

I hear the jingle of Mike's keys. "All I'm saying is …"

I don't wait to hear the rest. I bend and shuffle over to the kitchen counter and am relieved to find Katie's legs gone from the window. I only hope she went up instead of straight down.

Mike's key rattles in the deadbolt. I jump onto the counter and lean back. But my backpack, stuffed with my belongings, holds me upright like a couch cushion. Mike grumbles, the deadbolt clicks, sending an electric shock through me.

I can't get through the window with the pack on my back. But if I swing it around to my front, I won't be able to climb when I get outside. And I absolutely cannot leave it here for Dante to find, with my laptop and all my files and Sutton's notebooks inside.

The doorknob turns and I know I have one option. Quickly wriggling my arms out of the straps, I elbow the backpack out the window. Leaves and branches shake as it drops into the bushes below.

"What was that?" Dante asks suspiciously.

By the time Mike answers I have my upper body outside the window and one hand on the electrical pipe. I hear Mike's voice out here now, around the corner from where I'm dragging myself into midair. "Leaves, trees, wind!" he says irritably. "You work at the college. Haven't you learned *anything* over there?"

"Just open it," Dante orders.

Inside I hear the creak of the molding. I pull myself up and plant my heels on the window ledge.

"I said *open it*," Dante barks impatiently.

"I'm trying," responds Mike. I climb to standing outside the window. "It sticks sometimes."

"Move aside," Dante orders, and before I can lift my right foot to the top of the window frame, a loud CRACK-SNAP! splits the air.

Footsteps leave the landing around the corner and surge onto the apartment, within reach of where I'm standing.

CHAPTER 22

I pull my feet off the windowsill and perch my toes on the top of the frame. Gripping the pipe with my right hand and the edge of the roofline with my left fingertips I hold myself as still as a scarecrow, hoping they didn't spot my legs as they disappeared from the window.

I wait for Mike to shout, *"What the hell?"* and Dante to order to his guy, *"Grab those legs!"* But no one mentions my legs or feet.

"When was the last time you saw him?" asks Dante, stomping around inside.

"I told you," Mike says, "I hardly see the kid. He goes to work early and comes home late. Drops his rent in my mailbox."

"Was he here this morning?"

"How the hell should I know?" Mike snaps.

More footsteps, this time approaching the window. I remember Katie and look up. She's lying on the skirt of shingles, her face just two feet above mine and her feet pointing down slope toward the corner of the garage. She stares down at me with those electric blue eyes, devoid of seduction this time, full of uncertainty and fear.

"I'm warning you, Mr. Hollister, one word to the Committee and ..." Dante's voice is at the window.

I look down between my feet and see the top of his head emerge below. This close I can see flecks of gray in his short dark hair. I hold my breath.

"... you won't be happy with the results." He speaks to the air outside as he surveys the ground, missing, I hope, any sign of my backpack in the shrubs below.

Fear and fatigue tremble through my body. I try to drill a thought into Dante's head: *Don't look up. Don't look up.*

"Aw, screw that!" Mike says inside, getting Dante to draw his head back into the apartment. "You guys running around threatening ..."

Dante cuts him off with a sour threat. "You might want to think twice about that."

"What is this, communist China?" Mike protests. "Do as I'm told, say what I'm supposed to say *or else*?"

Footsteps shuffle inside until the voices emerge onto the landing.

Mike keeps complaining as he follows Dante and his man down the steps. "This may be Delphi territory," he says, voice fading with the footsteps, "but it's still America ..."

Katie's stare is hopeful, but not relieved yet.

Car doors open as Dante starts instructing Mike, "If he shows up here ..." I lose the sound of his voice, but I get the idea.

The car doors slam and I can imagine the disgusted look on Mike's face. The ignition starts and the car backs out of the driveway.

I look up at Katie again and heave a sigh of relief.

Her eyes are wide and hard. "How do we get down from here?" she whispers.

I tell her to do what I already decided is impossible— or at least dangerous. "You have to shuffle backward down to the corner and stand up. This ledge goes around to the landing."

With one elbow and knee hanging over the edge, Katie takes a glance behind her then down at the ground then back at me. She manages a tight shake of her head.

"Would you rather try to climb back in the window?"

She doesn't move.

"We're almost out of here," I say. "Just shuffle back a little at a time and make room for me. It's easy." I totally do not believe it's easy, even for someone comfortable with heights. But my legs are shaking and my arms ache. If I try to hang here much longer, I'll fall and break my neck in the shrubs below. If I lower myself back into the window and leave her out here alone I'm pretty sure she'll scream, bringing all sorts of unwanted help.

The ice in her eyes breaks a little bit. She's considering the possibility.

I nod. "Go for it. You can do it."

Another moment's hesitation and she moves. First, her hanging leg. Then her hanging arm. Then her other side.

Three seconds later there's enough room for me to start pulling myself up. As she crawls haltingly backward I hoist myself and swing a knee onto the ledge. I cringe at the thump and scratch my struggle makes, and realize how much noise we must have made earlier. I'm grateful to Mike for talking loud enough to cover our exit.

Once I'm on the ledge I look back to see Katie pushing herself into a crouch at the corner. She's gripping the siding like a baby pulling itself up by a couch cushion. When she reaches a standing position I can see how shaky she really is.

"Around the corner," I say gently. I'm trying to keep the urgency out of my voice, afraid it will spook her. But I can hear my impatience.

She looks toward the landing then back at me uncertainly, like she wants to say something but can't squeeze the words out.

"Go on, Katie. I'll be right there."

She shuffles along the ledge and disappears from the corner.

If she can do it, I can do it. I follow her path, keeping my eyes up and away from the ground that looks so far below.

"Zach," I hear Katie say from the landing, a little too loudly for my comfort.

"Almost there." I reach the corner, stand myself up, and immediately start shuffling sideways. In the corner of my eye I can see Katie standing stiffly on the landing.

I get to the railing and, steadying myself with one

hand on the rain gutter above the door, hop down onto the landing with a thump.

As soon as I turn around, I see what has frozen Katie this time.

Mike stands three steps down, staring up at us.

CHAPTER **23**

Mike's gray eyes are hard and suspicious. He has a foot propped a step above the other and his arms are spread open, one hand on the railing, the other pressed against the side of the garage, blocking the stairway and our escape route.

I stand dumbly next to Katie. I want to say something, give some explanation for why the Committee's security detail would *mistakenly* show up here looking for me, proclaim my innocence of anything bad. I also need to fill the silence, before Katie starts shooting her mouth off. I'm afraid of what she'll say to keep herself out of trouble.

But Mike speaks first, and his words surprise me. "Kid, I don't know what you did and I don't want to know." Rather than accusing and angry, his tone is helpful and concerned. "But you've really pissed off the Committee. They're looking for you."

This I did not expect. "You knew we were here? Why didn't you tell him?"

He takes a beat before answering, seeming to consider his weakness. "Unlike some people around here ..." he eyes Katie knowingly "... I don't want a police state running Arcanville. It's bad enough as it is ..."

"But Dante's gone," I say. "He believed you."

"Believes I don't know what's going on above my own garage? I don't think so." Mike glances over his shoulder. "He'll probably drive around the block and cruise by again. You've got maybe three minutes." He asks Katie, "Did you drive here?"

She shakes her head no.

Mike nods. "Good. You two can go out the back between the neighbors' hedges. Stay low and no one will see you."

"Thanks," I say.

Mike doesn't say, *"You're welcome."* He glares at Katie, not even trying to hide his suspicion, then back to me. "I'm counting on you not to cause me any more trouble."

"I won't be back," I say. "Just pretend you never saw me."

I bump Katie's arm to get her moving. I can't tell if she's scared stiff or contemplating saying something. Either way, I don't want her hanging around here any longer.

Mike has one more thing to say as he lets us pass on the stairs. "I haven't seen the Committee this riled up since ..." he trails off and I can guess he was about to mention my father's disappearance ten years ago amidst all the upheaval in the Committee. "Well, let's just say that if I were you, kid, I'd get the hell out of town."

I look back at Mike. "I'm working on it."

At the bottom of the steps I turn toward the back of the garage, Katie trailing me silently. I grab my backpack out of the shrubs far below my kitchen window, take one more look up at the razor-thin ledge I just climbed twice, and shake my head in disbelief. Then I lead Katie out of Mike's backyard and through the neighbor's hedges, crouching low.

Mike was right. This is good cover. The front of practically every house in town is the same—low brick walls and low-cut lawns. But the backyards on this block have thick gardens connected to one another by flowerbeds and mostly shielded by tall bushes.

Three yards down, we reach the end of the block and I stop.

Katie pokes me in the back. "What are you waiting for? Let's go!"

But I don't move, remembering Mike's warning about Dante. I wait ten seconds, twenty, and start wondering if Katie is right—we may just be sitting ducks here.

But after a few more seconds I hear a car engine round the corner. I duck low in the bushes and check Katie in the corner of my eye. Her eyes follow the sound of the tires passing by just beyond the hedge. When they're past, I peek through the branches and see Dante's black car turning the corner onto Mike's street.

Mike was off by a minute. But he was right—Dante didn't believe him. And he's hunting me.

CHAPTER 24

Ashley's bedroom is warm and the bedspread is pink. The princess styling of the room fits the softness I know is inside her. But I can only think that it was decorated a long time ago for a little girl, that she never had the chance to re-decorate once she became the hard-shelled teenager that the world knows. Or maybe she's kept it this way on purpose—to remind herself that despite the crushing horror she's been through, there's still a little girl who wants to live and be happy.

I slide my backpack off and set it on the end of her bed. A pillow with a bit of frill around the edges of the case lies at the head. I pick it up, press it to my nose, and draw a long breath. Lavender—the scented shampoo that Ashley and Katie use. The hint of Ashley all around makes my body ache.

Katie is downstairs. We came to her house so she could pick up her hospital ID. While she was busy I slipped in here just to be close to Ashley, or some sense of her. This is the longest Katie's been out of my sight since she showed up at my apartment, which makes me nervous. But I just needed a few minutes alone. The last couple of days have been a nonstop trip through the lowest ring of hell, and I'm afraid of what will happen to my mind if I don't get a break.

Worrying about my mental state is a habit from way back. Even before my mother took me away, she was acting strange. Dad's disappearance and supposed death broke something inside her. I was only seven, but I noticed it. And it got worse—scarier—as time went on. Her secret midnight visits to me at school, never saying when she was coming or when she would be back, and the constant whispers about "them" made me think she was schizophrenic. And if she could be, I could be.

Besides some money, the fear of mental illness was the only thing she left me when she died. Now I know she was sane for hating this town and risked a lot to take me away and disappear. So if she wasn't really crazy maybe I'm not crazy, but that doesn't erase the habit of worrying about it.

Thinking of Mom makes me sad and tired. I wish I could lie down on Ashley's bed and take a nap, but I don't have that kind of time. If I go to sleep here among Ashley's things, I'll never want to wake up.

I want to grab something that will remind me of her, something to hold on to until I can get back to her. I glance around, but there's nothing in this room that's personal to the Ashley I know.

I put the pillow down and step over to her desk, a white enameled thing with fancy brass handles on the drawers. Ashley's pink backpack rests against one of the curved legs. I bend down to pick it up. It's heavy, stuffed with textbooks.

She complained that her teachers were making her catch up on all the work she missed when she was in the psych ward last time. *"They punish you twice,"* she said. *"First they lock you up then they make you catch up on your schoolwork."*

Katie told me that Ashley was almost expelled from school for writing a paper about how a secret government runs the town and that the whole incident drove her to a nervous breakdown and a hospital stay. But I know what really happened. After a lifetime of testing and Pneuma experiments, Ashley was figuring out that the city government that picks up the trash and mows the lawns in the parks isn't in charge, that the Committee controls Arcanville, and she started talking about it. At the same time Sutton began asking questions about the Pythia Program.

The youth were getting out of control. They locked Ashley up to keep her quiet and juiced on those chemicals, hoping that the League's Board of Prophecy would accept her into the Pythia Program and she would be spirited off to the convent in Greece—a martyr to the cause and no longer the Committee's problem.

I unzip her pack and start shuffling through her books, hoping to find something small and portable among them. My fingers touch a wire binding and I pull out a spiral notebook. I glance around Ashley's desktop and see only three-ring binders for her school work. This one's definitely out of place, and its red cover is scratched and inked like one of Sutton's. Even though I can't find his name or initials anywhere, I'm sure it's his. The kid was obsessive about the kind of notebooks he used.

Another thing is different about this one. His other notebooks—the one I found at the coffee shop and the ones Ashley and I got from his backpack—sport weird blends of nature doodles and death art, blades of grass and leafy tree branches mingled with flaming sculls and staring black demon eyes. The etchings on the cover of this notebook, though, are just straight lines intersecting in an uneven grid, with one blank spot the size of a quarter near the center. It's not exactly like Sutton's others, yet it seems very familiar. It's a bad puzzle maze or maybe a map, like someone designing an imaginary road system.

I start to open the notebook when I hear footsteps on the stairs. Grabbing my backpack off Ashley's bed, I slip the notebook inside, vowing to examine it later. As I zip up my pack I see the half-open side pocket on Ashley's and tug the zipper the rest of the way open.

I quickly dig in, hoping to find a memento—a pen, a stick of lip balm. Anything that she held has value to me right now. My fingers touch something cool and bumpy. I grab hold and pull out a braided leather string with a knot on one end, a loop on the other, and eight small metal plates, each about half the size of my pinky nail, strung across the middle.

I turn the braid over against my knuckles and read the raised letters on the plates. N-A-M-E-L-E-S-S.

I smile as a tear stings my eye. It's Ashley's little joke. That day I cried on her shoulder in the rain outside Bobbie's back door, I revealed to her that Zachary White is not my real name. When she asked my real name I told her I didn't want to say because it could put her in danger. Sometime between that afternoon and the night we went into the library she made this bracelet for me.

I drape it over my wrist and feel the leather like Ashley's skin against mine. Lost in the moment, I roll my hand over and join the knot with the loop, pulling them tight so it won't come off. I turn my wrist up again and run my fingertips over the stamped letters, muttering the word, "Nameless," with a soft smile.

Katie's voice bursts the bubble. "Zach." She's at the doorway, staring in.

"What?" I snap reflexively, having forgotten about her footsteps on the stairs. The surprise in my voice announces I've been caught at something. Whether that something is finding a secret notebook or enjoying an intimate moment with an absent Ashley I don't know. Maybe both.

"We have to go." A purple courier bag is slung at her hip. She pats it with her hand. "I got us something to eat, but we can't stay here. My mom could come home anytime."

I don't know if Katie planned to lure me away from my memories of Ashley, but I can't resist. I haven't eaten since last night. With everything happening I didn't even realize I was hungry until now.

She notices me fingering the letters on the bracelet and eyes it suspiciously "What is that?"

I drop my hand out of view. "It's nothing," I say, meaning it's between Ashley and me and it's nothing I want to talk about with Katie.

She studies me for a long moment, accusation in her eyes, then shakes her head and turns into the hallway.

I take one last look at the bracelet, the gift Ashley made for me but never got the chance to present, and follow Katie out.

But the moment is tainted by a question in my mind. This notebook of Sutton's, covered with strange lines, was not in the backpack we took from his car. I haven't seen it before and Ashley never mentioned it, yet she had it in her things.

She told me that she never talked to Sutton because he was older and didn't talk to underclassmen. If that's true, how did she get hold of one of his notebooks? And why didn't she ever tell me about it?

CHAPTER 25

I munch on the sandwich and tiny carrots that Katie packed for me and try not to forget that I'm basically her prisoner. I also keep in the front of my mind that I'm pissed off at her in general. It's true she's doing something she doesn't want to do, going into the hospital to get my belongings, but I was planning to leave even without my stuff. She's keeping me around long enough to find out what I learned inside the library—and she's doing it with a threat to sic the Committee on me immediately if I don't do what she says. That's imprisonment of *some* kind.

If this works, though, it fits with my plan. We get my stuff, I tell her what she needs to know—and nothing more—then I leave. This isn't a defeat. I'll be coming back for Ashley later, stronger, with a better plan, and without Katie looking over my shoulder. It's a win. I have to think of it that way.

We sit on the bench, watching the back of the hospital. This spot across the parking lot is the place where the employees who smoke take their breaks and get some sun. It's empty now, between lunch and afternoon break, but I'm nervous that someone will see me sitting here and recognize me. I could be a legend around the hospital by now—or at least a topic of conversation.

It suddenly strikes me that this is a really stupid idea. I escaped from here just a few hours ago and now I'm back. People haven't even had time to forget my face, and I'm stepping right back into the place. I look at Katie, who's chewing the last bite of her sandwich and crumpling a paper towel in her hand. I think about sending her in alone with her pass card to find my stuff and bring it back. But I can't trust her. She's more than nosy, and all she'd need to figure out the importance of what I'm after is a computer to read the flash drive. Then I would be completely sunk.

Suddenly, her eyes focus on something by the building and I follow her stare. Three office workers step out of the back entry, one of them digging a pack of cigarettes out of her purse. Another, a man, already has a cigarette in his mouth, ready to light it as soon as they're far enough away from the building.

Katie stands up. "Let's go." She stalks off, away from the direction of the door and down the back row of cars.

I follow quickly and realize that she doesn't want to be seen by the people who just exited. I pull my hood over my head and hunch my shoulders, keeping my face down.

Katie turns left between two cars and glances back. "What are you doing?" she asks.

"I don't want to be recognized."

"That stupid hood will get more attention than your face," she hisses. "Pull it down."

I frown and slide the hood back onto my shoulders. She'd better be right or we're both in trouble.

Having dodged the employees who might have recognized her, Katie reaches into her pocket and slides out a plastic key card with a chrome clip attached. We get to the back entry, and without stopping, she swipes the card across a black box on a low post six feet from the door. With a blink of a tiny green light and a beep, the door clicks unlocked. It's all very smooth and proves that she belongs here.

As Katie reaches for the door handle, I glance up and see a small gray tube with a glass lens on the end pointing down at the entry—a camera. I can't help but wonder why she told me to pull my hood off when she must have known we'd pass under it. It could be clear photographic evidence later that she led me into the hospital. I realize that no matter what happens, Katie has the option of claiming that I somehow forced her to get me inside. So she doesn't care if my face is on video. I pull my eyes off the camera and follow her in, hunching my shoulders on instinct but knowing that it does no good.

Inside the entrance, Katie takes a sharp left and pushes through a heavy steel door with a slot of glass. The move surprises me and I wonder where she's leading me. I picture her marching me straight to the basement security office, shoving me in the door, and leaving me with a half-dozen scowling guards.

But she goes up instead of down. The big door slams behind us, sending a rumble through the stairwell echo chamber.

"Where are we going?" I ask.

She shushes me sharply. In a loud whisper she says, "To the third floor nurse's station."

"They took my stuff at the *Emergency Room*," I tell her.

"I know," she hisses back, "but it should have been brought up to the floor where your room was. If it didn't get to your room, it might have just gotten stuck at the nurse's desk."

"Are you sure?" I ask. I don't want to spend any more time than I have to in this trap.

"Yes!" Katie snaps back. "Do you think I do *surgery* when I volunteer here? I take people and their stuff from one ward to another and run files around. It's all they let us do."

At the next concrete landing, I know where we are— the second floor, which houses the hospital's psych ward and Ashley.

The memory from yesterday is as clear as a fresh nightmare. Ashley in her bed, begging me to get her out of there, me trying to unbuckle those heavy leather wrist straps, the nurse shouting at me, and them finally dragging me out as they jabbed her with a hypodermic needle and shot her out of her body again.

But yesterday I came down a stairwell on the other side of the building and navigated the hallways to get in. This is the back entrance and it must go right into the psych ward's hallway because a red-lettered sign on the windowless door reads:

RESTRICTED ACCESS
NO UNAUTHORIZED ENTRY
ALARM WILL SOUND

There's a black card reader next to the door, its tiny indicator light glowing red. I slow down and stare at the door, knowing what—*who*—is beyond it.

Katie rounds the railing and heads upward then stops. "What are you doing?" she asks.

I look up at her, feeling the nightmare jumping all over me. "Does your key card work on this door?"

She notices the door and what it means. "No," she says, pointing. "'Restricted.' That means not me—and not *you* either." She turns away as if erasing any thought of her sister. "Let's go."

In order to follow Katie up the stairs, I have to do a little bit of erasing too, just enough to drive the paralyzing ache out of my gut. Right now it's hard, but I worry that it will get easier every time I do it until, eventually, I forget about Ashley completely.

If I could talk to her right now I would tell her, *"I love you,"* and *swear* to her, *"I'll be back."*

CHAPTER 26

Katie stops at the third floor fire door. She takes the courier bag off her shoulders, sets it on the floor, and pulls her jacket off.

"Wait, this isn't the ward where you found me yesterday," I say. "They moved me overnight."

"I know," she says casually.

"You were keeping tabs on me?"

She ignores the question and I don't need to push it. Why should I be surprised she knows my moves? She probably came here this morning and found my new room empty then went straight to my apartment.

I watch anxiously as she straightens her hair and clips the plastic key card to the collar of her sweater. Now that it's turned around, I can see her picture and name—Katie Sloan—printed above the hospital logo. She reaches into her bag and produces a three-ring binder. She looks official enough for hospital business.

"What's the plan?" I ask.

She looks at me smartly. "I'm going up to the desk and ask for your belongings." End of plan. She sees the dismay in my face and says, "You stay here and watch my things. I'll be right back."

Crap! I don't want her going after my stuff alone. But I can't just go up to the nurse's station and show my face there. And I don't have a better plan, so I'm stuck watching Katie pull open the door and step through it.

I keep the door cracked as she goes. I don't see any staff or patients around to notice us sneaking around, just one nurse behind the desk halfway down the hall, leaning over some paperwork. The nurse looks up and sees her coming. My nerves spike, but Katie doesn't hesitate. She flashes her million-dollar smile, says a few words, and puts on a convincing show of checking an imaginary list inside the binder. She's good.

The nurse, a dark-skinned lady with white teeth, responds with a nod and a couple of words then disappears from the desk. Katie glances my way and, seeing me watching, snaps her eyes away. The nurse returns, handing Katie a big manila envelope—my stuff! Katie turns away from the desk with a smile. I close the door and wait.

A few seconds later the door opens and she slips through, checking the hallway behind her with a sigh.

The door clicks shut. I reach for the envelope, but she pulls it out of my reach.

"Hey," I complain.

"This isn't yours," she says.

"What do you mean?"

"Your stuff wasn't there. She wants me to deliver this."

"Let me see." I grab for it.

"No," she says, "it's confidential." She flips it, showing the red sticker that overlaps the flap. "If the seal is broken when it gets where I'm supposed to take it, I can get in trouble."

I eye her suspiciously.

"Do you think I want this envelope?" she snaps. "The nurse noticed I'm not here on my regular day. I told her I'm filling in for someone who's sick. Now I have to deliver this to someone else who'll notice I'm not supposed to be here and hope *they* don't give me an errand. They could keep me running until another volunteer sees me or I get caught by the volunteer coordinator."

"Then just get rid of it," I tell her.

"What, throw it in the garbage and pretend it doesn't exist? What happens when the nurse finds out I didn't take it where she told me? I'll get in trouble anyway."

I can see her point, but I'm still not happy about taking a side trip.

"I have to take this upstairs then we can go down to the ER and see if your stuff is there."

"What about the ward where my first room was?"

She shakes her head. "If it had made it there, it would have been passed on by now."

I don't know how this place works and she does. I just have to trust her—on this if nothing else. "Fine," I growl.

She points the envelope at me like a bayonet. "If you attract any attention and get me in trouble, I swear I'll scream for security and say you're holding a gun on me."

I spread my arms. "I don't have a gun."

"How could I know that?" she challenges me. "Maybe you told me there's one in your pocket and I'm so scared I believe you."

Jeez, aside from being afraid of heights, this girl has ice water in her veins. I shake my head. "All right," I grumble. "Where are we going?"

Katie reads the handwritten label on the front of the envelope. "Fourth floor, Intensive Care Unit."

ICU—that's where Screed is.

CHAPTER **27**

We stop at the fourth floor landing, outside the ICU. Katie hands me her bag and jacket and I don't have to ask about a plan. But this time when she opens the door the hallway is not empty. Dante and another guard—a man I've seen before—are walking straight for the door, both looking down at an open file folder in Dante's hand.

I reach for Katie's elbow to pull her back, but too late. She's out of the doorway and walking toward the two men. My mind says one thing: *She could tell them right now!*

My instincts take over. I step back. The door slams shut. My heel rocks over the edge of the step behind me. Dante and his man will reach the door in two seconds!

I turn and bounce down the stairs two at a time, throwing away whatever stupid trust I'd put in Katie. I'm trying to reach the first-floor exit and get out of the hospital ahead of them, but I only make it down one story.

My feet hit the concrete landing of the third floor and I turn the corner downward. At the same time, the latch upstairs snaps and the door opens with the metallic scrape of a jail cell gate, stopping me in my tracks.

I stand stiff, one hand locked on the railing, my head spinning, my lungs heaving. Half of me wants to keep running because Katie told them I'm here. The other half is afraid that if she didn't tell them, the echo of my footsteps will. I'm paralyzed with indecision. I wait to hear Katie's accusing voice directing Dante to see me, grab me, lock me up for kidnapping her.

Instead I hear a man's voice, murmuring with concern. No footsteps on the stairs, just shuffling as the two guards arrange themselves on the landing.

I force my breath to slow and look up through the angular gap between railings. I see a black-clad shoulder—Dante—then the back of his buzz-cut head then his ear then the side of his face. He's turning to look down and check if anyone's in the stairwell with them.

If I can see him he'll be able to see me! I push myself away from the railing. My foot slips off the metal edge of the step, but the door upstairs closes at the same time, covering the scrape of my shoe. I pull it back up, willing no noise to float up to them.

After a silent moment, Dante says, "It's clear." Then, "Well, what do you think?"

In the vault-like stairwell I can hear his companion's response like he's standing next to me. "Coma," he says hopelessly. "This is bad." I detect a trace of an accent but can't quite place it.

I can, however, put the voice together with the face I just saw in the hallway. This is the guard who was driving the security cart the other night, who stopped his partner from gunning me down with two words—"No! Alive!"

Dante sighs. "Tell me something I *don't* know, Poole. I didn't figure Screed for a car accident casualty. He's more of a knife-in-the-ear kind of guy." His voice is tired and worn, like he's sick of his life but can't stop living it.

"He's not dead yet," Poole points out.

"Tell the League that. It's Red Alert in Arachova."

I know from the letter I stole from Screed that Arachova, Greece, is where the League has its headquarters. It's near the original site of Delphi and the location of the convent where they keep the Pythias.

"What are they planning to do?" Poole's inflection is light and song-like—African or Caribbean.

"They said yesterday they're sending someone to take over." I read the frustration in Dante's voice. "Should be here in a couple of days."

"They didn't offer you the job?"

Dante's silence is his answer—no. I can feel his anger vibrating in this concrete cavern.

"Permanent?" Poole asks.

Dante remains silent. I imagine him shrugging in dismay.

"Help from headquarters," Poole says thoughtfully. "Game-changer."

"Yes, the game has definitely changed," Dante scoffs. "Quietest chapter in the League for ten years—now, boom, a possible intruder in the library and the security chief half-dead on the riverbank."

"*Possible* intruder?" Poole says.

CHRIS EVERHEART

"Yeah!" Dante says sharply. "Possible, *unconfirmed.* I don't care what Screed said, no one got through the entrances past us."

"You think he was going on a hunch?" Poole asks.

More frustration from Dante. "He wouldn't have hit the alarm on a hunch, knowing the hell it would raise from Arachova."

"But you just said …"

"I know what I said, damn it!" Dante snaps.

"OK." Poole speaks patiently, trying to soothe his boss. "I checked all the video. You were right. None of the cameras show anyone in the garage, the hallways, or the stairwells." The way he pronounces words gives his voice a quality of kindness that Dante doesn't have and doesn't respond to.

"But somehow Screed knew *exactly* who he was looking for," Dante says gruffly. "Gave me the description when he came out of the garage—young male, five-ten, dark hair. Too specific to be a phantom."

"That describes a third of the teen boys in town," Poole says. "Do we have anything else to go on?"

Dante pauses, seeming to think. "Last week, Screed had me pull a couple of computers out of the public library, didn't say why. Maybe it has something to do with that. He was working on something, trailing someone."

"Who?"

"I don't know," Dante sighs. "The bastard wouldn't tell me anything."

"You're sure this Zachary White kid is the one he thought was inside?"

"Do I sound like I'm *sure* about anything, Poole? We chase a kid across campus, he hurts a guard then gets away from you guys, disappears. Now, this morning I find out this kid was brought to the ER that night and later said he got hit by a car ..."

"Same kid," says Poole.

"Probably. But you got a look at him. You can ID him for sure."

"Eh, it was pretty dark," Poole hedges. "*Maybe* if I saw him in person again."

I think of that night when Poole and I saw each other. It wasn't *that* dark. I could see his face clearly. Maybe the conditions were in my favor, though, and I got a better look at him than he did at me.

Poole has another question for Dante. "Why didn't we know the kid was here, in the hospital?"

"The police found him limping around downtown the night of the chase. He was all scuffed up and incoherent, in shock. He was blocks away from Screed's wreck and didn't say he was hit by a car until he woke up yesterday. Police didn't put them together, didn't report him to us."

Downtown? I don't remember that. Screed's car flew over me as I lay on the sidewalk with his grill marks on my back. I can still see the black undercarriage crashing over the bridge railing and disappearing into the void. Then the sound of the car smashing and twisting on the riverbank below. Then I passed out. But I guess, even though my knee was messed up, I got up and walked into downtown. Where was I going? I only have one guess—to Bobbie's Coffee Shop to get my bike and ride to safety.

"Who found him?" Poole asks.

I hear paper shuffling—Dante looking through the file folder. "Uh ... Billings, squad sergeant, called an ambulance for him."

Billings, the cop who came to Bobbie's when Connor wiped out, who arrived at the bridge seconds too late when Sutton threw himself off, and now was responsible for getting me to the hospital after Screed ran me down. That cop might be the only adult looking after the kids in this town.

"Police patrols weren't looking for the kid?" Poole asks.

"They *would have been* if Screed had alerted them," Dante grumbles. "Cops didn't have a clue that we had a problem on campus. Screed didn't want anyone to know someone had gotten into the library."

"*If* someone got in," Poole reminds him. Then, "Wait a minute. If the police didn't report the kid to us, how did you find out about him?"

"Got a tip."

"From ..." Poole says expectantly.

"Text. From a blocked number," he says. "Same as the tip on the Sloan girl."

I know exactly who told Dante how to find me—*Katie!*

CHAPTER 28

My head explodes. After Screed's crash, Katie sent an anonymous text to Dante, telling him that Ashley had been in the library and was at home, getting ready to run away. It was the perfect opportunity to get Ashley out of her hair. Then, when I didn't respond to her threats yesterday Katie figured I'd never tell her about the list, so she texted Dante again this morning telling him I was the reason Screed crashed.

"As soon as I got the message I came over," Dante says. "Turns out the kid was here in the ICU half of the first day, three doors over from Screed's bed. If I had known, I could have locked him down then. But it's so messed up around here, the staff didn't even know what room he ended up in."

I guess Katie left out the details. Holding back information to use later? Smart.

Dante continues complaining. "By the time they figured it out, he was gone. Staff doesn't know what happened to him."

Katie is making some really tight plays. She came to my apartment to threaten me one last time and squeeze the names out of me, knowing that when Dante found

117

my hospital bed empty, he would be right behind her at my place to grab me.

"After I missed him here I did what Screed should have done night before last," Dante explains, "alerted the Arcanville police. Then Glenn and I went to his apartment. Nothing."

I picture Katie waving her cell phone in my face, threatening to call Mrs. Bradford. Then her innocent act when Dante showed up in the parking lot. *"I didn't call anyone."* Those big blue eyes ... I fell for it, the whole game. But she didn't plan on my counter-offer. I guess she decided the names were more valuable than seeing me taken away in handcuffs—valuable enough to follow me right out the window.

"Glenn's trying to track his identity and has gotten nothing so far," Dante says. "No parents either, by the way. I've got someone watching the place in case he goes home. When I catch him I'll squeeze him like sponge."

"But Dante, we don't even know that kid was inside the library," Poole says.

"You don't think the whole thing is suspicious? Seventeen-year-old living on his own? No known family in Arcanville? And he takes off from the hospital without being discharged, without saying anything to anybody?"

Poole responds calmly. "I'm just saying, maybe Screed got a false alarm from inside the office. Then a kid out past curfew, wandering through campus, gets scared by a bunch of amped-up security guys and runs to avoid trouble."

"Screed's dangerous," Dante says, "but he's not stupid. If he hit the alarm and then went and ran down a kid with his car, he had his reasons. Something's going on. I just don't know what yet. And I can't afford to be wrong."

Dante is silent a long time. When he finally speaks, his voice is determined. "Screed dropped the ball, Poole. If he was onto a possible threat, he should have followed protocol and reported it to Arachova."

"You're sure he didn't?"

"If they know anything, they're hiding it well. They sound as confused as we do. Screed should have at least told *me* about it so I could help. Then he screwed up again by not alerting the police department for backup that night. He let this kid slip away." Dante's voice turns bitter. "Whoever Arachova sends to help out, I'm going to make damned sure they know that Screed messed up."

"And that'll get you his job?"

"Not quite." Dante pauses. Their feet shuffle on the landing.

I press myself harder against the wall, praying they don't look down and see the tips of my toes parked a floor below.

When Dante speaks again, his voice is hungry. "I pulled you aside because you're one of the few people I trust around here, Poole. We have a couple of days before Screed's replacement gets here. I need to have that kid by then. And if he was inside the library the other night, he'll be a corpse within 48 hours of ..."

The fire door pops open with a steel SNAP! cutting Dante off. Someone has walked in on the conversation.

My mind goes off a cliff with the end of Dante's sentence. I'll be "a corpse within 48 hours of ..." *what?*

"Mr. Dante?" It's Katie's voice.

Dante doesn't answer. I cringe, waiting for my name to echo around this chamber. After two seconds of dead air, the door clicks closed. I think about running.

Katie speaks again, unsurely. "Um ... the doctor is asking for you at Mr. Screed's room."

After another stretch of silence, Katie's feet hit the steps and start descending. Knowing that she's in eye contact with Dante and Poole while I can't see them is torture. She could have passed a note while saying the doctor thing as cover in case I'm listening. She could be waving a silent signal to them now—*"Follow me. Zach's down here!"*

The shuffling of the men's feet adds to Katie's footsteps. The door opens. Instead of rushing down the stairs, though, it sounds like they're stepping back into the ICU hallway.

I let out a breath as Katie hits the landing a half-flight above me and her foot drops into view. She's out of their sight now and heading my way.

I think of the night I went to her house for our date and how hurt and angry Ashley was. But when Katie came bouncing down the staircase with her blue eyes and that million-dollar smile aimed at me, nothing else mattered.

But now, as she descends this sterile stairwell, there's no smile. She sees me on the steps and pins me with a glare.

Then I hear the footsteps above, starting to follow her down.

CHAPTER 29

When I see Katie's intense expression and hear the footsteps following her—Poole's, no doubt—I know I've waited here too long. I should have snuck down to the first floor exit while I had the chance.

I turn and move down the stairs, hearing her hiss behind me—not my name or any other word, just trying to get my attention. But I'm not slowing down for her. I turn the corner at the landing and catch a glimpse of her frantically waving hand. Trying to slow me down or speed me up? I don't care.

Halfway down the next flight of steps I hear muffled voices behind the windowless second floor fire door. The conversation is growing louder and I can tell that at least two people are coming toward the stairs. I speed my feet, trying to hit the landing before they do, but it's too late.

With the beep of an electronic lock, the door opens and the voices of two women echo into the stairwell. I see the fingers of the first one curl around the door's edge as she pushes it open. I'm trapped.

The red sign looms in front of me:
RESTRICTED ACCESS
NO UNAUTHORIZED ENTRY
ALARM WILL SOUND

I slip behind it and press myself into the corner. The lead woman in pink scrubs leaves the doorway, her back to me, and takes the steps down followed by another in a white lab coat and dress pants. Their banter sounds friendly, but I'm too panicked to actually hear what they're saying.

Footsteps echo off every steel and concrete surface. The two women have exited the psych ward and are heading slowly down the stairs. If I go that way they might recognize me from yesterday and scream.

I look up the stairs to see Katie swooping down on me. Her eyes are on fire and she's bearing her teeth in rage or frustration. Poole's footsteps follow her. I look from her to the women turning downward at the lower landing. I'm completely trapped, frozen in the corner and thinking any move I make will be a mistake.

I finally decide to go down the steps when I see Katie's lips move. Over and over she's mouthing the word "Wait!"

Wait?

Her feet hit the landing, Poole's sounding a half-flight behind. Without slowing down even a heartbeat, she grabs my elbow and pulls me out of the corner, stops the closing fire door and yanks me through it.

The door slams behind us and we're standing in the silent hallway of the psych ward. I take a breath to say so, but Katie holds up a silencing hand and points one ear at the door.

I stare at it, trying to listen along, but have to wait for the rush of blood to subside from my ears. Gradually I can make out the voices of the two women fading toward the first floor. Then Katie's shoulders tense and she goes stiff.

I hold my breath as heavy footfalls thump louder and louder on the stairs beyond. For one excruciating second, the sound is suspended. My mind's eye sees Poole stopping and staring at the other side of the door, convinced by some predatory instinct that we're standing just inches away, waiting to be caught.

The next footstep finally lands. Then the next and the next, getting quieter. Poole is following the women down the stairs. His echoing footsteps finally disappear and leave the stairwell silent.

"What the hell?" I whisper to Katie. "That guy was right behind you."

"What, was I supposed to stop him from coming down the stairs?" she whispers back.

"You were leading him right to me."

Katie shrugs. "I thought you'd be gone. Why didn't you run when they came out?"

"I …" I don't want to say I froze in panic so I let the sentence die. I should just be glad she pulled me out of Poole's path.

The hunter has passed us by, but I realize we can't stand here much longer. A staff member will show up within seconds and find two kids who absolutely do not belong in this high-security corridor.

Katie glances unsurely at the black box mounted on the wall next to the door, its tiny indicator light glowing red. She swallows hard and pulls her key card off her sweater collar.

I touch her hand to stop her, remembering what she said earlier—"'Restricted.' That means not me ..." If she's not authorized to access the door from the outside then her card probably won't work from the inside either. And worse, it might set off an alarm.

She gives me a shrug and a sharp glare that says, "What else can we do?!"

I have an idea, one that Katie won't like—which makes it all the more appealing to me. We can't get out of here until an *authorized* person opens this door. And it's time she sees what her sister has been going through, what she's done by turning her in. I grab her elbow and pull her toward the only room on this floor that I know—204. Ashley's room.

CHAPTER 30

Just a few steps from the fire door, we slip into Ashley's room and stop at a white curtain surrounding her bed.

I get a knot of anger in my stomach. The staff is trying to hide her from passersby and she has only a thin, blank wall to stare at when she wakes up. It must terrify her to be cut off from everyone.

I reach for the edge of the curtain but Katie grabs my arm, hesitation in her eyes. She doesn't want to see Ashley in here. I wonder if it's because she feels sorry for her or that she doesn't want to face what she's done to her own sister.

I shrug her hand off and pull back the curtain. I immediately wish I hadn't. Ashley lies dead in her bed — or she *looks* dead. Her face is a pale gray that I've only seen in zombie movies. Her eyes are narrow slits, crusted around the edges, and staring unblinkingly into infinity. The shallow pumping of her chest is the only indication of life.

Katie shrinks away with a gasp.

Ashley looks way sicker than yesterday. And there's something else that's new — a heart and breath monitor standing next to the bed, its tentacles snaking into her hospital gown. I wonder if that means she's dying. Or maybe as they flood her veins with more Pneuma, they need the monitors to tell when they're near killing her.

My body goes as dry as gravel, from my core outward. I might crumble into a pile on this spot. But I don't care. I reach for Ashley's hand, which is buckled into the same restraints as yesterday, though now they hardly seem necessary. Her skin is as cold as ice, but I thread my fingers with hers anyway, hoping to transfer some body heat. The ache in my chest presses a groan out of my mouth.

Ashley's eyes flutter and she turns her face toward the sound — consciousness!

"Ashley," I sigh.

"Zaaaach …" she breathes, her mouth opening barely wider than her eyes. "You … came …" Her weak breath runs out, or maybe the thought evaporated halfway through saying it.

Beside me, Katie comes out of her shock and reaches to the foot of the bed. She pulls Ashley's chart out of the box, and flips it open like a doctor. I ignore her. What good will it do? If she'd listen I could tell her exactly what's going on with her sister.

I try to stammer a few words of comfort to Ashley. "Don't worry …"

But before I can say anything more, the bed begins to rumble. First it's a low vibration. Then the side rails start to rattle. Some comical part of my brain thinks, *"Earthquake!"* But the quiver under Ashley's blankets tells me that she is the epicenter.

The monitor next to her bed beeps once, an alarm that sends a jolt through me. Noise, attention—we don't need it. I grip Ashley's hand, wishing to stop the convulsion. But the vibration rolls up her body in a wave, growing more violent the closer it gets to her brain, until her chest and head are rattling so hard I'm scared her neck will break.

The monitor beeps again and I lean close to Ashley's ear. "Shhhh," I try to soothe her, despite my own panic. She keeps rumbling. "Shhhh …" I whisper again.

After one more beep of the monitor, she responds. The rumble slows and the bed stops rattling. Her head and chest calm, taking the strain off her neck, and her body goes slack as she lets out a long breath. No more beeps.

I glance at Katie, who stares at Ashley curiously. With a sigh of relief, I stand up. We're quiet for now, but we need to figure out what to do next.

Suddenly Ashley comes to life. Without warning, her lungs vacuum in a huge, sharp breath and she snaps upright on the bed. The surge of her body and the piercing beam of her hot brown eyes shock me backward.

Katie gasps, slapping the metal clipboard against her chest like a shield.

Reanimated with a burst of energy, Ashley is stopped from flying off the bed only by the leather straps on her wrists and ankles. Her deathly gray skin is instantly burned through by a surge of pink, as if an inner light has been switched on.

When she turns her eyes to me, they are wide open and clear with the sight of eternity, focused on a dimension beyond this one. She looks at me like I'm a fascinating ghost. I stare back like she's a mirror-faced monster.

I want to run but her hand is a vise, squeezing my interlaced fingers at unnatural and painful angles. My knuckles are about to pop apart but I can't pull out of her grip.

I steal a glance at Katie, who stands petrified at the foot of the bed, unable to move, even if she is capable of forming a thought to run.

The heart monitor is alive again too, reporting the strain on its wires with a loud BEEP BEEP BEEP that doesn't stop. The lines on the screen are now spiking wildly. No nurse could ignore this alarm. Someone will be here any second.

Ashley twitches and a deep, fluttering groan rises from her chest. It echoes around the room, pressing my insides the same way she's squeezing my hand.

My mind drains of everything but *this, now.*

She stares deep into my eyes. Her lips move and words come out in a voice with the authority of the underworld. She recites a poem:

> *"Under the white stones of youth*
> *Eternal guarded you'll find*
> *The key to the secrets from Apollo's mind*
> *The gods give the brave a half-week's time*
> *To delve the deep ..."*

She jerks her head, locks eyes with Katie, and finishes her oracle.

> *"And save this line."*

I'm dumbstruck. My heart thuds against my empty lungs, demanding oxygen. Three feet away, Katie stands like a statue, staring at a version of Ashley she's never seen before.

Ashley pulls her eyes away from Katie and looks down to our interlocked hands and the "Nameless" band on my wrist. She lifts her gaze to me. A flash of the Ashley I know crosses her face with an expression of love and a small plea for help that stabs me in the heart. Then it's gone and the infinity-eyed prophetess returns.

She hovers a moment, staring into another dimension, then the switch is flipped again and all the energy and air holding her up vanishes. She deflates like a plastic bag and sags back into the bed. The color of life drains from her face, and her eyes drift back into barely open slits. Her lips keep moving though, muttering unintelligible words as if the flow of visions I triggered just keeps trickling out.

I pull in the breath that left me a minute ago and check the heart monitor. The spikes are slackening but not enough to stop the beeping alarm.

In the hallway a loud tone comes over the speakers, followed by a woman's calm voice. "Janice, please check a monitor alarm in 204."

Another woman's voice, too close to the door calls back, "I'm there, Nora!"

Katie's eyes are frozen on mine. I can see the calculations running in her mind but I don't have time to wonder what they'll add up to. That nurse will be here in two seconds to check on Ashley and she'll find us standing here like burglars waiting to be caught.

CHAPTER 31

I jerk my head toward the bathroom door's open a crack behind us. The inside is even darker than this dim room. Katie glances around, searching for an alternative, trying to stay in control. But if she stands there and gets me caught, neither of us gets what we want.

Another half-second of deliberation and two more footsteps outside. Katie blinks in frustration and turns to the door. It squeaks on its hinges, but the noise is covered by the sound of Nurse Janice's approach. I follow her into the cell, and ease the door closed, leaving a crack.

Janice enters the room and Ashley's heart monitor stops beeping, interrupting my fear with silence. I can hear Ashley's low, nonsensical muttering. It breaks my heart that this intelligent girl who was so right about everything has been reduced to a babbling puddle in a hospital bed.

"What is *going on* with you, young lady?" Nurse Janice asks Ashley gently. "You're sweating." Her tone is the one you use when you really don't expect an answer.

But Ashley manages to get a few words out. "I wanna go," she groans. "I wanna go with Z ..."

"Shhh." Janice cuts her off. "You're safe here."

I stifle a laugh at the idea that she's safe in the hands of these people.

Ashley moans. "Nooo, he came back for me. Zach came back."

I shift my eyes to see Katie staring at me in the minimal light. I give a small shrug.

"That was yesterday," says Janice. "He was trying to kidnap you. But we saved you. You're safe."

"Nooo," says Ashley, "he's here ..."

Another woman enters the room—Nora, who was giving orders from the loudspeaker. "What's going on?"

"She's agitated," says Janice. "Heart and respiration are up, she's sweating."

"It's that new compound they're giving her," Nora says. "It's stronger than the others, lasts longer too."

"She's getting harder to manage. The sedatives aren't working like they used to." Janice's voice has a note of hopelessness. "When she was younger, a small dose would put her out. Now ..."

How long have these nurses known Ashley? How many years of experimentation have they participated in, along with the doctors and the Committee and the League?

"I'll up the sedative," says Nora, her footsteps moving to the bed. I hear the hollow pop of a plastic cap coming off a syringe. She probably keeps the thing in her pocket all the time, ready to shoot Ashley down at any moment. A few seconds later, with a rattle of plastic on plastic Nora drops the empty syringe into the disposal box on the wall. It's done.

The room is quiet except for Ashley's fading mumbles.

Janice finally speaks. "Do you think everything she says is true?"

"I don't know," Nora sighs. "Even when you can understand the words, it's all riddles. Besides, it's way above our pay grade. You should know by now not to ask questions about this one." Nora's footsteps cross to the door. "The sedative should take effect in a few minutes. Get her cleaned up then you can go on break."

"It's just ..." Janice stammers, "... I mean ... is that compound *safe*?"

"I hope so," Nora says coldly, her voice fading into the hallway, "because they're doubling her dose tomorrow."

CHAPTER 32

My relief at hearing Nora exit the room turns to dread as Nurse Janice's footsteps approach the bathroom door. "OK, now let's clean you up," she says.

I squeeze into the corner, pushing Katie harder into the doorjamb. My heart thumps as the door swings in on us. The light snaps on, stinging my eyes. I reach for the handle to ease the door open and keep it from bouncing off the toes of my shoes.

A plastic tub thunks into the sink then the hiss of the faucet fills the tiny room. Man, I just want Janice to leave!

Now that we're this close to Ashley and I have help, maybe we can get her out of here. But it's way more than Katie agreed to in coming to the hospital. Rescuing Ashley was not on her agenda, and I doubt she's changed her mind.

Janice goes back into the room and drags a chair across the floor. Next comes the swishing and dripping of a washcloth being dipped into the tub of water and wrung out.

But Janice doesn't just wash Ashley. As she works, she talks to her patient. "What do you see, Ashley?" she asks gently. "Do you see the future?" This time she wants an answer.

And I'm hoping for a clue to where Ashley's words are coming from.

When Ashley responds, her voice is hollow and weak, like answering a question is not a choice, even though she doesn't have a single volt of energy left in her.

> *"In the invisible realm*
> *Past and future are dreams*
> *The wise one knows*
> *Beyond what is seen*
> *The Pythia considers*
> *The threads between."*

Katie shudders as she listens. It's like Ashley is speaking a foreign and mysterious language.

After a long moment, Janice says cautiously, "You know about romance. I heard you talking to the doctor about it."

Ashley doesn't answer. Water from the cloth rains into the tub.

Janice goes on, another notch of desperation in her voice. "You see, my daughter is engaged and I ... I'm not sure about him. Is he the right one for her? Should she marry him?"

Katie scowls at me as if to ask, *"Why is she asking Ashley all this stuff?"*

I shake my head, warning her not to react. She's still confused, doesn't understand the Pneuma compound or its purpose—giving sight beyond here and now.

This nurse knows it, though, and she's *exploiting* Ashley.

My heart sinks as Ashley starts another poem. Whatever takes over her mind through the Pneuma is talking in ways the girl never would, and she's a prisoner to it.

"All visiting must advance with care ..." Ashley moans.

Janice gasps. "That's his name ... Vance!"

> *"Who welcomes to the house hides a stranger there.*
> *The smile is to the window*
> *But a candle's glow*
> *The illusion of lightness*
> *And warmth all through."*

"I knew it," Janice breathes. "I just had a *feeling* about him."

With another squeeze of the towel the nurse continues her work. But she can't help herself. This time, I can hear the shame in her voice. "I've applied for a supervisor job. Will I get it?"

"Leave her alone!" I want to shout. But I hold myself in place, mouth shut.

When Ashley answers, her voice is thin, sleepy. *"A woman leading*

The most important one ..." she exhales,

"... Is followed by many ..." She trails off into silence.

"What? What does that mean?" Janice whispers desperately. "Is that a yes? Is there more?"

But it's no use. Ashley is asleep.

After a long moment, the feet of Janice's chair scrape the floor and her footsteps move into the bathroom. She sniffs twice before dumping the tub and runs the water for a few seconds.

Katie stares into the corner where she can see Ashley through the crack between the hinges.

When Janice turns the water off, she's still sniffling, crying softly. And why not? It sounds like her daughter is about to marry a creep. She heard what she asked for but she didn't like it. And she didn't even come close to finding out about her promotion.

I feel some satisfaction that she didn't get *all* of her selfish questions answered.

After a moment composing herself, she switches off the light and steps back into the room. She picks up the phone, takes one last long sniff, and dials.

"Nora, I'm going to lunch, heading out the back. See you in an hour." She hangs up the phone and sighs over Ashley. We hear the sharp slide of plastic guides on the metal rail as she pulls the screen around the bed. I left the curtain open and I'm glad they didn't notice.

When her footsteps head into the hallway, I bump Katie's elbow and tip my head. Not wanting to be seen crying, the nurse is doing us the biggest favor we'll get all day — heading out the back door.

Abandoning any idea of getting Ashley out now, I slip around the bathroom door. Katie follows me, one hand on my elbow. I stare at the white screen as I pass, resisting the urge to rip the curtain back and grab Ashley. My heart stings at the thought of leaving her here. But if

Katie and I hope to get off this floor without handcuffs on our wrists, we have to take this opportunity.

I hear the beep of the electronic lock in the hallway. Janice has waved her key card and let herself out. To me it's the crack of a starter pistol—the seconds to our exit closing start ticking down.

Five … I move to the door and glance into the hallway. Up by the desk, a nurse is walking away from our direction—Nora?

Four … I step into the corridor and Katie's hand leaves my elbow. I turn back to see her staring at the screen as if a monster is sleeping on the other side.

Three … I should leave Katie here, in the asylum she's doomed her sister to.

Two … I still need my flash drive, so I reach back and grab Katie's arm, pulling her along behind me.

One … We make it to the door within an inch of closing.

I jam my toe into the narrowing crack and shoulder it open enough for us to get through. We're on the landing and out of sight.

But just before the door snaps shut, I hear a voice in the hallway behind us yell, "Hey!"

CHAPTER 33

We can't afford to kid ourselves—Nora's cry of alarm was about us. On the landing, I move for the steps, wanting to bolt.

But Katie holds tight to my elbow, stopping me. I quickly understand why. Janice's descending footsteps echo below. We can't just go sprinting past her on the stairs. But the door behind us will pop open within seconds and Nora will be all over us. I look at Katie and wonder how long she'll keep us here.

When Janice's footfalls near the bottom of the lower staircase, though, Katie releases my elbow and follows me down. Luckily, Janice is in a hurry to get out of the building. I imagine tears streaming down her face as she rushes to her car where she can let it all out in private.

So that's what direct contact with an oracle can do, all that coded truth revealed to the asker can really break her down. I'm also experiencing the confusion of one of those cryptic messages, because what Ashley said to Katie and me didn't make any sense. The *way* she said it, though, convinces me that it's important.

I run it through in my mind so I can remember it:

"Under the white stones of youth
Eternal guarded you'll find
The key to the secrets from Apollo's mind
The gods give the brave a half-week's time
To delve the deep
And save this line."

What does it mean?

The first-floor door opens below. By the time we turn the corner onto the last run of steps Janice has gone out.

Above us I hear the psych ward door pop open and Nora call, "Janice?"

Katie snaps her eyes up at the echoing voice, but Nora can't see us as we slip out the door.

Out in the hallway, I turn toward the employee exit. Katie tugs my elbow the other way. I want to escape out the back, but through the glass I see a woman in scrubs—Janice—scurrying away toward the parking lot.

"Not yet," Katie says. "ER."

"But …" I poke my thumb back at the stairs.

"We're in deep either way. Come on." Katie pulls me toward the central corridor of the hospital, past two doctors and a couple of nurse assistants. One staff member recognizes her and nods then takes too long a look at me as we pass. I try to ignore it.

Katie stops at the corner where a line of folded wheelchairs stand next to the plastic railing. She pulls one free and pops it open. "Get in."

"What?" We'll be too slow if she has to push me around. I glance back down the corridor, looking for Nora poking her head out the door.

"Get in and shut up." Katie's impatient, confident in her idea.

I grit my teeth and sit down.

She yanks my hood over my head and orders, "You're sick. Act like it."

I slump in the chair, half blinded as she pushes me down the hallway. She knows the hospital better than I do, so I hope she's really taking me to the ER like she says. A manila file folder lands on my lap, startling me, and I realize she grabbed it from somewhere to complete our disguise. Now it looks like she's just doing her volunteer work—transporting a patient and his file from one place to another.

After a couple of turns, she guides the chair into a noisy hallway and slows down. It must be the ER. I'm ready to jump up and start searching for my stuff, but Katie puts a hand on my shoulder.

I lift my eyes just enough to see what she's slowed down for. Under the rim of my hood, I see two pairs of black boots and black fatigue pants strutting the floor in front of us. The security men are not speaking so I can't tell if either of them is Dante or Poole and I can't exactly ask Katie for commentary right now.

The chill of fear runs down my body as I wait. This plan—this relationship—is flawed, but it's all I've got right now. I have to trust her.

Katie pulls the wheelchair to a stop as the black boots keep walking out of my limited view. We've stopped at a corner. I turn my head in a question to Katie.

"Hold on," she says, lifting the file folder from my

lap and opening it. She's pretending to study the folder while surveying the activity in the ER.

After fifteen, twenty, thirty seconds that seem like forever, she speaks again, under her breath. "You see this corner on the right?"

I nod.

"When I say go, stand up and turn that way. Then, quick, walk about four steps straight ahead through the doorway. I'll follow you."

I nod again and wait. Every noise around me cranks up the tension. And wait. Every footstep seems to come straight at me. And wait. Every voice is about to shout my name.

Sweat itches my upper lip as I pray that someone who knows Katie doesn't stop for conversation or to give her an errand or to ask her what she's doing here today—or that the black boots don't come back and recognizing us. I'm about to burst with fear.

"Go," Katie says.

Without thinking I snap out of the chair. Keeping my hood pulled down, I turn right and walk forward quickly, hoping I don't run into a wall or trip over my own feet. Within a few steps I see the bottom of the doorway she described and go through it. The light instantly fades and I realize I'm walking into some kind of unlit closet. I stop when I see the shadowy bottom of a shelving rack at the back of the room.

Dead end. The door closes behind me.

CHAPTER 34

I turn around and peer into the murky light. Katie stands inside, blocking the glow from the narrow window slotted into the door. We stare at each other for a few seconds, waiting for our eyes to adjust to the dark.

After a minute, I can see well enough to make out the shelves and their contents. On one side, first aid supplies like gauze pads and elastic bandages, all wrapped in sterile paper and held in open boxes, are stacked to the ceiling. One compartment at the bottom is a parking spot for a waist-high laundry bin. In the shadows I can see that it's full of used scrubs. On the right side, clipboards and plastic-wrapped forms, pens, and office supplies fill the shelves.

"Is this the place?"

"Yes, and we have to hurry." Katie steps to the right, pulling out her cell phone to use the screen as a flashlight.

On the middle shelf, an open file box made of gray-painted metal stretches across one full section. Each of the four compartments is separated by five or six laminated cards with a single letter on a protruding tab. About half of the cards have one or more clear plastic envelopes behind them.

Katie pokes her fingers into the last compartment, behind the letter W and pulls out the single envelope. She stops and stares at it.

"What?" I demand.

She hands me the envelope and holds the glow of her phone over it. I peer in through the plastic. It holds a brown wallet, a couple of white letter-sized envelopes stuffed with papers, a few coins, and a gold ring the size of a fat finger—a wedding band. I stare in disbelief at the slip of paper inside reading "Walters, Charles E."

"No!" I snap. "Where's my stuff?"

Katie shushes me and glances nervously out the window slot.

I squint into the dim light and search the compartment, flipping every card from T through Z. I grope into the gloom at the bottom of the box to make sure my wallet and flash drive aren't lying loose in there. Nothing.

"What the hell?" I hiss at Katie. I dive into the neighboring compartment, checking M through S, just in case.

Katie stands there, looking helpless and confused. "I ... thought for sure it would be here. This is where they bring the patients' things."

"This is *bullshit!*" I wheeze, trying to keep my voice low, but failing. "You said it would be here."

"I said it *should* be here because it never got to your room," Katie hisses back.

"I can't believe it. Why would you do this to me? You brought me in here with security all around ..."

"It was *your* idea," she shoots back.

"You said my stuff was here." It feels like the hospital is pressing in on me. I'm trapped. My hope collapses and all that's left is rage. I can't control it. My jaw clenches and my hands twist into claws. I take a menacing step toward her. "I want my ..."

Before I see it coming, Katie's foot flies up and slams squarely into my crotch.

Jolted with a million volts of pain I drop to my knees, muffling a moan of deep agony.

"Back off!" she growls. "I didn't want to come here in the first place."

I press the heel of one hand into my lower gut as if it will stop the icy ache. The pain shoots up my body, through my stomach and throat, deep into my head. I want to curl up like a baby until my balls dislodge from my rib cage.

By the time I can speak, the physical pain has dragged out all the fear and emotional agony I've been holding inside. "I asked for one thing, Katie. *One thing.* I just want my stuff so I can leave."

My eyes fill with tears. I feel utterly defeated, crippled, and hopeless. For the first time, I want to give up. I want to just find my way back up to the second floor, curl up next to Ashley in her bed, and wait for Dante and Poole to come for me. They can do what they want, take me to the Committee's dungeon, torture me to death. I just don't care anymore. At least I'll be with Ashley a while longer.

"What is *wrong* with you?" she sneers. I know how much she detests weakness.

"You got me," I sigh. "I'm done. Just call the Committee and turn me in."

But the shrill blare of an alarm suddenly splits the air, telling me she won't have to.

CHAPTER 35

The screech of the alarm cranks up the pain in my body by a factor of ten. "What is that, the fire alarm?" A glimmer of possibility enters my mind. "Is everyone leaving?" If there's an evacuation, I could step into the hallway and blend into the crowd, get swept out the exit with them.

Katie frowns at the ceiling. "Security alarm," she says grimly. "They're locking every door."

I slump further to the floor. "You gotta be kidding me," I groan. I can use my full voice now because the commotion in the ER drowns us out.

"Maybe it was that psych ward nurse," Katie says in the gloom. "She saw us."

A man's voice barks outside the door, "Check all locks!"

Katie pulls back from the window slot as a shadow crosses it.

The door handle rattles. "This one's good," a woman says, her words already fading as she moves on.

"What difference does it make?" I sigh. "We're locked in here."

Katie grabs the handle and twists it slowly, shaking her head. "No we're not. These doors only lock on the outside." She returns the handle to neutral, not ready to pull the door open yet.

The glimmer of hope returns. I uncurl from my fetal crouch and stretch my painful guts. It still feels like a huge rubber band, connected from my nuts to every nerve in my body, is twisting and pulling inward. But I can stand, so I slide up next to Katie and let my eyes adjust to the shaft of light from the narrow window.

"That nurse waited ten minutes to sound the alarm on us?" I ask doubtfully.

"I don't know. This is crazy," Katie says. "I've never heard the security alarm go off before. They don't even do tests like the fire alarm. They just play the sound for us in training so we recognize it when we hear it."

The window gives us a view of the ER from behind the nurse's station. Staff members shuffle left and right. "Lock it down," a woman says. "Lock it all down. No one in or out."

As we look into the ER, a tall man in a dark blue suit steps in from a side hallway. "Who triggered the alarm?" he shouts over the noise.

I recognize him—from the coffee shop, from my childhood, and from the shadow standing in an upstairs window the night I stole Sutton's backpack from his house. It's Sutton's dad. "That's Mr. Bradford," I say.

"He's the hospital administrator," Katie says. "You didn't know that?"

No, I didn't. When I lived here before I never paid

attention to what the parents did for work. I never even knew that my dad was chairman the Committee.

Mr. Bradford looks around, "It came from the ER, who ..."

A woman's voice, deep, with an accent halfway between German and French, cuts right through the noise. "*I activated the alarm.*"

We can't see the woman yet. We can only see Mr. Bradford, who stares straight ahead. "And who are you?" he asks.

A tall, slim woman in a white trench coat steps into view. Her blonde hair is tucked behind her ears, tied back with a barrette, but flowing and wavy over the back of her neck and shoulders. With an expression of cold indifference, she reaches into her coat, pulls out a black wallet, and flips it open in front of Mr. Bradford's nose.

I glance at Katie, looking for some explanation, but she's bewildered.

Mr. Bradford stiffens as he looks at the information in the wallet. "Ms. Van Hook." He nods formally. "I'm ..."

"I know who you are, Mr. Bradford. Now you know who I am and that I have the authority to order a lockdown on this facility."

Van Hook's English is flawless but her accent causes her to over-pronounce the vowels and emphasize some consonants. I recognize the accent from a couple of boys at school, and her name helps me pinpoint her nationality — Dutch.

On all sides nurses, doctors, staff, and patients make a wide path around Van Hook. She pulses authority and she's staring their big boss down with dark eyes sharp enough to shred him.

If this is the "someone" Dante said the League was sending, I can see that they're not screwing around. And she's early—Dante said he had a couple of days, but the new security boss is here *now*.

A man in a gray business suit steps up behind Van Hook and whispers in her ear. She nods. The man thumbs a couple of buttons on his cell phone and the security alarm stops squealing.

The silence is a relief to my ears. But now the piercing power of Van Hook's voice is even clearer.

"Do you realize you have a Class-A candidate on the second floor, Mr. Bradford?" She's talking about Ashley. "She's to be protected with all available resources."

"Code One security alert," Mr. Bradford says as if reciting from a security manual. "The alarm system locks all doors. No one in or out. My guards each have an assigned exit to cover ..."

"After *I* sounded the alarm!" Van Hook barks. "The candidate has been here thirty-six hours."

Mr. Bradford stares back, oddly calm about the whole thing.

"Didn't you get a report from the doctor that she was admitted?" Every question the woman asks is like a knife slashing at him.

"I saw the name, but Mr. Screed has been ..."

She cuts him off again. "And unauthorized parties have visited the candidate."

Katie and I sink against the storage shelf. They know we're here, we're trapped, and this woman and her men will scour the building until they find us.

CHAPTER 36

I listen intently to Van Hook. She's here, she's taking over, she just told Mr. Bradford that she knows someone's been in Ashley's room, and Katie and I are stuck without an escape route.

"Yesterday," she continues, "a young man, a patient from another ward, broke in …"

Katie and I both let out a breath. Van Hook doesn't know that we're here now. She's talking about my visit to Ashley yesterday. I'm on her radar, but Katie isn't. Is this good for me, or bad? I can't tell anymore.

"*Snuck* in," Mr. Bradford corrects Van Hook. "There was no hard breach of security measures."

The familiar clock ticks in my head. Nurse Nora didn't sound the alarm, but how long before she's asked if anything strange has happened on the psych ward and she mentions seeing two kids *today* slipping out the back door?

Van Hook eyes Mr. Bradford with disbelief. "Un … authorized," she growls slowly, as if reminding him of the word's meaning. "And what have you done to increase security?"

Mr. Bradford shrugs. "Mr. Screed had control of security and he's been incapacitated since ..."

"When was the last time you reviewed your protocol, Mr. Bradford?" Her frustration with the hospital's administrator sharpens the edge in her voice. "You do not require approval from your Committee's Director of Security—conscious or comatose—to enact Code One lockdown on a Class-A candidate."

Dante enters, followed by another of Van Hook's gray-suited men. He holds his chin high, like a spotlight is shining on him.

"Who are you?" asks Van Hook.

"Curtis Dante, assistant director of security," he says proudly. It's the most energy I've heard him put into a sentence yet. He gestures to his left as Poole steps in from the side hallway. I don't know where he went after he sniffed at the psych ward fire door, but he wasn't anywhere near our trail. "This is my second, Mr. Poole."

"Mr. Dante." She sneers his name like someone has just dropped a bag of dog crap in front of her.

The look of pride slides off Dante's face and he drops his chin.

"You know the League's security protocol, Mr. Dante?" she stabs him again with his own name.

Dante's eyes flood with dismay. "Yes, ma'am. I've been assistant dir ..."

"Then why wasn't this hospital locked down to protect the candidate?"

"I ... we ..." Dante is disintegrating under his new boss's glare. He glances sideways at Mr. Bradford, half pleading, half accusing. "She's in a locked ward, ma'am. We're looking for the intruder ..."

"There should have been no intruder in the first place!" Van Hook snaps.

"Mr. Screed has been ..."

Van Hook takes a step forward, silencing Dante and forcing him to look up to meet her eyes. "The assistant director's duty is to enact the security protocol, Mr. Dante, not to wait for his superior to wake up and give orders."

Poole stands back, out of the fray, and watches. He's smart enough not to try rescuing Dante. They would both go down.

Dante is barely treading water now. Sweat glistens on his forehead and his lips work nonsensically before any real words come out of his mouth. "Mr. Screed didn't allow ..."

Before Dante finishes, Van Hook turns her eyes on the hospital administrator and stings him with a suspicious glare. "Mr. Bradford, you're relieved of duty." Then to Poole: "Mr. Poole, lock down all exits and post double guards. Check IDs of everyone entering and exiting."

Dante eyes his underling, realizing that his own moment in the spotlight is vanishing.

Poole nods confidently. "Already done, ma'am."

She gives Poole a nod, the only generous thing she's done since she got here. "Then take Mr. Bradford into custody."

Poole glances unsurely at Dante then at Mr. Bradford, whose jaw hardens.

"Uh … ma'am?" Poole says unsurely.

As she examines Mr. Bradford's face—looking for what?—she tells Poole, "No outside contact. He doesn't leave until I'm finished with him."

In the window's glow, Katie and I exchange looks, imagining what that could mean.

Mr. Bradford's eyes go hard. He stares defiantly at Van Hook as Poole reluctantly grabs his elbow and pulls him away.

Van Hook shifts her attention to the elevators. "Mr. Dante," she announces, "take me to the candidate."

"Don't you want to check on Mr. Screed first, ma'am?"

"The *candidate*, Mr. Dante," insists Van Hook, her accent chilling her disregard even more. "Mr. Screed is not going anywhere."

Dante points to the elevators. As Van Hook and her men brush past him, the statuesque woman swings her head, expertly surveying the ER and sending the rubberneckers shrinking away.

When her eyes pan over the storage room door Katie pulls away and I step back, fading farther into the dark. There's no way she can see me in here, but she seems to look me right in the eyes. The jolt it sends through me crowds out the pain of Katie's kick.

"Candidate?" Katie asks.

"Ashley," I say. "They're going to see Ashley first. The nurse will tell that she saw us. We have to get out of here. Now."

CHAPTER 37

The ER fills with thumping footsteps as Van Hook leads her four short-haired, gray-suited men toward the elevator. They'll go directly to the second-floor psych ward where they'll stand around and stare at Ashley like the science experiment they've made her into.

Dante, in his black fatigues, follows the group as more guards swarm the hallways.

I glance around the dusky storage room, trying to find an escape route. There's no back door, no secret panel, no side window, just the door in front of us. I look up at the ceiling. We could push up a white panel and crawl over to another room …

"Forget it," Katie says, watching me. "There're too many wires and tubes."

I flash her a questioning look.

"They tell us in training not to try and hang anything like decorations from the ceiling because there are electrical wires and gas tubes and stuff up there. If we try to climb up it'll be like crawling into a spider web."

I slump against the shelf. "We'll have to wait for …" My thought trails off. I can't think of any advantage we'll get from more time inside this closet. Someone will open the door sooner or later and catch us sitting here.

I'm about to give up, but like a dog hearing a silent whistle, Katie tilts her head and pierces the dark with a distant stare.

I'm shot with curiosity. "What is it?"

But she doesn't answer. She's frozen in thought for one, two, three seconds. Then without a word, she pushes me aside and pulls out the laundry cart from below the shelf.

"It's not big enough," I say, knowing on sight that we can't both hide in there.

She scoffs and shakes her head. "Zach, you're so dumb."

Ashley said the same thing to me when she was trying to tutor me on the workings of the Committee and the League. These sisters have a way of making me feel like I know only enough to cause them trouble.

As Katie picks quickly through the used scrubs, I hear the siren—an ambulance, maybe a block away, approaching the hospital—and I get her plan.

She shoves a blue cap into my hands and yanks pink pants and a shirt out of the pile for herself. Within seconds, we each have a full set of scrubs and are scrambling to pull them on before the ambulance reaches the entrance.

"The guards ..." I say, imagining Dante's men doubled-up at every door, checking IDs.

Now dressed head-to-toe in pink, Katie reaches behind me and grabs a clipboard from the shelf. "They won't stop us at the ER door." She peels some hospital forms out of a stack and clips them on.

I pull the surgical cap down, covering as much of my dark hair as possible.

The siren screams louder then cuts off. The ambulance is pulling into the driveway.

"Just stay close to me," Katie says, peering out the window slot, "and act like you're right where you belong." She puts one hand on the door handle. With the other, she hoists the clipboard in front of her chest, looking official.

As I look at Katie's hospital-issue clipboard and the patient forms on it, I think about what she just said — "... *like you're right where you belong.*" A bare sliver of a notion jabs into my mind. Too tantalizing to ignore, the thought turns into a hunch, pushing me back to the file box on the shelf.

In the dim light I reach for the first compartment, which I left unchecked earlier, flip back the fourth card with the letter D, and find a clear plastic envelope. My heart skips a beat as I lift it out and read the name— White, Zachary. It holds my wallet, my flash drive, and my cell phone.

"Okayyyyy ..." Katie mutters at the window, anticipating our chance to move. She doesn't notice what I'm doing. She's focused intently on the action in the ER. "Now." She pulls the door open and slips out like a puff of air.

I squint against the light stabbing into my eyes and follow, holding the envelope at my side. A nurse sits at the ER desk, but her back is to us and she doesn't notice when we round the desk and fall in behind the two nurses and one doctor rushing for the door.

My eyes are still adjusting to the glaring light so I just lock onto Katie's pink blur and count on the fact that she's as desperate to get out of here as I am.

Ahead, the ER doors slide wide open and my clearing eyes spot the guards, one on each side watching the action. I crowd close to the group, focusing on some imaginary medical duty.

Just as the guard on the right turns to scan me, I pull my eyes off him and flip the clear envelope to my left hand, hoping he doesn't notice I'm only carrying a patient's belongings.

One of the rear doors pops open on the ambulance. The paramedic inside is tending to a man on a stretcher whose alarmed eyes hover just above an oxygen mask.

Katie says something to the guard on the left. One of her words—"contagious"—pushes the guy two steps away from the door, like the air wafting in could kill him with one sniff. A hard shove wouldn't have been more effective.

Just outside the door, she bumps my elbow and moves to the left as the little emergency team reaches the back of the ambulance.

"We have a contagion?" the doctor asks the paramedic.

"What? No. Heart attack."

As we duck to the driver's side of the ambulance, one of the nurses asks, "Then who said 'contagion'?"

I follow Katie around the open hatch and see the driver stepping out of the ambulance's front seat. He eyes us suspiciously, probably wondering why we're not at the back, where the emergency is.

Without missing a beat, Katie waves the clipboard. "Driver," she orders, "give these forms to the admitting nurse."

The driver takes the clipboard and frowns at the empty forms.

Katie spurs him, "Hurry, she needs them!" She keeps moving as the driver jumps for the ER desk as ordered.

I follow her out from under the ER entrance canopy and into the parking lot. As we thread between cars, Katie pulls off her cap and I do the same, dropping it on the pavement.

Then I open the clear envelope.

She glances back. "What's that?" she asks.

"My things." I stuff my wallet, cell phone, keys, and flash drive into my jeans pockets under the scrub pants but leave the identifying sheet of paper in the envelope. When we reach a curb, I throw it down and kick it into a storm drain.

Katie's eyes are quizzical but she doesn't have time to ask how I ended up with my stuff.

I'm glad she doesn't, because I don't want to explain that instead of being stored under W for White, the envelope with my belongings was stored in the file box under D, where someone would put it if they knew my *real* last name.

CHAPTER 38

For the past two hours, Katie and I have been sitting in this stand of bushes next to someone's garage waiting for nightfall. Once out of sight of the hospital we ditched the scrubs and went to where I'd hidden my backpack, in a trash bin behind the Chinese restaurant a few blocks away. Then we sat there in the alley, not knowing where to go. Any move we made could be unsafe.

I finally got an idea and we started walking again. We steered wide around the Arcanum campus, taking the long way back here to Larry's neighborhood. I've kept the idea to myself because I'm not sure this is the smartest move and Katie might argue about it. But it's the best I could come up with.

I stare into the waning daylight, across the street at our destination. Larry's little cabin is a hundred yards back from the street, by the bank of the Shadow River, and obscured by the dense woods. But this time I'm not here for Larry. He thinks I'm on my way out of town and I don't want him to know any different. I'm interested in the abandoned house at the front of the lot, whose roof is crusty with age and whose yard is overgrown with many seasons of neglect.

I've passed it a few times coming and going on the path into the woods. Even when I was here this morning, with as much as I had learned about the town and my family, I still hadn't put together what the house really meant to me.

Every few minutes, Katie shifts and grumbles. Her legs are stiff, it's getting cold, she has to pee. She has a thousand questions but I shush her every time she starts one. She huffs and acts like she'll leave but I know she won't, not until I tell her what she wants to know.

I'm not talking, though. As soon as she finds out who's above her on the list in the library she'll have no more use for me. She'll start the clock ticking—twelve hours until she calls Mrs. Bradford and gets Van Hook and every buzz-cut in town after me. But I'm not ready to start running yet. I need rest.

And there's another reason I don't talk, don't just blab to Katie. As I watch the street in front of me, I have one foot back there in Ashley's hospital room, staring into her cosmic eyes, and hearing her words echo in my head like an epic poem:

> "Under the white stones of youth
> Eternal guarded you'll find
> The key to the secrets from Apollo's mind
> The gods give the brave a half-week's time
> To delve the deep
> And save this line."

It wasn't just babbled nonsense. She woke up from a near-dead stupor to say it. The intensity in her face burned every detail into my brain. I saw only flashes of the Ashley I know, but enough to prove that she was in there, that the message was not random—it was for *me*.

And the way she looked straight at Katie when she said the last line of her poem—*"And save this line"*—I know that Katie is important to whatever I do next, even if I can't see how yet. Is it a prophecy, an *oracle* like in ancient times? I'm stalling until I can figure it out.

The lots across the street aren't just deep, they're wide along the river's edge with thick woods standing between the houses. Bordering the front of each yard at the sidewalk, though, is a classic-Arcanville, standard-issue low brick wall capped with yellow limestone and short iron spikes. The path I usually take to Larry's cabin—which I'm now guessing was once the servants' quarters—cuts into the woods to the left of the house.

Behind our little hiding spot is a regular neighborhood, with houses lined up close to one another. Dense population—lots of eyes and ears. That's why I'm being so careful. We're not just going to go traipsing across the street in daylight for any citizen to see us.

I also watch for black sedans or anyone creeping around—any indication that the Committee knows about this spot and is watching it, waiting for me to show up here. I want to know with absolute certainty that we are not seen.

I'm starting to shiver now from the cold, but force myself to be patient. I run Ashley's words through again, like a song repeating on my iPod.

Every line—every word—must have meaning to me.

"Under the white stones of youth"

"Stones of youth" could mean the bricks of a school building—the high school? But its bricks aren't white.

"Eternal guarded you'll find"

Something important enough to keep safe forever.

"The key to the secrets ..."

Some decoder or a master code ...

"... from Apollo's mind ..."

Apollo was the patron god of Delphi.

"The gods give the brave ..."

Gods could intervene for or through humans in ancient times.

"... a half-week's time"

This is more than the twelve-hour head start Katie's giving me.

"To delve the deep"

Someplace deep—hidden?

And the last line was delivered directly to Katie.

"And save this line."

Why did she look at Katie when she said it? If it's an oracle for *me*, why did she make sure that Katie got the last line? All I can figure is that Katie's more important—to the prophecy, the plan—than I want to admit. Whatever Ashley is telling me to do I can't do it alone. I need Katie, her sister who ignores her suffering and even turned her in to the Committee.

Katie played along today, got me in and out of the hospital as promised. Maybe Ashley's telling me to trust her. Hasn't she earned it? But I still have a bad feeling about partnering with a girl who just yesterday said she'd stab me in the back first chance she got.

CHAPTER 39

The dinner rush hour is over, and the street is quiet now. When Katie leans over my shoulder and speaks, I can see the fog of her breath in the vanishing daylight. "Zach, it's been over two hours. It's cold …"

She doesn't have to say any more. It's time.

I turn to her with my finger across my lips then tip my head for her to follow. With one last quick scan, I leave the bushes and step into the street.

Not wasting a second, I sprint to the opposite sidewalk and up to the black iron gate. My feet rustle in the uncut grass that hangs over the walk. I hear Katie's steps right behind me as I push the gate. With a stubborn squeal of its rusty hinges, it swings open and we're in the yard. The overgrown hedge running inside the low brick wall gives us cover. No one will see us if we're quick.

I close the gate and pick my way through the grass to the brick house.

"What are we doing?" Katie whispers.

We reach a big window at the front. It's large and multi-paned, a checkerboard of smaller glass panels. The row along the bottom has hinged sections that a person might fit through. But when I push on them they don't tilt open. Locked tight. If I try forcing a window I'll risk the noise of one squeaking open or, worse, breaking.

I abandon it and move on around the corner. In the shadows, I almost snag my eye on the branch of a large apple tree, neglected for years and hanging toward the house. The leaves are yellow and falling off. Katie bumps into me and grunts angrily. The mystery and the conditions are pissing her off.

I duck under the branches and see what I was hoping for—a window with the sill at chest level. The upper section is too high to see if the latch is locked, so I have to just give it a try.

Katie stands aside and glances toward the unruly hedge at the street. "It better be warm in there," she growls.

I push up on the window and feel some play. It's sticky, though, so I push harder and hope the lock is unlatched. I stop, pull down on the window and see that I've made some progress.

"Zach ..." Katie warns as headlights sweep across the front of the house.

I stop and look that way. The headlight beams are broken into a thousand tiny lasers by the leaves and branches of the hedge and apple tree. The sound of a car engine and tires on the pavement move slowly by. A neighbor running an errand—or someone searching for me? When the white light fades and the glow of red taillights disappears, I know we're safe.

I turn back to the window and push harder. I'm as sick

of being out in the cold as Katie is. This time it slides a couple of inches. I pull it all the way closed again to get a running start then give it a hard shove upward. It slides open with a wood-on-wood scrape.

I step back and wave my hand, giving Katie permission to enter first.

She just stares at me.

I chuck my backpack into the opening, brace both hands inside the frame and lever myself up. Seems like I'm spending too much time climbing in and out of windows today. But I must be getting good at it because in three seconds I'm standing inside and reaching out for Katie.

She swats my hands away, sneering "I got it" and hoists herself in.

When she's inside, we stand shoulder to shoulder and peer into the darkness. It's full night inside now. The streetlights bleed faintly through the sheer curtains that cover the hazy windows.

I can see the ghostly outlines of furniture covered in white sheets, like someone threw on the dust covers and left for the summer but never came back. The air is dusty and stale, but the smell of rot that I expected isn't here. From outside, the place looks as gross as an old piece of cheese, but inside it's dry and clean.

I strain to remember this place, try to imagine a tiny version of me crawling across the floor, playing among the now-covered furniture, sitting in a chair and opening a birthday present. I should know it, recognize it, but I don't.

I'm sure Katie's been wondering for the last two hours, but I wouldn't let her talk. "Whose house is this?" she finally asks.

"It's mine," I say.

CHAPTER 40

Katie scans the dusty shadows. "If this is *your* house, why have you been living in that crappy apartment?"

"I didn't know it was mine," I tell her. "I just figured it out."

I put it together after we left the hospital this afternoon. I was racking my brain for a safe place to hide and coming up empty. Then I remembered my first conversation with Larry a few days ago, back there in the woods. When I threatened to tell the owners of this house that Larry was squatting in their cabin he wasn't worried, just said, *"We have an arrangement."* His casualness perplexed me. Then yesterday, he told me that he's my uncle. Why wouldn't he be worried about me telling the homeowners that they had a bum living in their old servants' quarters? Because he knew the owners weren't around.

My dad's parents died when I was three, so I don't remember them. And even though I'm sure I had visited here when they were alive, I certainly did not come here after they died. Larry was gone by then, wandering the world. Our house was only a mile away, but no one lived here so there was no reason to visit.

With my grandparents gone and Larry officially listed as dead in the *Chronicles*, the house would be owned by my father. When he supposedly died in the plane crash on his way to Europe, the house would have gone to my mother. Now she's dead, so ... I'm the heir to this dusty little castle.

I don't even want to think about the complications of ownership since I saw my father listed as "Missing" in the *Chronicles*. We buried an empty casket—isn't that legally dead? Larry is back but seems content living in the cabin, so I'll take the house—especially since I need it so badly right now.

Katie steps toward a doorway and reaches for a light switch.

"No," I say. "No lights." I'm hoping that Larry having electricity and water out back means the main house has it too.

I take out my phone and turn it on. Still has some battery power. I pan it around like a flashlight. The dusty furniture covers glow like a moonscape. I work my way across the room toward the black hole of a hallway and find what I'm looking for on the wall—a thermostat.

Katie steps up behind me, rubbing the cold out of her arms. She's wearing a thin jacket for daytime. With these autumn days never really getting hot, the house feels like a walk-in cooler. The sweat from running all day cooled off when I sat in the bushes for two hours, and the chill is seeping into my bones.

I examine the thermostat in the minimal light, flip the control switch from "OFF" to "HEAT" and wait. A second later an electric click sounds in another part of the house. A mechanical shudder rattles the vents.

One second, two, three. Nothing more. Then, just as Katie and I exchange doubtful glances, a puff of dusty air surges into the hallway, hitting our eyes and noses, blowing us back like a sand storm. We stumble into the living room, airborne crud swirling all around.

"Ack!" Katie chokes. "Turn it off!" She pulls the collar of her sweater up over her nose and mouth.

I do the same. "Just give it a minute," I say. A little dirt won't kill us, and I'm tired of being cold.

In a few minutes the house is warming up and the dust is settling. Katie rubs her eyes and I think about opening more windows. But don't want to risk it. Someone outside might see signs of life in the house and get curious.

Time to check the other utilities. I go to the big front windows and pull the heavy drapes closed over the sheers. Next I find the nearest bathroom and turn on the faucet. The pipes groan dryly and hiss for a second or two before water comes out. There's no window in here so I close the door and flip up the light switch. One of four round bulbs above the mirror lights up. It's enough light for me to see the rusty water swirling in the sink. After a minute, ribbons of steam rise from the water. The rust is diluted and clean hot water flows from the faucet. I breathe a sigh of relief. There's electricity, heat, and water.

I look up at the small mirror, at my eyes staring back through the fog of dust and steam. With a swipe of my hand my whole face is revealed between the smears.

I pull back my hood and stare at a person I barely recognize. It's the first time I've seen my reflection in a couple of days. My eyes are hollow with worry. Have I been eating? Because my face looks thinner than last time I saw it. And the frown creasing my chin is as grave as the one I'll wear to my funeral. I look angry, beaten, exhausted, hopeless.

With a grayer tone to my skin, I'd almost be there with Ashley—a living mummy. A bubble of sadness wells up from my chest and clogs my throat. I don't have the strength to stuff it back down this time. My resistance melts and the pressure of tears pushes up into my eyes.

A knock at the door startles me, evaporating the emotion.

"Zach," Katie says to the closed door. "Does the toilet work? I gotta pee."

I turn off the faucet and stare doubtfully into the toilet. There's a tiny pool of old water in the bottom of the bowl. It obviously hasn't been used in years. But when I press the handle it springs to life, flushing itself with orange water. I flip off the light and open the door.

"It's fine," I say, hearing sticky emotions in my throat. "Just don't open the door when the light's on."

I step out and Katie squeezes by. As she pushes the door closed, she pauses a moment, examining my face in the shadows. Her eyes register concern for what I just saw in the mirror. I don't like it either—a grim mask of doom.

CHAPTER 41

A half-hour later Katie and I are setting up camp inside the house. While she finishes rolling the dust covers off the furniture, I check every possible crack in the drapes to make sure no light can seep out. Then I pull a coat from the closet, and trying not to think about which of my dead grandparents wore the garment, I hang it from the front door's top trim to cover its little windows.

Next, I get my laptop from my backpack and set it on the coffee table in front of the couch. I dig out power cords and find an outlet in the wall, hoping the fossilized thing doesn't zap me. No deadly sparks fly. I plug my phone in next to the computer but turn it off in case anyone's trying to trace the cell signal.

When I turn back to the couch, Katie is sitting there pinching her lower lip, lost in thought.

I sit down, resisting the urge to ask what's on her mind. She's not Ashley, and I don't have any obligation to listen to her worries or try to comfort her. The less I have to think about right now, the better.

I open my laptop and watch it wake up, lighting the screen with my background picture of the French Alps— green foothills with the white cap of Mont Blanc towering in the distance. I went climbing there on a school trip last year. I wish I had stayed, gotten lost in those hills. I could have learned to ski then started teaching it. I could have spent the rest of my life in complete, happy ignorance of any of this mess.

But, no, I had to come back here. Despite every way that Mom warned me, I came back. Now I know why she drilled it so hard into my head. *"Whatever happens, Zachary,"* she said on her last visit, a cold midnight in the darkened school chapel, *"remember that Arcanville is not your home. You are a citizen of the world now."* After everything that I've seen in this insane asylum of a town, I wonder if *"the world"* will have me back. That's assuming I can ever leave alive.

I'm desperate to escape now. But I'm haunted by what Ashley said today.

> *"The gods give the brave a half-week's time*
> *To delve the deep ..."*

That's for me. I'm supposed to *do* something. And running away isn't part of it. The gods themselves are supposedly giving me half a week. That must count for something.

But at the same time I'm sure that Larry is right. Run now, regroup, come back for Ashley strong, with a plan. She's not in her right mind. If she were thinking clearly, if I could explain it, she'd agree. I know it.

And after seeing Van Hook today, I'm ten times more worried what will happen when this new security chief catches up with me. I'm sure she'll figure out about the tunnels—and throw a net on Larry too. That'll be my fault. With that many wound-up Committee security guards around, plus Van Hook's razor-heads on the prowl, something bad will happen. They're capable of anything I can imagine—and probably worse.

A war of words is raging inside me. It reminds me of the day I told Ashley how alone I was, that my mom had died, and that I'm not who I say I am. She didn't judge me, didn't reject me. I cried on her shoulder in the rain. I struggled so hard, wanting to tell her the rest of my story but afraid of the consequences.

I'm not *"the brave"* Ashley talked about in her oracle. Instead, I've been looking to cut the best deal I can get and run. Katie helped me get my stuff back and I owe her. If I give her just enough info to chew on tonight— some insight into the truth about the Committee and the League of Delphi—maybe she'll give me a break and let me stay here overnight. Then tomorrow I'll tell her the rest, give her the names on the list, and make my escape. It's the coward's way out, but it's the best idea I have.

I hover my fingers over the keyboard, wondering what I should show Katie, what she's most likely to believe. I think I'll start with the conspiracy stuff about the League. I owe it to Ashley to punch a couple of holes in Katie's wall before I leave.

I slide my finger across the track pad and tap the Wi-Fi network icon. I'll need to mask my location before I jump on the Internet and browse sites that are unflattering to the League—that's how Screed tracked Ashley and me to the public library a few days ago and almost caught us.

Katie reaches over and stills my hand. I'm surprised by how tentative her touch feels. "What *was* that?" she asks.

THE DELPHI DECEPTION

I point at the computer screen. "What, you mean Mont Blanc? It's ..."

"No," she says, her blue eyes glowing in the light of the screen. The questions I've forced her to hold in come spilling out. "At the hospital—Ashley." She pins me with a look of genuine curiosity that might rise to the level of *concern* for her sister. "What was with the spasms and that weird poem she told you? And why was that nurse asking her questions about her *daughter*? Why would Ashley know anything about that?"

I take a long breath, stalling for an extra couple of seconds. She's asking about the stuff I was planning to leave out. If I tell her everything, she'll know I have way more information than I should and keep me here longer to find it all out. Plus it all sounds so crazy that she might think I'm just making it up to con her or scare her. But I have no play. I'm more trapped than she is.

"It's the Pythia Program," I say, watching her reaction.

Katie's eyes narrow and drill into mine. When I don't squirm, don't give any sense that I'm lying, her eyes widen. She *knows*!

But then Katie throws her head back and lets out a long, howling laugh.

CHAPTER 42

As Katie laughs, I go from shocked to suspicious to confused to humiliated in three beats of my heart. Now I'm seething, thinking of Ashley in that hospital bed, trapped by the League while her sister laughs it off, and how hurt she would be.

Or would she? As Katie holds her belly and howls, I realize that Ashley *knows* her, better than anyone. She's not confused about who Katie is. And yet she looked right at her when she said, *"And save this line."*

After a minute of convulsions, Katie's cackling winds down and she catches her breath. "Did *Ashley* tell you that?" A tear of hilarity glistens on her cheek.

I don't answer. Maybe I won't tell her a goddamned thing now. And maybe that's part of the plan—be "the brave," don't do the easy thing here. Don't just blurt out everything I know, trying to change Katie's mind or punish her.

Katie sniffs and wipes her eye, a huge smile on her face. "Oh, Zach," she says pityingly, "that's the oldest myth in the book."

I turn to the computer screen, thinking of the flash drive in my pocket. I could show her the letter from the

Board of Prophecy, prove it to her in five seconds. Then she wouldn't be laughing.

"A bunch of girls saving the world with psychic visions," she says, wryly. "Don't you remember that story from when you lived here? That's like telling you she's a *fairy princess*." She snorts into her hand and melts into another laughing fit.

She thinks I'm as crazy as Ashley. It's like the League has no secrets from kids like Katie, letting all the really bad stuff masquerade as rumors and horror stories they tell each other when the adults aren't around. It must be quite a shock when they grow up and find out it's all true.

Katie wants to be president of the League of Delphi, but she doesn't even know what she'll be the leader of—doesn't *want* to know. Ashley said there's a *"key to the secrets"* that we can find. If we find the key and the secrets, it won't be necessary for *me* to convince Katie of anything.

"How do you laugh at the idea of the Pythia Program but believe in the ranking list?" I ask. "That's a myth too, isn't it?" Dante said so to Poole in the hospital stairwell: *"Every kid in every town in the League knows that story."*

"Sutton told me," Katie says. "He couldn't keep his mouth shut when he was high or drunk. He came over to my house after Connor's one night and blabbed about it."

"How did he know?" I ask.

"He wouldn't say, but I know his mom told him. He was on top so she didn't have anything to worry about—

except keeping him there. It wouldn't look right for the chairwoman's son to be any lower than number one."

I think about what that means to me. If my dad were still in Arcanville and chairman of the Committee, what would my life be like? How much pressure would I be under to be the best at everything, to keep up the family image?

"But the *Pythia Program*?" Katie scoffs.

I still don't know why it's so hard to believe— especially after seeing Ashley like that. Is Katie in some kind of denial? Can she compartmentalize that easily and leave out evidence she just saw? Or maybe she just hates Ashley so much that she wouldn't give her the benefit of considering it.

After another minute of giggling, Katie gets up off the couch. "So," she says, pulling her jacket tightly around her, "you got your stuff. Now I want mine. Who's on the list?"

I open my mouth but nothing comes out. My promise and Ashley's oracle are fighting for my voice.

Katie lowers her chin. "Are you going to tell me?"

Ashley's last line rings in my head: *"And save this line."* She looked at Katie when she said it.

"No," I say, "I'm not going to tell you."

She shifts on her feet as the last trace of laughter drains from her eyes. "We had a deal," she coldly.

"New deal," I say.

She draws her phone from her pocket like a gun. "One phone call ..." she warns, stepping toward the front door.

"No." I ignore her threat and point to the window we came in an hour ago. "We can't use the doors. Someone might see or hear. That window is covered by the old tree outside. Use it."

She hisses in disbelief. "You think I *care*? That blonde bitch and her agents will be here five minutes after I make the call."

"I'll take you inside."

Katie stiffens at the words. Her face in the shadows, but mine is lit in the computer monitor's glow. She can see that I'm serious.

After a long silence, she asks, "When?"

"'A half-week's time,'" I quote Ashley as I run the calculations. A half-week would be three and a half days, using this afternoon as the starting point. "Three nights from now."

Katie's head tilts.

I shrug. It's all I've got.

She's trying to decide if I'm for real or if I'm trying to trick her.

I don't need to rearrange her world view. I only need to nudge her enough to get her to follow me. "If I could prove to you that everything Ashley says about Arcanville is true, show you that Mrs. Bradford is hiding more from you than she's telling you, wouldn't that information help you get ahead around here?"

She doesn't answer, just looms in the dark, calculating. She may not believe me. Ultimately, I'm counting on Ashley's gift for seeing the future and Katie's hunger to see the list—and the rest of the Committee's secrets—with her own eyes.

By the time she unfreezes herself, I still don't know what her decision is. But when she reaches for the front door's knob it's my chance to test her.

"Uh uh," I say and point to the window.

She sighs angrily and steps toward the window, stomping her feet a bit to demonstrate that she doesn't like it. But now I know. The promise of getting inside is more powerful than any reasonable suspicion she has of me.

When she gets to the window, she turns and points at me. "We have a deal. Don't try to skate on me, Zach." She pulls the window up and tries a couple of awkward angles to get her body out. I don't get up to help. She finally decides to swing one foot out then the other and slide through on her butt. Then she's gone in the darkness.

I sit here a long time, feeling the cold October air pushing in through the window. I eventually let my head sag against the couch cushion. I wish Katie would never come back and I could just ride out the window on the breeze, out over the Shadow River to freedom, carrying Ashley in my arms, and never ever return.

CHAPTER 43

I wake up lying on the couch, wrapped in one of the dust covers like a burrito. The room is completely unfamiliar and it takes a minute to register where I am. My grandparents' house—*my* house now.

The shades drawn across the big front window muffle the morning sun, but the side window we used as an entrance lets in some shady daylight. Katie left it open when she left, but it's closed now. I must have gotten up in the middle of the night and pushed it down. It's nice and warm in here.

Sunlight also glows in from other parts of the house— the hallway that looked like a black hole last night and the room through the doorway, likely the kitchen that we didn't explore.

When I stir, my shoulders are sore—probably from the crutches. The decorative pillow I used all night didn't help my neck any, and when I slide my hand down my face I can feel the dimples its beaded cover has pressed into my cheek.

I also feel an ache in my knee and instantly think Larry's witch doctor remedy didn't take. But I sit up and stretch, working my leg a little bit, and the stiffness goes away. I marvel at it. The guy is weird but he really knows his stuff.

The house is quiet, much quieter than the hospital I woke up in yesterday. The only thing I hear is Ashley's voice echoing in my head. My brain has been replaying her oracle all night long, over and over, so many times that the words have practically lost their meaning.

"Under the white stones of youth ..."

I was thinking of the high school, the bricks being the "stones." But that doesn't seem right. Could it mean a headstone, like at Sutton's grave?

"Eternal guarded you'll find ..."

What did Sutton know that needed to be kept safe forever? Maybe that weird notebook with the lines and numbers that I found in Ashley's room has some code—

"the key to the secrets from Apollo's mind."

"The gods give the brave ..."

This is supposed to mean me, I guess. But Katie might be the brave one—she hasn't been inside the library and gotten the hell scared out of her yet.

"... a half-week's time"

I don't know why not last night or today or tonight, but I can use a couple days rest before another assault on that now extra-fortified fortress they call a library.

"To delve the deep"

I can only imagine that this means the tunnels. Is there a deeper place in town that we could get to within three days?

"And save this line."

I was totally baffled yesterday by those last few words.

But I dreamed an answer overnight that's sticking with me. In Sutton's backpack, Ashley and I found an unusual textbook with a simple black-and-white cover called *People of the Prophecy*—no subtitle, no explanation. The book wasn't filled with stories or lessons, only lists of names that I think were genealogies of the men who came from around the world to help Jan Van Arcan found Arcanville. Back in the family histories of the Europeans were some big names that I recognized, including Leonardo da Vinci, the Roman emperor Nero, and Joan of Arc—the girl knight who saved medieval France, and then was burned at the stake for saying *a voice from beyond* directed her to do it.

The first name, though—all the way at the beginning of the book and the one from which all the others branched—was Deucalion. I had never heard it before and neither had Ashley, so I dismissed it. But I saw the name again the other night. The Board of Prophecy's letter that I stole from Screed's computer said they *"have identified, in the line of Deucalion, one Arcanville Chapter candidate for induction into the Order of the Pythia"*—Ashley.

So this Deucalion may be the founder of the League of Delphi, a bloodline stretching around the world and threaded into many cultures, but leading all the way back to one person at ancient Delphi. Is this the "line" that Ashley intends Katie to save?

I hope not, because I honestly don't care about the Pythias or the League and their line of Deucalion. I have no intention of saving them. They can all go to hell as far as I'm concerned.

I feel weird that the oracle is starting to make a

different sort of sense to me. This is the priests' job at Delphi, deciphering oracles into something usable. The prophecy is like a puzzle—you examine what the Pythia says and compare it to everything you know, check and re-check, looking at every tiny bit of information in a way you never have before. And then, when you're done, you're still left with a best guess. It's maddening.

I stand up and stretch, trying to untangle the mental tension from the physical. My stomach growls. Food—I hadn't thought about it all night, but now it seems like the main thing.

Through the doorway that leads to the back of the house I find a big formal dining room. The wood floor creaks in spots. Everything is covered—long table, six chairs, sideboard against the back wall. Even the chandelier is draped in plastic. I check the window, trying to judge if I can be seen from the outside. I really need to be careful. I'm assuming that Larry doesn't use the house, but if he was wandering by on the path in the woods and saw movement inside, I don't know what he'd do.

The kitchen beyond is huge compared to my apartment's kitchen, with dark hardwood cabinets and caramel-brown granite countertops veined with gold. Three tall stools stand at the island, facing the stove and sink. They're covered with white sheets.

Then there's a smaller table and chair set—all covered—and past that a family room with a couch and two big chairs under dusty sheets. A bulky white thing stands under cover as well, and I recognize the shape as a big old tube-style TV. The house was closed up before flat screens came around. A set of glass doors to the right are covered by sheer curtains, letting in a flood of screened daylight from the backyard.

I try to imagine Grandma and Grandpa in here, eating, talking, living. I can barely put together an image of them in my mind, can't remember the last time I saw even a photo. It's been so long ...

At the sink, I turn on the faucet and let it run the rusty water out. The horizontal blinds above it are about one-quarter open, letting in some warm light. There's no way I could be seen from outside. I peek out the window onto the deep backyard, the overgrown lawn, and the trees that are changing color. I can't even see Larry's cabin from here.

Checking the cupboards, I find plates and glasses but no food, not even a box of old crackers. Then I remember my backpack. I grab a down-turned glass from a cupboard, blow the dust off the bottom and flip the faucet handle to cold. After a few more seconds of liquid rust, I fill up with clear water.

Back in the living room I flop down on the couch and pull my bag into my lap. In the front pocket are what used to be two granola bars that in yesterday's running, bouncing, and banging got pulverized back into granola.

I tear one open, dump half of it into my mouth, and chomp on the sweet apple flavor. I'm so hungry right now that it tastes like a full breakfast buffet. A big swig from the water glass washes down the whole-grain goodness.

When I lean forward to set the glass back on the coffee table, I see something to my right that I didn't notice before—a waist-high bookcase with a stack of dust covers next to it. Katie must have found the shelves when she uncovered the other furniture.

I slide off the couch onto my knees and shuffle over there. One shelf in the middle is lined with leather-bound volumes that remind me of the *Chronicles* that Ashley and I saw in the library. But these are of various sizes, thicknesses, and ages. I think I know what they are.

With two fingers I tug one out of the row. When I open the cover my suspicion is confirmed. It's a photo album.

CHAPTER 44

The album in my hand has pages of black-and-white photos that look like they're from the 1920s and '30s, maybe the '40s. There are women in simple dresses and men in Army uniforms—World War II?—group photos of friends and family at picnics, dances, parties. Here and there a face looks kind of familiar—the eyes or the smile—but I don't really recognize any of these people.

In the next album, babies appear with one of the couples. As I page forward, the photos change from mostly black-and-white to color. I can practically watch the kids grow up from the '40s and the '50s, through high school, college, and work in the early '60s.

Then I recognize one of them—a young man in a business suit, standing next to a red Mustang convertible, smiling proudly. I squint at his face and focus on the eyes—same as my dad's, same as Uncle Larry's, same as mine. This is my grandfather.

Within a couple of pages a young woman appears in the photos close to Grandpa—Grandma. I can see the high cheekbones that would show up later in Dad. I touch my face, realizing that I have them too. And there are shots of them with babies—one, my father, then another when

Dad is five or six years old—his little brother, Timothy, who calls himself Larry now.

While the boys smile and laugh, Grandpa frowns. Soon Grandma is frowning too. Not all the time, but in the background when they think they're not seen by the camera.

I turn the page and find blank spots. *What?* Photos are missing.

By examining the pictures that are here—Grandpa and Grandma on a cruise with friends in the '70s, Grandma showing off a new necklace at a birthday party—I can tell that the ones missing are of Dad and Larry. I flip pages and find more of the same, blank spots interspersed with photos of Grandma and Grandpa and various people I don't know.

Someone has removed the photos of the boys. Larry? My mom? I can't even be sure they were here before my dad left and disappeared, so *he* might have taken them. But why? Then there's the League's security force—Screed. Knowing that Larry and Dad had disappeared, they could have taken the photos for identification.

There's space for two albums at the end of the shelf but no books there. Those could have held pictures of me. Mom may have taken them to protect my identity.

Then something dawns on me. I stand up and walk to the dining room door. Two framed photo portraits hang on the wall above the sideboard—Grandma and Grandpa from the 1980s, around the time Dad graduated from high school. I step closer and spot what I had missed before—the dusty outlines of two portraits that had hung next to them. The photos of Dad and Larry are missing from the walls too.

I work my way around the house, up the stairs to the four bedrooms, and find more blank spots. No full family shots hang on the walls. The bedrooms are all pretty generic—no indication which room belonged to Dad or Larry. And aside from the few pictures of them as little boys in the albums, there's not a single photo of Larry or my dad in the whole house, no evidence of their identities past ten years old.

I hear a thump and stop to listen. How many times has it sounded that I didn't hear? After a moment, another thump. My heart spikes. Someone's downstairs.

I consider the window in the closest bedroom. I should jump out, climb off the roof, and run. But I can't leave my backpack and computer down there. Even if my plan to reenter the library is blown, I need the rest of my stuff to help Ashley.

Instead, I creep over to the stairwell, my senses narrowing to a tight tunnel, and wait. Hearing nothing I start down, praying that the steps don't creak and give me away. If it's Dante or Van Hook and their men I need to get a head start on them.

Distant footsteps stop me at the bottom of the stairs. I peer into the living room and spot my laptop and backpack. No one has found it. Can I sprint over there, grab them both, and get out the front door before the guards can react? Will the front door even open? Maybe the window we used is a better bet—I know it works and I'll be able to get out.

But it may not be the Committee snooping around. What if the noise is Larry just doing something random inside the house? If I startle him he might club me with a frying pan or something.

I can't just stand here on the stairs like a raccoon in headlights. The footsteps stop. I have to move. I take a couple breaths to pump myself up, and then jump. I hit the floor running directly for my backpack. Now my footfalls are the loudest thing in the house. A woman yells—Van Hook?—as I reach my laptop and snatch it up, nearly knocking the table over.

I snag the backpack strap with my arm and stand up to run for the window. I'm in luck—it's open. I don't stop to wonder how, just spear toward it.

I'm nearly there, almost out, so close to freedom when a body jumps in front of me.

CHAPTER 45

"Zach, stop!" Katie yells, dodging out of my way.

My loose backpack strap trips me and I pitch forward, letting my knees strike hard on the wood floor to keep my forehead from slamming down. The sting in my right leg instantly punishes me for it. I skid to a stop and the house is dead quiet.

I look up at Katie, giving my terrified brain a moment to register her. I listen for other footsteps, any sign of co-conspirators in a plot to trap me in my own house. Silence.

"What are you *doing*?" She stares down at me in disgust, a box of crackers in one hand and a bottle of orange Gatorade in the other.

"I thought ..."

"What?" she demands.

I swallow hard and catch my breath as the sweat cools on my forehead. "I thought you were ... someone here to ..."

Katie doesn't wait for the rest. She turns and walks back through the dining room doorway, shaking her head.

191

I feel ridiculous. I'm so on-edge I never thought of Katie bringing me food. I'm trembling from adrenaline and hunger—and from the chill of learning that my father and uncle have been erased from the house they grew up in.

I get up, put my laptop back on the table, and drop my backpack on the floor next to it. After wiping my forehead with my sleeve, trying to calm myself, I follow Katie into the kitchen.

She's pulling the last of the groceries from her shoulder bag—not just breakfast. There's more Gatorade, a jar of peanut butter and one of grape jelly. Potato chips—two flavors—a box of granola bars, a fistful of candy bars, four cans of soup, and a bag of Oreos. I stare at it in awe.

She looks up at me. "About three days of food ..." she says.

I could kiss her. She gives me a look of disapproval, like she's reading my thoughts. But she does generously step aside and wave a hand at the plastic-wrapped buffet.

Two things I'm still not quite used to since moving back to the States—all-you-can-eat food and plastic wrappers. We didn't eat like this in France. I learned to enjoy food that was fresh and ... *alive* is the best word to describe it. Most milk is raw there, not pasteurized. Same with cheese, which is actually still full of the live bacteria that make milk into cheese. Meat doesn't come in vacuum-sealed plastic baggies. We get a full cut that's roasted or cured and slice lunch right from it. I hated it when I first moved there. Took almost a year for my stomach and taste buds to get used to it. I also miss food being *important*. Here it's almost an afterthought. Still

I can't complain about the taste of Oreos. My bachelor existence has even gotten me to enjoy peanut butter and jelly.

Too hungry to be picky, I dive in, opening the crackers and peanut butter first. I pull a knife from a drawer and a plate from up above, rinse them off, dry them with a paper napkin from Katie's grocery kit, and make myself some cracker sandwiches, adding jelly, then head for the small table with a bag of chips.

I set my plate down on top of the dust cover, plop into one of the chairs, and start eating. I twist the top off a Gatorade and chug some, depleted from my panicked dash across the living room.

While Katie rearranges some of the groceries on the counter I think of Sutton's weird history textbook, the Board of Prophecy's letter, and how they may relate to Ashley's oracle. Without turning around, I ask, "Does the name Deucalion mean anything to you?"

The plastic rustling stops and I'm sure Katie has turned to stare at me.

"Where did you hear that?"

I shrug. "Around." The name is something I'm not supposed to know about and I love that she's disturbed by it.

Katie hesitates and I can tell she's thinking about lying to protect something. But when she finally speaks, her words register as truthful. "Before written history, Deucalion and his wife, Pyrrha, were the only survivors of the great flood that Zeus unleashed on Earth to cleanse it. They rode out the storm in a wooden chest that Deucalion built and landed on Mount Parnassus ..."

"Delphi ..." I mutter in realization.

I turn to see Katie nodding. "They restarted the human race," she says.

"Like Noah," I say.

She looks blankly at me for a moment. Then her eyes pop with understanding. "Oh, from the Bible," she says. "Yes, they obviously copied that story from Deucalion."

"'Obviously?'"

"Yeah, in Alternative World History we studied the Bible and other mythology."

Now I'm interested. I don't know of a single public school in America that teaches the Bible. And it's certainly not labeled "mythology" in most places. "What makes you so sure that Deucalion wasn't copied from the Noah story?"

Katie's answer is utterly sincere. "Everyone copied the Greeks. And the Greeks learned everything important from the Oracle at Delphi in ancient times."

"But the story is way older than the Bible or Greek history, you know. Ever heard of Gilgamesh in Mesopotamia? Maybe the Greeks stole the story and lied that it was theirs."

She stares at me with genuine concern for my well-being. "Delphi is the seat of all wisdom and virtue, Zach," she explains as if quoting a textbook. "That's where mankind returned to the purified Earth. It's what makes that sacred ground the navel of the world, the center of the universe. They couldn't lie about that."

The astonishment in my face must mirror Katie's dismay. But can she see it through the haze of "facts" crammed into her head?

And all this time, I thought I was the crazy one.

CHAPTER 46

Katie joins me at the table, preferring to pull the cover off a chair before sitting in it. I expect her to argue more about Deucalion and his wife restarting the human race at Delphi after the Great Flood. But she's unfazed by my insistence that the story is much older and more universal than she's been taught, with different names and details in every culture. She's convinced and there's no room for doubt, so she says nothing more about it.

Something else is bugging her, though, and after an appropriate pause she asks me the most obvious question she can. "You really believe Ashley, don't you?"

Where's this going? I drag my wrist across my mouth, wiping away cracker crumbs. I don't answer, but she can see the *"yes"* in my eyes, in everything I've done lately.

"Zach ..." She reaches for my hand to pat it sympathetically, but hers falls short on the table halfway between us. "Ashley has always been ..." She stops before saying "crazy" because of how I've reacted before.

She tries a different tack. "Look, I know you ... *care* for her. But she's not ..." Katie searches for a palatable word, one that won't make me throw Gatorade in her face. "... *stable*," she finally offers.

Taking my non-reaction as permission, she goes on. "I was thinking about it last night—that stuff Ashley said in the hospital. It didn't make sense. Even what she told Janice, that nurse, didn't make sense."

I still don't answer.

"Janice was crying," she says, "so it meant something *to her*."

I nod.

"Like the candle thing ..." Katie explains.

"*'All visiting must advance with care ...'*" I mutter, Ashley's voice echoing in my head. "*'Who welcomes to the house hides a stranger there.'*"

I'm amazed at how effortlessly I recite the oracle word-for-word, even my inflection is the same as Ashley's. "*'The smile is to the window but a candle's glow, the illusion of lightness and warmth all through.'*"

"Right," Katie mumbles. She stares at me curiously, equally surprised by my easy recall of the words. She regains her footing and gets back to her point. "That's right," she repeats firmly. "So, Janice heard that her daughter's fiancé is hiding something."

I nod slowly in anticipation.

"But Ashley didn't say any of that. She just spat out a random poem about windows and candles and '*advance with care*' and Janice assumes it's about this guy named Vance. It fits in Janice's mind because she asked about something that's bothering her and *wanted* to hear something in all that random stuff."

I watch Katie, waiting for her to drop a piano on the whole thing, and she delivers.

"Does that seem *real* to you?" It's a question but she doesn't care about my answer.

I think of what Larry told me yesterday morning — *"Just because there's a paranormal aspect to something doesn't mean it's not real ..."*

Katie delivers her conclusion with a piercing gaze into my eyes — an accusation, a warning, a call for me to come out of Ashley's illusion. "It's like Ashley is just sucking people into this little world that she lives in," she complains, "and people are desperate enough to believe it."

I'm frozen in disbelief. Seeing her sister — whacky or not — wrecked in that hospital bed and channeling prophecies would convince the average girl that something deeper really is going on. But Katie is not average — and she's blinded by her agenda, won't even admit that she'll profit if Ashley's right about this town.

She's smart enough to play every angle, but somehow doesn't see that I'm taking her into the library not because *she* convinced me to, but because *Ashley* told me to do it in her oracle. Katie's getting what she's wanted, a gift from her sister who she shits on every chance she gets. But it's not *"real"* to her.

Katie smiles solemnly as she beams those laser-blue eyes into mine. "I'm just afraid you'll get hurt."

I refuse to react. I hold every muscle in place. I could go either way right now — explode or melt; launch or sink; rage or sob — but I won't show it, not to Katie. She has been trying to push me away from Ashley since the start. Not being able to control me throws her world plan off by a tiny fraction that she simply cannot tolerate. There's something twisted about that.

I've learned from Ashley and our research that the oracles are confusing. They're cryptic and misleading, always have been. They're that way on purpose. Someone who goes looking for an answer out of selfishness—whether it's Nurse Janice or King Croesus—deserves what they get. The wisdom of Delphi says that only the pure of heart, those honest with their deepest selves, can correctly decipher an oracle and be helped by it. All others bring upon themselves dismay, despair, and destruction.

And just like that, something clicks in my brain, sending my mind into a vast inner space. I have the sensation of standing on the gear of a giant clock as it ticks one second forward in time—and I *get it*.

Katie sees the realization in my eyes and her gaze lightens with hope. She thinks I'm coming around.

"You're right, Katie," I say at last. "Janice only heard what she wanted to hear—that her daughter is engaged to a creep."

Katie smiles triumphantly, feeling she's won me over.

A swell of knowing rises from my gut and shoots up into my head, lighting my brain with an idea not my own. "But what she heard was wrong," I say. "What *you* heard was wrong."

Katie's smile drops into a frown.

"The oracle *does* mean something, but not what Janice

thought. *Her daughter* is hiding something," I explain. "*She* shouldn't be trusted. What's going on in her face?" I draw a circle in the air around my own. "That's the *candle to the window*, and it's only an *illusion. Vance* is headed for heartbreak."

The revelation doesn't stop with the oracle to Janice. An icy wind of understanding blows through my brain, uncontrollable and driving everything else out. I drop the bottle of Gatorade on the table and stand up.

Katie stares at me like I've just regained lost sanity then thrown it away again right here in front of her. And maybe I have.

I wander out of the kitchen on rubbery legs. Ashley's ethereal voice and infinite gaze crowd my head. I don't know what's happening to me. I don't know why I'm still in this town, hiding in this house, eating the enemy's food. I only have one guess and I don't like the answer because it makes me suspect that I really am insane—I'm not in control of my destiny, the Oracle has spoken to me, and I must fulfill her prophecy.

CHAPTER 47

I stumble through the dining room, past its missing photos, and reach the living room. I press my fists to my temples, trying to stop the ringing in my head. The resonance—the pain—is so loud that it smears my thoughts.

"Zach," Katie pleads, trailing closely behind me. "Zach, I ..."

"Don't say anything," I beg. "Don't say anything. Just let me be."

I sit down on the couch and fold myself onto my thighs, slide my hands over my ears. But nothing reduces the confusion of a thousand images blurring across my mind—Sutton's grave, Ashley's eyes, rows of ancient books on towering shelves, Mom's hollow face in Rochemont's shadowy chapel, my father's status in our *Chronicle*, the huge marble disk looming over twelve council chairs in the library's inner chamber.

The static clears just enough for me to make out the golden letters on that disk, the ones I recognized only as some ancient Greek script that I couldn't read. Now I see them clearly: *Γ-Σ*. The initials for the Oracle at Delphi's most famous command: *Gnōthi Sauton*—Know Thyself.

If Ashley were here, she'd be telling me to "know myself," trust my instincts, my purest heart, and to trust *her*. She woke up and gave me an oracle. I didn't ask for it, like Janice selfishly did. I didn't ignore Ashley's situation like Katie has. She trusts me and gave me this gift. And I know what to do with it.

The pain drains from my head into my gut. Still doubled over, I start rocking myself and chanting, letting Ashley's words bubble up from deep inside me.

> *"Under the white stones of youth,*
> *Eternal guarded you'll find,*
> *The Key to the secrets from Apollo's mind.*
> *The gods give the brave a half-week's time,*
> *To delve the deep,*
> *And save this line."*

I mutter the phrases over and over to myself. It's somehow soothing and maddening at the same time—like when you really listen to the words in a nursery rhyme and realize how terrifying it actually is.

I rock and chant, rock and chant, *"Under the white stones of youth, Eternal guarded you'll find, The Key to the secrets from Apollo's mind. The gods give the brave a half-week's time, To delve the deep, And save this line."* Rock and chant.

I hear Katie's voice far off, echoing with concern. "Zach, are you OK?"

I don't answer her, just rock and chant. It means something. Every word means something. A gift from Ashley to me. Nothing wrong, nothing wasted. *Know Thyself.*

The first answer that comes is *the key*. It's not a code. It's an actual key to a lock. But a lock on what? The answer is so close …

Rock, chant, ignore Katie, rock, chant. "... *to the secrets from Apollo's mind ... secrets from Apollo ...*" I think back on the old history book illustrations of the Pythia in her chamber, sitting on a tripod and waving her arms. In ancient times they said that the Pythia actually entered the realm of the gods and that Apollo spoke to mortals through her—this is what an oracle from Delphi actually was, a message directly from Apollo.

So behind a door somewhere are the oracles—maybe recorded or cataloged.

"Under the white stones of youth ..." I mutter "... white stones ... of youth ..." A school? No. A grave stone? No.

The stones emerge from the shadows in my mind—a bag of oddly shaped white rocks, a pile of stones inside a cloth wrap like a sack. "Under the white stones of *youth eternal!*" I pop out of my crouch, sending Katie backward a step.

Fear colors her eyes as she stares at me like she looked at Ashley writhing in her hospital bed yesterday.

"Not *'eternal guarded,'*" I say, raising a finger of discovery. "*Youth* eternal! It's not the guarding that's eternal—it's the *youth*—and that's where we'll find *the key!*"

Katie shakes her head, unable to follow where my head is going.

I know now that there's a key and where it is. But where do we have to go to *use* it? Suddenly I know that too.

I've been wasting my time trying to understand what the oracle means by *"save this line."* Only Katie can figure that out—and *she* doesn't even know it yet.

My wonder and joy of discovery start melting into dismay. The place that Ashley is telling me to lead Katie could easily become a trap—one way in, one way out, no room for error. In that place, mistakes are permanent.

CHAPTER 48

I lie back on the couch, exhausted. I don't know if it's from the mental herky-jerky I just went through or from the physical exertion of the last couple of days, but I can barely move. I was in pretty good shape when I woke up, but now I feel like I've been run through a rock grinder.

Katie wanders around and babbles for a while about Ashley and the oracle—she keeps calling it a poem—how she doesn't accept that it's anything but a delusion and insists that I'm falling for it.

Lacking the strength to argue, I drift in and out of sleep as she rants. A hundred different dreams play in my head at once and run together. I try to follow one to see if I can learn something from it, but it crisscrosses with another and I lose it. Sometimes I think I'm linking up with Ashley, sharing a dream with her. She's there, standing by and watching or doing something in the dream. I try to talk to her, but I can't.

Sometimes I half wake up and realize that I have incorporated what Katie is saying into my dream.

At one point I hear her swear. I crack my eyes open to see her sitting on a chair at the end of the coffee table with my laptop open. She's trying to unlock my computer.

"What are you doing?"

She's not startled, so I have the impression she's not snooping. "I'm trying to get on the Internet. But this thing won't unlock. What's your password?"

"Use your phone." I reach over and close the laptop.

At some point Katie leaves—maybe to go to school, which is where she's supposed to have been the last couple of days. I don't care.

Sometime later, I roll off the couch. It's dark and I'm groggy. The daylight has disappeared from the windows, leaving the bare outlines of furniture and doorways to navigate by as I shuffle into the kitchen to drink some Gatorade.

Then I pick my way upstairs to one of the bedrooms and pull the dust cover off a full-sized bed. I find a quilt and pillow in the closet, wrapped in plastic. I tear the bags open and throw the pillow on the bed, wrap myself in the quilt, and lie down.

I'm out cold in a few seconds. The dreams don't stop.

CHAPTER 49

Sun streams in through the bedroom window. It's late morning. I slept all night and part of the day, my brain and body trying to process the physical strain mixed with the mental storm caused by Ashley's oracle. I still don't feel right. I cover my eyes as long as I can, but I can't drift off again. I have to get up.

I roll off the bed and head for the bathroom, glad to know that there's hot running water to shower with. Finding stacks of plastic-wrapped towels in the linen closet, I tear one open and am hit by the freshly laundered smell. I think of the housekeeper—or maybe my mom—closing up the house after Grandma and Grandpa died, pulling the towels out of the dryer, bagging them, and leaving them here for me to use these years later, somehow knowing I would be back and need them. It's just a fantasy, but a comforting one.

I turn the water on in the bathtub, run downstairs, and grab clean underwear, pants, and a shirt from my backpack. By the time I get back, the water is running clear and hot. I step into the shower, hoping the steam will settle the dust whirling around my mind. Everything is mixed together and only slowly sorting itself out. Some of the especially strong dream images I don't want to let go. I want them to have meaning, and I'm afraid if I forget them I'll miss something important. But as my brain wakes up, most of them dissolve. I can't hold onto them.

I step out of the shower, trying to rub the fuzz out of my head with the towel, when I hear an electronic ping somewhere in the house. I wait a few seconds and hear it again. It's not my phone. I've never heard this tone before. I know the house doesn't have a burglar alarm, but it could be a smoke detector.

As I pull my pants on and tuck in the front of my shirt, I hear the sound again and realize what it is. I turn from the mirror and run down the stairs to the living room. On the coffee table, my laptop is open but the screen is dark. Katie must have reopened it after I went back to sleep. I hit a key and enter my password. When the screen wakes up, I see the message box:

RAMPER!

It's the French word for *crawl*—one of Anton's jokes. His little group of hackers call themselves *les Vers*—the Worms. So when they're successful breaking into a network or altering a code, they shout *RAMPER!* online to let everyone know they're making progress. Now this one French word announces that my trip into the library was not a waste.

I had tried to get into the League's computer network from outside but hit dead ends—no direct connections to the Internet. It's one-hundred-percent isolated, the most effective anti-hacking security measure.

When I asked Anton and *les Vers* for advice, they

agreed it was weird that there's no back door into the network. None of them could find it anywhere on the web and they didn't like it. They took it as a personal insult and a professional challenge.

Their response was to give me the code for a bot that would rove the network from within and find an open node—a desktop computer connected to both the isolated League network and to the Internet at the same time. The main catch was that to plant it, I had to get to a network node directly connected to the League's mainframe—one *inside* the library. That was my best excuse for wanting so desperately to get inside. Everything else Ashley and I saw and did in the library that night was a bonus—if you can call it that.

I wasn't expecting to see the word "RAMPER!" on my computer screen for a while—a few days at least, and more likely weeks. But that insane gambit that pulled the house of cards down on Ashley and me is paying off sooner than I thought.

My heart races. I want to jump online and shout to Anton and the Worms, "RAMPER!" but I realize one thing—I'm connected to the Internet through the city's free WiFi network, the one Ashley said the Committee uses to spy on everyone. I didn't mean to log on, but when I opened my laptop, it must have connected automatically. If this alarm showed up on my laptop, there's a possibility the Committee's cyber-spies know about it.

If they're watching it and looking for me they could trace which WiFi node I'm accessing and figure out what part of town I'm in. They wouldn't know exactly which house, but they could define the neighborhood. That would narrow my location and give them a search area, making my life very difficult very quickly.

I know a countermeasure that could hide me for a while. Online, I easily find the junction for the WiFi connection and follow the link to the city's WiFi central hub. If someone *is* watching me they'll know what I'm doing. And even though this is an easy hack, it's probably setting off alarms at the central server right now, so either way I'll be on the radar within a couple of minutes.

I work fast, finding the network's tracking software. This is the set of codes that monitors which receivers are most active and feeds bandwidth to the right places. I can see that right now the campus and downtown are most active—another strike against me. I'll stand out even more because the residential receivers, one of which I'm on, aren't very busy now.

But I think I can mask it if I tweak one of the codes. I lock onto the master code for the switching station and change one simple command. Instantly, the whole network reacts, snowing the reporting channel. The program that feeds alarms to the town's computer technicians is now maxed out. They won't be able to see me because every receiver will be reporting full capacity. They'll know it's a mistake, but it's buried so it will take them up to a couple of days to figure it out.

Next I jump over to the central archive and find my IP code listed. It's the address of my laptop computer that would be as recognizable as my face to someone who knows what they're looking for. Good news—there's no record of an administrator accessing it, so the Committee probably doesn't know I've logged on. This one will be a little trickier, and I don't have time to jump over to Anton or the Worms to ask advice.

I simply erase myself from the archive list. It's not the only record, but it's the one that reports to the systems administrator who would report to the Committee's security team if they spot me. I'll still show up on a report somewhere, sometime, but, I hope, I'm erased from real-time monitoring. It's the best I can do.

The fact that Dante and Van Hook aren't breaking down my front door right now is a good sign that I'm still invisible.

CHAPTER 50

Now that my location is masked, I follow the bot's alert through the Internet to the open node. I don't have a choice in which node to access. One office worker, against what I'm sure is a strict League policy, has left their computer on with the mainframe connection and the Internet browser open at the same time.

In seconds I'm at the open desktop computer. I crack the personal password quickly and I'm inside, knocking down the permissions settings and giving myself a picture of their screen. Now I'm seeing what I would if I were sitting in front of their computer. It's that easy.

I find the computer's camera and turn it on, revealing an empty office. On the wall behind the desk hangs a small plaque embossed with the same letters as the marble disk in the Arcanville Committee's chamber: Γ-Σ.

I wonder how this Committee's temple is designed. Is it disguised like Arcanville's, or is it just a fortress that doesn't bother masquerading as a library? Maybe it's some old office building that no common citizen can ever enter without getting shot. It must have a town built around it like Arcanville. A college too?

I poke around the desktop, looking for clues to this

computer's location and see that most of the folder names and document titles are in Spanish. Or is it Italian? I'm pretty good with both languages, but the words I'm seeing aren't matching up to either. I glance through them for a minute and start to suspect that the League has its own Latin-based language when it hits me—it's neither Spanish nor Italian nor some secret language. It's Portuguese.

So I've cracked into a PC at a Committee office in Portugal? But the sun is glowing in from a nearby window. It's nighttime in Europe now. Sunlight indicates the Western Hemisphere, where Portuguese is the dominant language in only one country—Brazil. Cripes, the League really is *everywhere*.

Opening a couple more files, I see references to Sao Paulo and Belo Horizante. I look at the clock in the upper corner of the screen—mid-afternoon. It's still working hours in this office. That's not ideal. But do they siesta there? Am I lucky enough to hit this office at their after-lunch break? Just to be sure, I dig into the systems settings and black out the monitor. This way, if the owner comes back to their desk, they'll find the monitor blank and think their PC broke down. I'll be safe for a few minutes.

The files look like pretty standard office stuff. I can't read Portuguese but it doesn't matter. I'm not looking for their Committee's specific business, I'm looking for links to Arcanville's business and to anything bigger that I can use against the League.

With a couple more moves I find the window into the League's network. Here, the code is all standard—no translation necessary. The main file codes indicate that everything I'm looking for is here. Now that I'm on their network from the inside, the security is simple. Only basic password encryptions keep people from entering unauthorized areas. I can break any of them in seconds with Anton's code cracker.

But one file grabs my attention. Written into the title line is the word "Financius." It's Latin for money or finance. A grin creases my face. I came looking for their secrets and found their balance sheets.

I pull the flash drive from my pocket, plug it into the USB port, and run the decryption program. It breaks through the security with ease. My palms are sweating as I wonder what information I'll have access to. If I can learn how their businesses track money, maybe I can disrupt their hidden economy. One altered number on one ledger could throw them into panic. I could burn Maryellen Bradford and her Delphius Group—the people responsible for the drugs Ashley is on right now—just by moving a decimal point on an income report. And it would only be the start of the mayhem I cause them.

Past this password prompt is another, double-encrypted. Not a big surprise—a society whose bloodstream pumps money would want to be careful with the numbers.

I punch in the decryption code again and let Anton's program do its work. But it's not breaking through as fast I thought it would. I can see the decrypter working, running line after line of raw code, trying a million different letter-number combinations. It's not working.

I'm about to pull out of this dead end and go back to the main file when the scrolling code stops and cracks the password. Before it rolls over I see that the password is *nine characters* long. I can't even do the math, but with digits and letters combined the number of possible combinations is in the *billions.*

Anton, you are my superhero! I type a command to save the password. There's no guarantee it will work from any other node but, if it does, getting back in will be a lot quicker.

Once inside I start looking for report headings, business names, and chapter locations. But I don't see any of that. All the headings are in Latin, the official language that all Greek institutions adopted once Rome's takeover was completed in the fourth century. I easily recognize the words for Deposit, Transfer, Balance. My antenna goes up. This isn't a financial statement for businesses, like I thought.

I tab through, opening and closing a few files, perusing the numbers—millions, hundreds of millions, billions of U.S. Dollars, Euros, Yen, Bat, Rupees, Roubles, Renminbi. And this is not an external user interface where reports can be read and shared. This is a mainframe session.

My heart thumps. Everything is pointing to one conclusion so unbelievable that I can only count it as a suspicion, a figment of the broken part of my mind.

Questioning my own thinking, I scroll back up to the top line in the file and read the words I missed before: *Argentaria Delphi.* I recognize the Latin word *Argentaria* and my suspicion is confirmed. I'm inside the League of Delphi's bank!

CHAPTER 51

I stop scrolling and catch my breath. I am in the League's banking system. This is like getting into a bank vault without a gun or a ski mask, and without anyone knowing you're there.

There's one other difference: if it were a real safe, a person would be limited in the amount of cash they could take by how much they could physically carry out. Inside the computer, though, someone could easily transfer huge amounts.

A new world of possibilities has opened up in front of me, unveiled by Anton's brilliant hacker codes. How much damage could I do to the League by not just shifting numbers on balance sheets but by moving rafts of cash out of their system? *Chaos* is the only word that comes close.

Everything I need to ruin them is at my fingertips. I could move money to the bank account in Switzerland where Mom saved my college fund. Or I can open an anonymous account in the Cayman Islands. I can take money now and ask Anton to find someone who can help me hide it and cover my tracks.

But a question stops me: is the transfer potential

really unlimited or are there alarms on certain sized transactions?

My fingers hover over the keys as I consider the hidden risks. I'm far from an expert in finance and banking. There may be a hundred triggers built into this system that could start slamming shut windows like the one I've accessed. Once I move a dime, how long will I have to escape? And what would Van Hook do to anyone caught playing around inside the banking system—and to anyone associated with such a thief?

It's *so* tempting. Enough money would do major damage to the Committee and the League and get me far away from here. But safe? That's another problem altogether. I think of Ashley, trapped and helpless. Money won't help her right now.

A crazy fantasy floods my mind—a thousand mercenary soldiers from all over the world filling the streets of Arcanville, paid by me, loyal to me, taking over the city and rescuing Ashley. Then we'd move on to the next chapter and the next, building an army like Genghis Khan's as we sweep across the world, gathering support. I would conquer the League with its own money.

"*Quê?*" The voice of a frustrated man pierces the quiet, bursting my conquest fantasy like a bubble.

I look around my living room in surprise then realize the voice is coming from my laptop speakers.

He speaks a few more words, of which I can only understand the word "*quê*"—"what?"—and I'm guessing he's asking "*What's wrong?*"

I slide the cursor over to the camera icon minimized at

the bottom of the screen and open the window. The tiny picture box is filled to the edges with the scowling face of a man. His eyes are hard under heavy brows and he glances angrily around his computer screen.

On instinct, I duck away then remember that he can't see me. His screen is blacked-out, which is why he's frowning.

He looks off to his left, calling, "*Claudia!*"

I'm guessing Claudia is his IT expert, which means I have a couple of minutes at most.

I go back to the mainframe window and get out of the bank network. Desperate and short on time, I jump out to the main menu and type in a search command for "Van Hook." With a worldwide network, I can only imagine how many cycles it'll take to find one name, but I have to try.

Within two seconds, I get a ping and Van Hook's name populates several lines. She wasn't hard to find after all. And my nerves go icy when I see why—she's one of the League's heads of security, at a number-two or -three position in the world. They're not screwing around, sending her to clean up Screed's mess. Or maybe she wanted to come here personally, which gives me another idea.

Inside the files with Van Hook's name I search "Sloan" and get several hits. In a secure email box, Ashley is mentioned in a number of subject lines. One stands out, reading "A. Sloan Candidate Transfer Order."

A woman's voice sounds over the speakers. "*Um momento, Senhor Cardoso!*" It must be Claudia calling from the hallway. Her boss's name is Mr. Cardoso. She's on her way to help him.

I open the Transfer Order in Van Hook's account and my heart jumps into my throat. It says they're going to move Ashley two days from now—the day after I think her oracle tells me to take Katie into the library. *Ashley knows*. I seriously doubt they told her when she'll be moved, but she knows anyway.

Larry was wrong—way off, in fact. He said I had months, but Van Hook is moving Ashley *this week*.

Claudia's voice sounds again, louder and closer, but I can't understand the words.

Mr. Cardoso lets fly a stream of Portuguese complaints about his computer.

Claudia responds gently, her voice on top of the microphone now.

I hear a chair roll away from the desk as Mr. Cardoso grumbles.

Claudia mutters thoughtfully to the sound of keys tapping. She'll turn the screen on within seconds.

I scramble to get out of the mainframe session, backing out and closing every file I've been in. I could just make the window disappear by clicking the X but the files would stay open, leaving evidence that I was in there.

I close the last file and click out of the mainframe window just as Claudia says, "OK."

The mainframe window disappears, revealing the video feed and I'm face to face with a pretty young woman—blonde hair, soft blue eyes, small pink mouth.

The face is not only pretty, it's familiar—I *know* her! My shocked brain quickly opens and closes every file in my memory until it stops in France. She was in the girls' school, St. Jeanne, outside Auberjons. She was captain of the girls' programming club. Claudia!

We worked on joint projects with her and the girls from St. Jeanne a few weeks out of the year. She spoke French with a Latin accent so I always thought she was Spanish, but now I realize she's Brazilian. Anton had a huge crush on her. She was nice, but she was older and barely paid attention to us.

Claudia's eyes widen in alarm. She sees the video window on Mr. Cardoso's monitor and my face staring back at her. I turned his camera on without disabling my own—*stupid*! Startled, I move my mouse and click my camera off. It's too late. She's seen me.

I freeze, waiting for an alarm.

But Claudia doesn't scream. Instead, she glances cautiously over her shoulder. Mr. Cardoso sits in his office chair behind her, grumbling. I can see his shoulder but not his face. He can't see me either.

Claudia looks directly into the camera and, in French, mutters, "*Faire attentione.*"

"*Quê?*" asks Mr. Cardoso.

"*O nada,*" she says, dismissing her boss's question. Then she says something to him that sounds like "repaired."

She flashes one last cautioning glare at the camera and clicks it off.

Mr. Cardoso's desktop disappears from my screen and the video feed goes with it. I'm no longer connected to Brazil.

I lean back into the couch, my mind unspooling. Getting caught snooping through the League's system was a possibility I didn't want, but one I could imagine. Seeing Claudia's face on the other end, though, was *inconceivable*. I can't make sense of it.

She works for the League. Has she always been involved? Now I wonder if she was spying for them in France, looking for me. But if so, wouldn't they have come and found me on her tip? Maybe she wasn't looking for me. Or maybe she didn't know about me.

This all has to be a weird, *weird* coincidence. But could it be an accident that I know her from the past, that I'm searching for a way into the League's network, and that her boss's computer was left open and connected like that? No. No one high enough in the ranks to have mainframe access, like Mr. Cordoso, would be that careless. It should have taken me weeks to get lucky and find an open link. It took *two days*.

Claudia caught me, and instead of yelling in Portuguese, *"Hey, someone's hacking us! Call Van Hook!"* she said softly, confidentially, in French, *"Faire attentione,"* knowing that I would understand.

In English the words mean simply, *"Be careful."*

CHAPTER 52

A tap at the window startles me. I see a hand waving then the window starts grinding open. Katie's face appears in the gap. The clock on my laptop screen says it's an hour past school closing.

I shut the computer and get up to help with the window.

Katie drops a backpack inside and I kick it out of the way. I can tell that this time it's not full of groceries but clothes. I wonder if they're for me or if she plans on staying overnight.

Next, she passes in a white paper cup from Bobbie's Coffee Shop capped with a tight lid. My heart sinks into my stomach. Even though I have good reasons, I feel bad for not being at work.

Katie pulls herself through the window easily, now that she's done it a couple of times. She reads my face and says, "What's wrong?"

I hand her the cup.

"She asked about you, wanted to know what happened to you and Ashley."

"Me *and* Ashley?" My pang of guilt turns to a jab of suspicion. I can see Bobbie wondering where I am, but why would she ask Katie? "How did she ask? Did she ask about Ashley by name, or did she say 'Zach's girlfriend'? Did it sound like she knows anything else?"

"She said, 'Where are Zach and *your sister*?'," Katie grumbles. She hates answering questions about Ashley. "Said she hasn't seen you in a couple of days."

"Sister …" I repeat. Bobbie once told me that she lives over in Woodbridge to stay out of Arcanville's politics and society. It sounded like a smart idea, but she seems to know more than she was letting on. "I didn't think Bobbie paid attention to that kind of thing."

Katie shrugs. "She's known us since we were little, opened that place when I was in third grade. My dad takes us there every Sunday."

It bugs me that Bobbie asked about Ashley and me together. That means she's been paying enough attention to know that we're a couple. Who else has noticed? If someone on the Committee figured it out before we caused all this trouble, they could have been watching us, even manipulating us.

Or—this is crazy but it makes a kind of sense—what if Bobbie has been *spying* on me? The coffee shop is a perfect place to watch people. It's one reason I liked the job so much. So many people come through there that it's been a great place for me to get reacquainted with the town. If she keeps an eye on people for the Committee and told them I was up to something, they could have been way ahead of me, knowing that I would do something—or at least that I was messing with their precious Pythia candidate. She did try to get me to talk a couple of times about what's been going on.

I think back on how I got the job there. I searched online for student apartments and found Mike. The day I rented the apartment from him, he told me to go downtown and talk to Bobbie because she was looking for part-time help at the shop. It was exactly what I wanted. And it was so easy—maybe *too* easy.

I feel a net closing around me. Was all this arranged ahead of time? Mike seemed to have no problem with renting an apartment to a lone teen then helping me dodge Dante. And how does Bobbie live somewhere else and run a business in this isolated town without being under the Committee's suspicion?

"What did you tell her?" I ask Katie.

She waves her coffee cup dismissively. "Nothing. Ashley's in the hospital again—big surprise—and I don't know what happened to you."

"Did it sound like she knows about the library?" I ask.

"*Nobody* knows about the library. It's our secret."

That's no consolation. If Bobbie was in on some kind of plan to trap me, or at least to keep an eye on me, then no mention of the library isn't proof that she doesn't know. All the conspirators could be keeping the break-in a secret, especially if they were supposed to keep me out, or keep me away from Ashley, and failed.

"Don't talk to her again," I order Katie. "Don't say another word to her or anyone else."

Katie scowls. "I haven't said anything to anybody."

The possibilities fly around my mind, colliding and breaking up, creating new possibilities. Now there's the video feed from Brazil—Claudia giving me access to all the League's secrets? I thought I was accomplishing these things, but every advantage is starting to look like someone else's trick. My mind is scattering, trying to follow every thread of suspicion.

I shake my head to stop the tailspin, and point at Katie's backpack on the floor. I need a change of subject. "What's this?"

She hesitates, unsure if my question is conspiracy related. "My clothes," she says, lifting it off the floor. "Black. For tomorrow night."

The mention of going into the library makes my gut tighten. Or maybe it's hunger. I haven't eaten yet. I woke up and got sucked right into Brazil before I had the chance. It may be another reason I can't think straight.

I walk into the kitchen, checking windows as I go. It's my house but I still feel like a burglar, or more like a fugitive holing up.

Katie follows, watching as I reach the food pile and dig into a bag of chips and open a Gatorade. "I've been thinking," she says.

Uh oh.

"Why wait until tomorrow night to go in?"

I tense up. Nothing Katie is about to say will be helpful. And my only answer—"*Because Ashley said so*"—will not satisfy her.

"There's not that much I don't know, anyway," Katie goes on.

I stare at her in the waning afternoon light. She only knows about the list. She has no idea what else she'll see in there. She won't be prepared for it—I'm counting on it.

"Unless you want to just tell me who's on the list …" She's baiting me but I can tell she's nervous.

I'm tempted to just blurt out the names. I now have access to a bank with billions of dollars in it. I'm sick of being shocked and terrified. I could get enough money to screw the League, change my identity again, and disappear forever. But there's also a sadist inside me who wants revenge and is willing to endure a little more of this nightmare just to put Katie through it too. Maybe that's part of Ashley's plan—"Welcome to my world, sis!" I smile at the thought.

Katie sees my smirk. "What, you don't trust me?" she asks.

I shrug and turn to the counter, picking out a can of soup—vegetable beef. "I trust you to be who you are, Katie. That's all." I dig through a couple of drawers until I find a can opener and start cranking it on the can's top.

"What's that supposed to mean?"

I take my time, letting her twist. I open a cupboard, grab a bowl, and rinse it off. Then I dump the soup into it and pull the sheet of clear plastic off the microwave oven, hoping it still works. When I open the door, the light comes on—a good sign. I put the bowl in, close the door, and hit a button. The oven turns on and starts counting down from two minutes.

When I turn around, I've already decided not to

answer her. "We're not going in tonight."

She frowns. "Why not?"

"Because this isn't your show," I say. "You're not giving the orders and going in isn't your idea."

"*I've* wanted to go in all along," she snaps.

"Yeah, but you were willing to take an easier deal. All I had to do was tell you who's above you on the list and you'd let me go."

"Then why don't you just ..."

I cut her off. "Because we're working from *Ashley's* plan now."

Katie's eyes harden into icy diamonds that could cut right through me. "Ashley hasn't had a sane thought since she was five years old," she hisses, "maybe never. That *fable* she told you the other day, you think that *means* something? 'A half-week's time?' Because she says some nonsense, I have to wait three days to get my end of the deal? I should ..."

The microwave bell rings, interrupting her threat. She was about to say for the tenth time that she should just call Mrs. Bradford and sic the whole League on me, yada yada yada.

I turn around and pull the soup out of the oven. There must be a spoon in one of these drawers. I find one in a tray of silverware that's been zipped into a big plastic storage bag. I take my time and stir the soup. It's steaming as much as Katie is.

"It doesn't matter what you get or when," I say, lifting the bowl off the counter. "I'm not ..."

When I turn around, Katie is gone.

CHAPTER 53

A couple of hours later I'm back in the front room, finishing a second bowl of soup and anxiously thinking ahead to tomorrow night and the library. Maybe Katie was right—waiting another day is a peculiar kind of self-torture. But I remind myself that I'm honoring Ashley, what she said, and forcing Katie to do the same.

Katie left without a word and I wonder if she'll call to yell at me or send threatening texts. But she doesn't do much of that anyway, probably doesn't want an electronic record that we've been talking and planning. It's OK with me.

Is she finally mad enough to stop threatening and actually pull the trigger? No, I decide. She didn't take her bag of clothes when she left. She'll be back for the infiltration tomorrow night. She's desperate to get inside and won't do anything to blow the opportunity. She knows it, I know it, and Ashley knows it. In the meantime, she's off scheming or silently punishing me— or both. I don't care anymore. I have an inexplicable faith in Ashley's instructions.

I nervously arrange my things on the coffee table, making a just-in-case pile that will, I hope, make all the important stuff easy to grab in an emergency. I learned my lesson yesterday, getting spooked by Katie.

I move papers to free my laptop cord from snagging on anything. Then, as I pile the notebooks into a neat stack, the weird one ends up on top. Sutton's uncharacteristically straight cover art of intersecting lines grabs my eye. After I found it in Ashley's backpack I vowed to look at it later, but I didn't get back to it until now.

I examine the cover again, the tight grid with a blank spot above and to the right of center. When I finally open it I can see that it's filled with more intersecting lines—page after page—with numbers noted alongside them. Is this some kind of geometry class work?

I leaf through, letting the mysterious contents soak into my brain. There's something familiar about this … Then it hits me—I know what it reminds me of and where I can get confirmation.

Before I can talk myself out of it, I stand up and leave the living room, heading through the dining room and kitchen straight to the patio door. It's dark now—outside and inside—so I feel safe opening it to launch a mini recon mission into the backyard.

Over the last couple of days, I've half-expected Larry to come and scope out the house at some point. He's usually way ahead of what's going on, seems to know what I'm up to before I do. But I've been checking the windows constantly and haven't seen even a shadow of him, leading me to think he has no idea that I'm still in town or that someone's hiding in here.

It's possible that he knows but is leaving me alone for

his own wise reasons. Or maybe something has happened to him. Whatever it is, my curiosity about the notebook is overriding my better judgement and pushing me out into the dark.

I step onto the patio and pull the door closed. It's cold and mostly cloudy tonight. The moon peeks out and casts fuzzy shadows across the overgrown lawn. There's fifty yards of high grass between the house and the woods then another fifty yards of woods to Larry's cabin at the riverbank. I know I'm cutting a noticeable path through the untended grass, but after tomorrow it won't matter because I won't be hiding in the house anymore, I'll be gone.

The breeze is freezing my ears so I pull my hood over my head. As I get closer to the trees at the back edge of the yard, I can see points of dim light from one of Larry's cabin windows. The tiny slivers glow unevenly through the leaves, branches, and tree trunks. I crouch as I walk, even though I doubt Larry could see me stalking around up here.

When I hear footsteps in the woods I stop, but realize quickly that it's just branches and leaves rattling in the wind. A few more steps and I'm at the tree line looking for a path. If my grandparents' servants stayed in that cabin, there must be a way to get from there to the house.

I shuffle off to my right, looking for a gap but find only more thick woods. Then I track back to the left and there it is—a dark opening in the trees with a stone path winding away from the yard. After a quick glance over my shoulder at the house, I duck into the woods.

The path feels spongy under my feet—moss between

the stones. Who knows the last time anyone walked on it. I pick my way through the dark, tripping on a ridge of moss every few steps. I keep an eye on Larry's cabin, ahead and to the right, its one lighted window peeking through the foliage.

Reaching the end of the path, I stop at the edge of the little patch of undergrowth that could be called a yard. A couple of weeks ago I stood on the opposite side watching Larry feed sparrows a bag of crumbled muffins he took from the trash at Bobbie's. I had followed him here trying to find out who he was and why I kept running into him. I thought I was pretty stealthy, but Larry knew I was there and invited me to come out and talk to him.

As I tried to be subtle with him, dancing around the edges of my agenda, Larry practically detonated a bomb, saying a bunch of stuff that proved he'd been watching me since I'd returned to Arcanville. He knew who I was even though I was convinced my secret was safe from everyone in this town. Like the other morning when he fixed my knee, he manages to peel back another layer from me every time we meet.

Tonight the cabin looks empty. No movement inside, which is good because I don't want to talk to Larry, I don't want him peeling back another layer. I only want to see that notebook he put in the carton of electrical supplies last time I was here. The glimpse I got was enough to be intriguing. Then for one like it belonging to Sutton to show up in Ashley's bedroom is just weird. I want to get a closer look at it, to see if Sutton's version is a copy of Larry's, a companion to it, or if I'm just imagining that they're alike.

I stare at the light in the window a few yards away—a small lamp in the little living room. I have no idea what Larry's schedule is, if he has one. Is he in there right now sleeping, ready to get up any minute or will he stay in bed all night? If he's out, when will he be back?

Crap! I didn't think this through at all. As soon as I saw Sutton's notebook I should have made the connection to Larry's and started planning a way to examine them together. Then I could have been watching him the last couple days to figure out his pattern. Now I'm flying by the seat of my pants again, right before I go back into the library—bad timing.

I'm taking my first step off the path when I hear a crunch in the woods on the other side of the clearing. I shrink back in the shadows and listen. Footsteps are coming from the direction of the riverbank.

CHAPTER 54

I think about turning to run, but the footsteps aren't coming at me. They're cutting through the woods in the shadows beyond the clearing. I wait a few seconds and see a murky outline emerge from the riverbank path— Larry.

I'm so lucky right now. Thirty seconds later and he would have come out of the woods to find me staring into one of his windows.

He shuffles across the yard toward the cabin, hunched and looking exhausted. Where has he been? He opens the front door without a key. I feel stupid, because I might have gone breaking a window when I could have walked right in the front door.

The screen door slams and he flicks on another lamp, casting a new shaft of light onto the front steps. He stalks across the floor to the kitchen table and the carton filled with electrical supplies, wires, little metal junction boxes, and the strange notebook. But he doesn't touch it. Instead, he turns and paces back to the front door then wheels around and stalks back to the table, obviously agitated. Then he shouts and knocks the carton over, sends it tumbling to the floor with a swipe of his hand.

I twitch with surprise. I saw the anger the other day when I prodded him about not helping me and Ashley. Now it's back—times ten. Before this week, I hadn't seen him mad, didn't think he was capable of it. The first time we met, I yelled at him and he responded with a peaceful *"Namaste."* Now something is driving his fury. It can't be me—he hasn't set eyes on me in three days.

He bends over the table and snatches up a short stack of papers. As it flails in his hand I realize it's the notebook. He curses and slams the pages down like he's trying to pound some information out of them.

Pressing both hands to the tabletop, he hangs his head and tries to calm down. Then he lifts one hand and starts paging through the notebook, studying it closely, thumbing pages carefully at first. He grows frustrated again, flipping pages harder, practically ripping them from the binding, until he snarls and sweeps the notebook off the table, pitching it against the wall and to the floor.

He turns and scans the little kitchen before stepping over to the cabinet and opening it. He pulls out a couple of bottles of herbs and shakes some of the contents of each into the ceramic bowl on the countertop. Then he crushes the herbs together, working them hard with the heavy staff that goes with the bowl. When he's done pulverizing the stuff, he draws half a glass of water from the tap and dumps the mixture in. He swirls the glass a few times to blend it all together and knocks it back, wiping his lips with the back of his hand.

Larry straightens up, the exhaustion evaporated from his body. He seems to have regained some control, but he's still seething. For a moment he lifts his eyes and gazes out the window. I shrink away, even though I know he can't see me. After a minute of staring, he takes a deep breath and shakes his head, pulling himself together.

He slouches again, grabs the cardboard carton off the floor, and sets it upright on the table. He picks up the little metal boxes and spools of wire and drops them back in. He comes up with the notebook and drops that in too. Then he tucks the container under his arm and strides across the floor. He steps out the door, closing it behind him, and walks off into the woods on the path along the riverbank.

I stand a while, listening until Larry's footsteps fade. I can't tell where he's gone. He could have followed the path back to the tunnel entrance a half-mile upriver or he may have turned left and gone out to the street.

Either way, I'm screwed. Larry's angry and I don't get to see the notebook.

CHAPTER 55

The next twenty four hours are a blur of restless sleep, pacing the floors, checking the windows, and running through every possible thing that could go wrong between my house and the inside of the library.

Katie arrives at eight p.m., changes into her black clothes, and paces along with me, trying to ask questions that I don't want to answer. I shut her down over and over. When she finally gives up, it makes for tense silence between us. But it's better than trying to explain my plan.

It's after eleven when we finally leave the house and head toward campus. We're exposed. We're not on the footpath along the riverbank, the most hidden entrance into the tunnels and the library. Completing phase 1 of Ashley's oracle would take too long if we went in that way and would not get done at all if we got lost inside.

Instead, we walk through the old village, taking the alleyways. Katie gripes a couple of times about the smell of garbage behind restaurants but she stays close, not wanting to get left behind.

I'm tempted to lead her into the tunnels and leave her there, let the Committee claim one more victim. But unlike the kids Larry told me about, who went missing years ago, Katie may be smart enough and persistent enough to find a way out. Then I'd be in real trouble.

When we reach the end of an alley at the edge of the village, I stop and lean against the corner of a building, watch the rear campus gate on the opposite side of the street. I peer into the dark for any sign of a roving guard inside. I can see only a sliver of space beyond the six-foot wall. A black-clad guard will be hard to see in the shadows. Plus, the other day the guards and police didn't know yet that I was on the run, so I got away. Now I have to be as careful as I can under the circumstances.

"OK, so what's the plan?" Katie asks for the tenth time. Once, while she was changing into her black clothes at the house, she called the question through the bathroom door. I pretended not to hear her then, and I ignore the question now.

I don't want to answer for a couple of reasons—one: she doesn't know yet about the tunnels, so possessing the rare knowledge of how to get into the library keeps me in charge; and two: she still has the option of taking anything I tell her about schedule, route, and objective and turning it over to the Committee, destroying my ability to fulfill Ashley's prophecy. But once I get her into the tunnels she'll need me, and running away or betraying me will be a mistake more costly to her than to me.

Another even more personal reason is the creeping sense that my analysis of Ashley's oracle is wrong. The way I figured it out wasn't logical, it was more *psychic*. I don't know how this new dimension works. I'm going on what I *believe*, not on what I *know*. If I announce a plan that's based on some sort of imagination and things don't go that way, Katie will try to take over and I'll have no authority to stop her.

I don't see anyone along the street. So far, no bodies move around inside the gate, either, so I step onto the sidewalk. I walk casually toward the street corner that lines up with the gate.

"Zach ..." Katie complains. She can't stand not knowing the plan and being in charge.

At the corner I pause only a moment for a quick glance through the narrow gate. No shadowy figures move around inside, so I step into the street and hustle across. I hear Katie's footsteps on the pavement behind me. She has stopped complaining and is now probably as nervous as I am. We're under the brick arch and on campus in seconds.

I immediately leave the walkway and step into the grass. This wide park-like field lies between the brick wall and a line of trees at the outer ring of campus buildings. I take it at an angle, getting distance from the main walk as fast as I can.

In half a minute I reach the closest tree and stop to lean against it, letting Katie catch up.

"Where ..." she starts.

I hold up a hand to silence her and turn my eyes to the walkways between the buildings ahead. A lone man steps into view a hundred feet out, on the other side of a classroom building, moving diagonally away from us. I can tell by his silhouette that he's a guard—his pant legs are tucked into his boots and a rifle hangs from his shoulder.

I'm guessing all the guards are carrying rifles now. I shiver at the thought of a long gun aimed at my chest.

I wonder how many guards are on campus tonight. If Van Hook doubled security at the hospital the other day, she would certainly do the same here. I hadn't thought of that. I guess I just figured it couldn't get any worse around here. I'm wishing now that I'd taken us in by the river. That route is slow and has serious risks, but flying bullets aren't among them.

We're only about three blocks from the library, but I think about turning back. Once outside the wall, we can work our way back through the village, to the trail by my house and the riverbank.

I turn around and scan the dark lawn we just crossed, calculating how long it will take us to get to my neighborhood now that we've come this far. If we go now, we may still have time to get into the library and out again before dawn.

Katie watches me in the slivers of light. She knows I'm doubting myself. My plan is unraveling already.

I decide to lead her back to the gate. But when I scan wider I see a shadow strutting along the walkway—another guard. If we had stayed on that sidewalk we would have run right into him. Now he's headed to the gate. He'll see us if we go back that way. I clench my teeth in silent frustration, knowing I only have one choice now.

Katie reaches over and grips my bicep. She's seen him too.

Ignoring her, I turn around again. I do a quick scan of the shadows and lights between the campus buildings then jump, moving deeper in—no going back.

CHAPTER 56

We dodge in and out of the shadows between buildings, taking the long way to our target. The more direct path will take us down wide avenues and I can't risk exposing us like that. The other day, guards stalked the roof of the library with rifles, so I want to avoid any direct line of sight as long as possible.

Crouching next to a building, I hear the putt-putt-putt of a motorized security cart. I get a flashback to the night I ran from the guards. They had two carts chasing me down. Poole was on the one that almost caught me. He stopped his partner from shooting me because Screed wanted me alive. Why Screed told them not to hurt me and then tried running me down with his car I can only guess—because he wanted to be the one to kill me.

This cart sounds like it's moving away from us. Knowing we have a few seconds of clear passage, I step around the corner of the building and start running for the alleyway on the other side of the narrow street.

Three steps out the beam of headlights cut across the near intersection and stops me in my tracks—the other cart! Katie slams into me, almost knocking me to the pavement. The motor of the cart throttles louder toward the intersection and the lights grow brighter. For a second, I'm frozen, trying to decide what to do.

I check the distance to the building ahead of us and judge the sound coming to the corner. I can't beat it. As the cart's motor whines louder, I shove Katie back and follow her off the street, into the shadow we just left.

I make it to the building's corner and hear the cart reach the intersection, maybe in time to see us. I press myself against the brick wall next to Katie, panting steam into the cold night air.

The cart's motor and wheels wind down then growl louder as it turns onto our street. I think about retreating but there's no time. We won't get to the back corner of this building before they reach the front. I see a shallow nook in the wall next to Katie and shuffle that way, bumping her along ahead of me. We reach it and tuck ourselves in.

The headlights cast a glow onto the street. The cart putts by slowly. A black-clad guard in a jacket and baseball cap drives. Next to him sits one of Van Hook's men in a heavy black trench coat. He shines a big flashlight into the gap between the buildings that Katie and I were just heading for, sees nothing. Then he turns in his seat to shine the light on our side of the street. We push ourselves harder against the wall, trying to become part of it. The cart is already moving past our position and the light misses us, flashing the opposite wall then the front of the next building as it rolls down the avenue.

Katie sighs and starts panting. I do the same. But we can't hesitate. The closer we get to the library, the more frequent the patrols. We're barely a block away now and someone will come by here again in a couple of minutes.

I lean out to see the cart turn the next corner in the direction of the library. That was close, but we didn't get caught. Ashley's oracle keeps driving me. Whatever happens will happen. I can't stop it.

The street is clear for the moment so I nod to Katie and spring out, crossing and running between the two buildings. When I get to the rear I stop and hunch in the shadows. I recognize the stand of trees rising up a low incline toward the next street.

Beyond the trees is the horseshoe shaped ring of bushes that Ashley and I hid in just a few nights ago. After I said "Run!" and pushed her, she came this way, running for her life. I went the other way to distract the guards. And it worked—until she got home and Katie turned her in.

Tonight, the library is lit up like a night soccer game. I have a disturbing thought—has Ashley told the doctors at the hospital the same oracle she told me? The whole point of their experiments with the Pneuma compound is to get prophecies. Do oracles only come out once or can the Pythia recycle them, tell them again and again to anyone listening? If I was only the first to hear this prophecy—or the last—then they may be expecting some kind of attack in "a half-week's time."

Or this is just Van Hook's way of doing things. Knowing that I'm still out here somewhere and that they need to safely move Ashley tomorrow, she has her whole army on Red Alert.

The putt-putt-putt of a security cart pulls me out of my worry. The headlights' glow passes the bushes and the library beyond. There's our opening. I move for the trees but Katie grabs my elbow.

When I look back, her eyes are wide with alarm. "What are you doing?" she hisses. "We can't go straight up to the library!"

I shush her and tip my head, ordering her to follow. I crouch as low as possible, shuffle along, and pray that no one on top of the library is looking down at us right now. The streetlights and the library's exterior lights shine in all directions, but the trees and the shadows work in our favor.

I thread through the tree trunks and slip into the horseshoe of bushes, keeping my head low, then turn to guide Katie to a spot an arm's length from me, her back against the shrubs.

A guard coughs and walks by just a few feet beyond the hedge. We're so close! I shut out all distractions and work my fingers through the short grass beneath us. Finding the seam in the roots, I jab my fingers deep into the thick, damp carpet. I see the confusion in Katie's eyes. She thinks I've gone crazy. But she goes from doubt to astonishment as a disk of grass starts moving in front of her.

I've found the edge of the iron manhole cover beneath the turf. Working my fingers into the slots at the rim, I lift one side of the plate and the sod on top. When I get a few inches gap, I nod to Katie and she reaches in, helping me widen the opening. With four hands, we're able to hinge the heavy iron cover back and let it drop upside-down.

Katie cranes her neck and gapes into the black hole. The rush of musty subterranean air pushes her back for a breath. Then, as if she has X-ray vision, she traces an invisible underground line from the manhole to the library across the street.

She looks back to me with a hopeful question in her eyes.

Knowing it's not as easy as a straight line into the library, I shrug.

Her face lightens then shifts into a greedy smile. But as she thinks it through her grin slides into a frown. She glances in the direction of the guards. Yeah, she's getting it. She's about to go into the belly of the beast. And it might digest both of us.

CHAPTER 57

The sound of the guards walking and talking just a few feet away sets the clock ticking in my head. The damp air from below ground is warmer than the autumn night and it steams faintly as it rushes out of the hole. It's not the smoke of a forest fire, but it'll be noticed if the light hits the column of vapor right.

I nod for Katie to climb down and she hesitates. I don't know what she expected—some *clean* secret way in?— but she obviously was not counting on a dank, black hole in the earth. She flashes her eyes side-to-side, seeming to consider it. I prompt her with a quiet grunt. We have to get moving!

She shifts toward the hole and I point to the iron ladder rungs on one side. She sits in the grass and dangles her feet, cautiously probing the shaft. Her right foot catches a rung. A little surprised, she probes with her left foot and finds the same rung. Then she takes her first step down. Soon, Katie is confidently dropping into the hole step by step.

When she's out of sight, I drop my legs in and reach for the manhole cover. I have to work the heavy disk up and hinge it forward on top of me while lowering myself.

It's hard work, hoisting a hundred pounds of iron. I grunt once, louder than I want to. I stop and listen for an alarm from the guards. Nothing. I pull again, levering the weight up until it tips toward me. Now the challenge is walking myself down the ladder without slamming the lid down on my head, crushing my fingers, or just closing it loudly enough to call the guards over.

I look down into the blackness. "Psst," I whisper, "I need help."

Katie climbs up beside me, sharing the ladder rungs. She presses herself against me as she reaches up for the cover. Her body is warm and soft. It's an almost intimate position that we both have to ignore.

"Careful," I whisper.

We let the lid down gently, crouching on the ladder to keep the cold iron from knocking into our heads. When the light disappears from the crack in the grass, we're close. I guide the lid the last few inches and seal us in total darkness.

I hope the seam doesn't show on the outside. Before Ashley and I ran from this place, I was able to brush away any dirt and blend the grass to hide the ring. Now, I don't know what it looks like out there. I can only hope no one wanders by and sees a perfectly circular mess on the lawn.

Katie untangles her body from mine and disappears downward. After a few seconds, her feet scrape on the floor of the shaft and there's a sudden flare of light. She has turned on her flashlight. First she aims it up, blinding me with the beam. Then she shines it down into the opening at the bottom.

She won't like what she finds. The duct doesn't point toward the library like she's expecting. A hundred yards long and barely wider than two feet, it runs at a downward diagonal deeper into the ground, angling *away* from our target.

Ashley and I tracked the smell of fresh air and the faint street noise to this spot. We had wandered so long underground that I was hoping we'd found an exit off campus and out of danger. We crawled the last hundred yards to freedom—or what I *thought* was freedom—climbed out of the manhole, and found ourselves just a few feet from the library and the guards.

My feet reach the bottom of the ladder and I take a second to brush dirt from my "NAMELESS" wrist band.

We can't go any farther until Katie moves. She looks up in the low light, her eyes unsure.

My voice echoes dully in the narrow cavern. "We can't stop now, Katie. And we can't go back up. Move or we'll be stuck here."

She hesitates, about to say something, but abandons the thought. Then she reluctantly crouches and pokes her head into the shaft. "It goes *down*," she says. Her voice is laced with worry. The weight of the library is already pressing in on her mind.

"I know, just go," I urge her. There's nothing I could have done to prepare her for this, but if the dragon girl totally loses her nerve now, we're screwed.

After another paralyzed moment, she moves. Her light disappears into the hole first, then her head and body. Soon her legs are gone too.

I follow her in, scraping down the slope on hands and knees. Katie scurries to escape the tight space and the heavy smell of earth. She gets farther ahead of me but I can hear her breathing, harder and harder as her flashlight and shadow shrink in the distance.

I worry that she's edging into panic. "You OK?"

She doesn't answer. But she doesn't slow down either, just rushes on into the dark.

Knowing that this is more a marathon than a sprint, I let her go, choosing to conserve my energy for the long night ahead. Panicking and rushing now won't make things easier.

There's no map of these tunnels that I know of. Ashley and I found this passage because I got us lost on the way out. But having been all around down here once, I think I can navigate our way to the underground library entrance from here. When we're done in the library, I'll use Larry's original directions to get us out by the riverbank. I hope it works—because failure means being lost in these tunnels forever.

After a few more minutes of crawling, Katie is way ahead of me and nearing the end of the duct, desperate to get out.

I open my mouth to warn her about what's on the other side of the opening, but she and her light disappear from the pipe. It's too late.

Katie screams.

CHAPTER 58

I crawl faster toward Katie's screams. I'm almost at the end of the tube when her light pokes back into the tunnel, stinging my eyes.

She follows its frantic beam. "Zach, there's a *guy* in there, a *dead guy!*"

"Go back!" I snap. "You can't come this way."

But she doesn't stop until we're nose-to-nose. "No," she says, "there's a guy ..."

"I know what's in there. Now be quiet or they'll hear you." I point up, indicating the guards on the surface. I don't really think anyone can hear us through thirty feet of rock but it has the effect I want, shutting Katie up.

Her eyes spark and her breath is quick and shallow.

I can't blame her for freaking out about what she's just seen, but I have to be firm. "Calm down," I say, not giving an inch to her retreat, "and back up."

She shines the light in my face and sees how serious I am. When she starts moving backward I start to think she actually trusts me.

I follow her out the end of the channel to a small chamber about four feet long and wide and barely six feet high. Her light is trained on the "dead guy" she was screaming about. It's the skeleton Ashley and I found on our way out. And it's an important part of her oracle.

The lumpy pile of white bones is wrapped in a dusty and tattered shirt with the logo of the disco band the Bee Gees printed on the front. As soon as I saw the band's logo the first time I knew what it meant. I have a couple of their record albums in the small collection of vinyl my dad left me. The logo dates the body—this kid has probably been down her since the late '70s, the last time the Bee Gees were popular.

More importantly, Ashley's and my first impression was that we were looking at a bag of white rocks. The giveaway to its true identity as human is the skull, lying lopsided on one side of the pile and staring empty-eyed at us. Then the flattened blue denim of his jeans extending from the pile makes sense—his fleshless legs leading to the white ankle bones and sneakers at their ends.

"Is it real?" Katie asks.

I nod. "Kids from town who went missing over the years wandered into these tunnels and never found their way out." This ghost story of Larry's turned out to be true.

Katie groans.

"Yeah," I agree. Judging by the size of the skeleton, this kid was barely into his teens when he ended up down here. I feel sorry for him, a future wasted, and such a lonely way to die. I also remember my silent vow after Ashley and I found him to search for his identity, though I doubt that will be possible in the time I have left.

I bend down, staring right into the empty eye sockets, and reach behind the skeleton feeling for the back pockets of his jeans.

"What are you doing, stealing his wallet?" Katie moans, showing what a low opinion she has of me.

I feel it—not a wallet, a hard square in the pocket closest to me. I slip two fingers in and clamp the object, sliding it out easily. When I hold it up to Katie's light she squints at it—a light gray plastic rectangle, barely thicker than a credit card.

"Is that ..."

"'Under the white stones of youth eternal,'" I recite, "'guarded, you'll find the key ...'" The same sickening ring enters my head as when I deciphered the oracle, though it feels dull and distant now. It's like a remote connection directly to Ashley.

"A key card," Katie sighs in astonishment. "How did she ..." she trails off.

I don't bother telling her what I think—that Ashley stole it from the Committee's office while I was distracted and hid it here before we went into the final leg of our escape through the hole. When I tried to rescue her from the psych ward, she kept saying she'd done a bad thing and gotten caught. I thought she meant our going into the library. But this must be what she was talking about, stealing from the offices of the all-powerful Committee.

I have Katie on the ropes, off balance. And I intend to keep her that way until she learns what Ashley wants her to learn.

Katie shakes her head. "If this isn't a tunnel into the library then where are we?"

I chuckle, because somehow the explanation seems ridiculous now. "These are old steam tunnels," I say, repeating the history that Larry told me. "They were dug in the mid-1800s when Arcanville was building a big steam plant to power the town. They were going to put pipes down here running to every building on campus then dig under the town. But something went wrong with the plant and they never finished the project."

"Steam power ..." Katie mutters, looking around. She asks the same question I did when I first learned about it. "How come no one knows about this?"

I give her Larry's answer. "A fire burned up the maps and people just forgot all about them."

"But you ..."

"Yeah," I interrupt her. "You know Larry, that crazy bum you've seen around town? He told me about it."

"Why? Why would he tell you?"

I don't tell her that Larry is really Timothy, my uncle. But I have to give her some explanation. "He explored them on his own and knew I was curious. He doesn't like the way the Committee keeps secrets. So he told me how to get into the library."

Katie points to the duct we just crawled through. "And this is how you came in?"

I debate for a half-second and decide not to tell her about the other entrance by the river. I just let her question be the answer she wants.

I slide the key card into my back pocket. "Come on," I say, shining my light on the bigger opening across the chamber. I don't give Katie a chance to object. I duck into the low tunnel and expect her to follow me. She does.

CHAPTER 59

I lead Katie out of the skeleton chamber through a cramped passageway, and turn left into a small side tunnel. It's roomy by comparison but the ceiling is low and I have to stoop to keep the top of my head from banging on the granite. I remember this section, where the tunnels seemed to shrink the farther away from the main passageways Ashley and I walked.

My light points out oncoming footprints on the dusty floor—I'm following Ashley's and my steps in reverse. This is great! All I have to do is retrace our footprints back to the library.

My stomach sinks, though, as I realize I could have done that the other night and gotten Ashley and me out more quickly and safely by the riverbank. I just went from genius to idiot in two thoughts.

A few paces ahead the ceiling starts to rise, allowing me to stand straighter.

"Ugh, thank God," Katie groans. "I'm starting to feel like a hunchback."

Another half-minute of shuffling and I can stand up

to my full height. We're getting back to the main tunnels and the footprints are still here, making our mission a lot easier.

We reach an intersection and I stop.

"What's wrong?" Katie asks. "Are we lost?"

"Not exactly." I pan my light on the floor of the junction. The branch we're standing in has only two sets of footprints, but the other three are trampled with overlapping and barely distinguishable tracks. I assume most are Larry's. Some—the smaller ones—must be mine and Ashley's. We really were lost if we passed by this intersection multiple times before I sniffed out the exit.

I try to remember the direction we came from—right, left, straight?—to get into this side tunnel, but I can't. All I can remember is that I was following the faint sound of air and traffic.

"Well, which way is it?" Katie asks. Her voice is either panicked or annoyed. I can't tell which.

I don't want to choose, for fear I'll be wrong and we'll wander these tunnels all night—or worse. Damn, this is stupid! How could I be so convinced that I'd be able to just pick my way through and find the library on instinct?

"Zach, if we can't find the way ..."

"No," I say with all the confidence I can muster, "it's this way." I point my light to the right, down the branch of the tunnel where it disappears into darkness.

"Are you *sure*?"

I have to be sure, even if I'm wrong—as idiotic as that sounds. "Yes. Come on."

The bedrock hallway curves. Our feet shuffle and tap on the floor, echoing deep into the labyrinth. I'm already worried that we're going the wrong way. I was lucky, getting Ashley and myself out of here once. Even if I do get Katie into the library by dead reckoning, will I really be able to find the riverbank exit once we're done? I shut out the doubt. I'm building some sort of workable map in my mind—I hope.

Katie is falling behind, her footsteps echoing out of sync with mine.

"Keep up," I tell her. "I don't want you getting separated."

"I *am* keeping up," she says over my shoulder.

Her voice is so close it startles me to a stop. She stops with me and when our feet are quiet, the echo continues faintly behind us, or up ahead—I can't tell for sure.

I click off my flashlight and stand still.

"Do you hear that?" Katie asks.

"Yeah," I whisper.

We wait and listen thirty seconds, forty five, one minute as the footsteps fade. Then they're gone.

"Who was it?" Katie's voice is barely audible.

I shake my head as if she can see it in the dark. It's probably Larry, up to whatever he's been doing the past few days. It's possible, though, that Van Hook has sniffed out the tunnels and sent in a patrol.

"Are they gone?" she asks.

"I think so," I say, but I really don't know. If there are

guards or Van Hook's suits down here, we could walk into the barrel of a loaded gun around any corner. I'm soaked with cold dread. "Let's move ahead. But keep your light off, just in case."

"How are we supposed to see?"

"There's nothing to see," I hiss. "It's a *limestone hallway*. Let's just be careful for a few minutes, all right?" The nerves crackle in my voice.

Katie sighs and puts a hand on my shoulder, following me as I step forward into the black with one hand on the tunnel wall for guidance. I reach into the darkness with my ears, listening for another odd echo. I hear only our footsteps, quicker and more confident, scratching over the layer of fine sand on the floor.

Two minutes into our blind excursion my feet scrape pebbles. There's some kind of gravel on the floor. I definitely have not been to this section before. I keep shuffling and feeling into the dark, wondering about the change in landscape as my toes kick larger stones. In another few steps my hand reaches a jagged edge of wall. I stop.

"What?" Katie asks.

I have a decision to make. Try to feel my way blind or risk turning my flashlight on.

There's nothing typical about this tunnel corner. Its edge is not straight or even, like the well-carved corridors we've been walking. It's ragged and haphazard. I couldn't be any more creeped out touching a fuzzy spider in the dark. This hole doesn't belong here.

"Hey." Katie shakes my shoulder. "Are you OK?"

"I'm fine," I say softly. "We're at a corner. I'm listening for footsteps."

The hard echo of the tunnel gives way to hollowness beyond this gap.

"I don't hear anything." Katie says.

"Me neither." I switch on my light.

A ragged red brick outline interrupts the yellow limestone wall. Inside is a black chasm that drains the sound and light away. I shine my flashlight on the floor. The gravel we've been walking on is the rubble of smashed bricks and mortar. Surrounding the brick edging is a finely cut limestone arch. This was once a tunnel branch that was closed off with the town's standard-issue red bricks. Now it has been reopened with a sledge hammer.

I point my light in as Katie steps up and turns hers on. She pans the light around inside. Another tunnel, three times as wide as any under the campus, stretches off in a straight line so long that I can't see the end. Every few yards a clean hole like a doorway interrupts the wall of the limestone vault—tunnel branches, an expanded network of underground corridors.

"What is this?" Katie asks.

I suddenly understand—Larry lied to me. "More steam tunnels," I say. "Under the whole town."

CHAPTER 60

I slouch against the jagged edge of brick. Larry kept this from me. He insisted that the tunnels only run under the campus, that the project was scrapped before they could dig under the whole town.

"Look." Katie beams her flashlight at the ceiling.

I look up at a thin black cable snaking out the top of the dark hole and making a sharp turn in the direction we've been walking. The wire is attached to the ceiling with silvery brackets every few feet. I add my light to Katie's and draw the beam along the arch about twenty yards, where the black line turns left and disappears into another tunnel.

We trace the cable back toward us and into the hole. It's clamped firmly to the ceiling on the other side and runs twenty yards into the big tunnel where it meets an electrical junction box. Two more lines snake out of that and into the closest archways on either side, while a third runs away into the dark and repeats the pattern.

"What the hell?" I mutter.

Together, Katie and I follow the line of wires and junction boxes with our lights until it finally fades into the shadows.

"They're wiring the town?" Katie says vaguely.

I shake my head. It's not the city or the Committee who's been working down here. I've seen this kind of cable and junction box before—at Larry's cabin the other day, and again last night. The cardboard carton with the funny writing on it.

Larry is wiring the town. But, *for what?*

"Looks like video cable," Katie observes.

Surveillance! Oh, my God, this is how Larry knows so much. He's got audio or video or both running through this entire town. He's plugged into a matrix of information here. He's way more sophisticated than he lets on. His control room must be somewhere inside this deep cavern where the wires originate. I imagine a Bat Cave in there with monitors glowing and servers humming 24/7. How could he keep track of everything? How could he filter everything? And what does he plan to do with all the information? Maybe he's already doing it.

"Come on," I say, stepping away from the hole.

"Aren't we going in there?" Katie asks.

"No," I say, pointing my light to the single cable on the ceiling. "This way."

I walk out of the rubble, Katie trailing. At the next corner I turn left and follow the black line. I know exactly where it will lead.

CHAPTER **61**

After another five minutes of walking and several lefts and rights, the cable reaches a junction box and turns into a side tunnel that I recognize. I know where we are now. I led Ashley in here last week by Larry's simple instructions, only we approached this turn from the other direction. Although I got lost coming out last time, I won't make that mistake again. If we go forward from here and follow the directions in reverse, we'll get to the secluded entrance at the riverbank.

The other night, I crossed this intersection instead of turning. I don't know why. I guess I was so freaked out by what we saw inside, then by Screed and his men chasing us, that I lost my bearings—the fog of war that soldiers talk about? We were lucky to get out. Now here I am going into the library again, this time not following Larry's *directions*, but his *wire*.

A thousand suspicions open like doors in my mind— the mystery of Larry, why he lied to me, what else he's keeping from me, and what he's really been doing down here. I can't deal with it right now, so I immediately slam them all shut and turn right into the narrow tunnel.

"You just followed that wire in here the other night?"

Katie asks.

"It wasn't here the other night."

"What about that hole in the wall? Was that there?" she asks.

"I guess so. But we didn't go that direction."

"What do you mean? You came in through that manhole and the place with the skeleton …"

I stop and shine my light in Katie's face. "We didn't come in that way," I admit. "That's how we got out when we were lost. We didn't pass that ragged hole in the wall."

My own words answer one of my thousand questions. Larry's *very specific* instructions for getting in and out plus his terrifying warning of lost kids never escaping the tunnels—he didn't want me wandering around down here and finding that hole. Now he thinks I've left town, and he's been back down here to finish his secret project and run a wire from his network under the city to the library.

"Zach, this is a dead end," Katie says. Her light shines past me onto the limestone wall at the end of the passageway.

I nudge her shoulder and point my flashlight up at a two-foot-wide hole in the ceiling. The black cable wraps over the rim and follows the shaft upward at a forty-five-degree angle.

Katie's mouth drops open and her eyes widen.

I nod. "You first."

CHAPTER 62

I follow Katie and her wobbling light as she shimmies up the shaft under Larry's wire. She reaches the top and crawls out of view. A few seconds later I find her sitting against the wall in the chamber beyond, catching her breath.

She shines her light around this little vault. Eight feet long and four feet wide with walls of heavy limestone blocks stacked five feet high, it looks more like a tomb than the utility chamber the Bee Gees kid's skeleton rests in.

"Where are we?" she whispers nervously.

"Almost there," I say.

She shifts off her butt and perches on her knees, excited for what's next. But I also see apprehension in her eyes. As much as she wants to see what's inside, she still has to break some major rules to get there. It must be a conflict, even for someone as ambitious as her. I put my hand over her flashlight's lens. She gets the point and, after one last glance around, clicks it off.

I crawl to the front of the chamber and the rectangular, two-by-three-foot door, outlined by the minimal glow from beyond. Without wasting a second I run my hands over the rough planks and find the crossbar at the top. I dig my fingernails into it and pull. The hingeless hatch scrapes lightly at the corners and pulls away, dropping toward me. Warm, fresh air and shady light rush in from the gap.

Katie shuffles up behind me as I gently set the door aside.

"Oh …" she breathes.

I glance over at her face. Her eyes glow like she's looking up into a glass-bottomed aquarium — and she hasn't even seen *anything* yet.

I press my forefinger to my lips for silence then wave her through. She swallows hard and crawls slowly, scanning all around like a curious cat. I follow, joining her in the awkward space inside, then pull the hatch loosely into place behind us.

The slim enclosure is about ten feet long with a limestone block wall on the left. The back of a massive wooden bookcase curves sharply inward on the right, narrowing into one of the yellow limestone pillars that enclose the space at each end. This void is a perfect cover from any library authorities.

The long, horizontal tails of the bookshelves stick out two inches from the back panels like ladder rungs. Some of the dusty footprints on them are Ashley's and mine. The rest are Larry's. He discovered the way in and told me about it after using it himself I don't know how many times. He's been in town over two years, so he has probably secretly explored the entire library using this entrance.

I nod at the footholds on the bookcase's back and Katie stares at me, puzzled. I don't want to open my mouth to explain so I just start climbing. Halfway up I look back to see her grab one of the ribs with her fingertips and pull herself up a foot. By the time I reach the top of the case, she's halfway up and climbing easily.

The view she sees when she joins me at the top is exactly what I saw when Ashley and I snuck in last week—another curving line of eight-foot-tall bookcases, just like the one we stand on, across a circular aisle with pools of low light gleaming off the floor. The ceiling pattern of foot-wide recessed octagons stretches into the dark beyond.

I freeze when I hear muffled chatter—someone talking in the chamber beyond the bookcases? But they're too forceful to be whispers. If they were inside, they'd be loud, so I know they're outside the doors—in the hallway or the offices.

This is the Committee's inner sanctum. People don't usually hang around in such places, but I listen another minute for any indication of someone close by—footsteps, a chair rolling on the floor, the rustling of paper. Nothing.

Satisfied, I step up and rest my belly on the bookcase's top, demonstrating for Katie how to spin around and use the front of the shelves like a ladder down. Only this time I do something I didn't think to do before—I pull the sleeve of my sweatshirt over my wrist, covering my new bracelet, and wipe away the yellow foot dust as I descend.

Katie follows my lead, wiping her footprints on the

way down. At the bottom she does what I did the first time I got inside the library—she stares at the thousands of aged books lining the shelves. "What the ..."

I look up at the top of the case to make note of a landmark. Ashley and I almost got caught by the guards because we didn't pay attention to which case we came over on the way in. Ashley found our dusty footprints and saved us. But Katie and I have just erased that evidence, so I need a better marker.

It's obvious, now that I'm looking for it—the two pillars enclosing the cubby are at the very back of the chamber. If I could draw a straight line from this spot through the inner ring of bookcases, it would hit the front doors. We're at the top of the arc in the semicircle of bookshelves. I won't get lost in here again.

Katie touches a book with a dark red leather binding, slides it off its shelf, and looks at the cover. Running her fingers under the embossed Greek letters, she reads in a whisper, "Kronika Delphoi, Agkos seven thousand seven hundred fifty one ..." She contemplates it a few seconds then turns to me, saying, "*The Chronicles of Delphi*. They're real."

I nod, giving her a silent suggestion to open it.

On the thick, yellowed pages inside are recorded family histories that stretch back thousands of years. The earliest entries are written in an ancient Greek script. Then, following the shift to Roman influence about one-third of the way through, the words change to Latin.

In Greek I can read the letters and sound out some of the words, making sense only of the ones that we still use as root words in English, Spanish, and French. I'm better with Latin because I took a year of it at Rochemont.

Katie must be good with both Greek and Latin—she didn't puzzle even a second over the book's title or the lettering inside.

On every page are four columns, each with a heading. The later Latin page headings say: *Nomen* for name; *Natus* for birth date; *Locus* for place; *Mortuus* for date of death.

Occasionally under *Mortuus*, instead of a death date the word *Absentis*, meaning "Missing," is recorded. Most of those are scratched out and have a date of death entered next to them. A few, like the one I found next to my father's name in our family's chronicle, are still there—no date of death for a person who went missing and was never found.

Each book holds lists upon lists of names, page after page, volume after volume, shelf after shelf—thousands of volumes in this archive alone. I can only imagine how many there are in all of the League's chapters, assuming they each have an archive.

Katie slides the volume back into its place and scans up and down the bay of books.

I know what she wants. I point to where Ashley found their family's chronicle. "Two cases down on the right. Eye level."

I stand where I am, watching silently and giving her space to do what she needs to do. If I hear any sign of someone coming in, we're still close enough to climb to safety before they could reach us.

I wait for a hint that viewing her family's chronicle

267

has an effect on Katie—satisfying some curiosity, scaring her out of her blind drive for power, confirming the truth of a childhood myth. Two minutes later, she's done. She puts the book back on the shelf and looks over at me. Her eyes glisten with the beginning of tears but they don't spill over like Ashley's did. Katie won't give me the satisfaction of seeing her cry.

And she won't give me credit for showing her that the mythical *Chronicles* are as real as the ranking list Sutton told her about.

After another short moment of contemplation, she steps up to me and asks, "OK, what now?"

CHAPTER 63

Now that Katie has seen her family's chronicle, I'm ready to follow Ashley's instructions and fulfill the oracle. And Katie is about to fulfill her part, whatever that is, whether she wants to or not.

I can't resist the pull of voices outside the chamber, so I signal Katie to follow me around the left-hand curve of the bookcases. When I reach the end of the archive shelves, I glance to my right into the Committee chamber.

The room is simple yet opulent. About fifty feet wide and enclosed in the inner ring of bookcases that form a 240-degree semicircle of a wall, it resembles a classic courtroom, except that it's round and there's no jury box or witness stand. Also, instead of one judge's chair at the long, crescent-shaped bench on the riser, there are twelve facing two tables and several rows of benches. Volumes of books, either *Chronicles* or documents of other League secrets, line the inside of the wall up to the edge of the riser.

Behind the bench on the smooth, curving wooden wall is the marble disk, buffed to a mirror shine and inlaid with the two golden Greek letters—ΓΣ. A low yellow flame flickers in a shiny bronze cup below it.

Katie drinks in the scene, looking up to the high ceiling, and exhaling a sigh of astonishment.

I let her stand there, ogling, as I move over to the huge wooden doors. The things probably weigh a ton each, but when Ashley and I visited I found that they swing easily—a marvel of engineering, considering this place was built over three hundred years ago.

I won't be opening them tonight, though. On the other side I can hear the voices more clearly now. They're not close enough to be in the hallway. They're likely across the way in the office.

I tune in to the sound and make out Van Hook's voice. Her strong accent is obvious. There's another woman talking too, arguing—Maryellen Bradford. The office door must be open or I wouldn't be able to hear them this well.

"...move a candidate before the final clinical rounds," Mrs. Bradford is saying. "It's not proper ..." she breaks off, frustrating me. It's like she's pacing the office, reversing direction every few steps and projecting her words away from me. "... new compound," she continues, referring to her latest Pneuma formulation. "The final dosage will ..." I lose the sentence but I get the idea. They're talking about moving Ashley. Mrs. Bradford is against it and I can think of a lot of reasons why, besides proper procedure. She comes back "... now would be *dangerous*."

When Van Hook responds, her voice is clear and steady. I'll bet she's standing tall and stiff, watching Mrs. Bradford pace angrily. "For three thousand years, the Board of Prophecy has managed Pythia candidates ..."

"I don't care about three thousand years!" shouts Mrs. Bradford. "It's reckless. They can give us the standard two weeks to stabilize …"

I hang in the gap and calculate. Two weeks—that's much shorter than the eight to ten weeks that Larry said was standard. Does the new compound work faster than all earlier ones, or was the timeline Larry gave me just more disinformation?

Mrs. Bradford returns. "… is extraordinary."

"These are not ordinary circumstances, Mrs. Bradford," Van Hook replies. "Your security has failed. The candidate is at risk."

"*My* security?" Mrs. Bradford cuts in. "Screed is *your* man. I did what I said I would do. The Delphius Group pulled together the funding and found the lab …" she fades out.

Her big investment group abandoned high-tech research a couple of years ago and went into pharmaceuticals to create a better Pneuma compound. It's very efficient at extracting prophecies from young girls. At the same time, they're marketing a version of it as a prescription drug for ADHD and autism. It's making them a fortune and gives them a perfect cover story.

Mrs. Bradford returns, "… then that idiot nearly killed himself chasing down a couple of *teenagers!*"

"They were inside this facility," Van Hook says, sounding like she wants to knock Mrs. Bradford's head off.

"Admit it," Mrs. Bradford snaps. "You don't know how they got in or how much they saw."

"This is serious, Mrs. Bradford. There may be agents of resistance inside this community."

"*Resistance*," Mrs. Bradford sneers. "You think that girl and whoever she was with are *agents*? She's a kid. And she's not lucid enough to even tell us *why* they came in."

"This is not simple teen mischief," Van Hook insists.

"Well, whatever it is, it's not my fault. If your people had done their jobs properly, the candidate *would be* secure."

"Nevertheless, I declare that Arcanville is under a security threat and that the candidate is in danger," Van Hook says. "I have orders from Arachova to move her immediately, so tomorrow ..."

A hand on my shoulder shocks me from my concentration—Katie behind me, resting an ear against the door. The look in her eyes says she heard it too—or heard enough.

"But, moving her now could *kill* her," insists Mrs. Bradford.

A bang like a gunshot—Van Hook's fist on something hard and hollow—announces the end of the argument. "We are out of time, Mrs. Bradford!" the security chief shouts. "The Board of Prophecy is *desperate*. Our society is fracturing. Release Miss Sloan to me or I'll ensure that everyone knows you held back the most promising Pythia candidate in a century while the League's last useful oracle expired!"

CHAPTER 64

My knees feel weak as I reel from the door. Katie keeps her ear pressed to the panel but follows me with her eyes. I stagger back a couple of steps and lean against the last bench row.

Van Hook's words, "... *the League's last useful oracle*" echo in my head. She also said, "*We're out of time!*"

It was in one of Sutton's notebooks. He had written part of a sentence—"*running out of time!*" I thought he had figured out that the League was chewing up girls with the Pythia Program and their Pneuma, and that he ran out of time before he could stop his mom from doing it to Ashley.

But it's bigger than that. He found out that the League of Delphi's oracles—the tools they've used to stay ahead of the rest of the world for 3,000 years—are running out. They are out of time and they're desperate. Maryellen Bradford's new Pneuma compound is their last hope.

Larry told me Mrs. Bradford didn't care about the money she would make from the new formulation. He said the entire League would owe her for creating a substance that would produce oracles more efficiently.

Now I understand how big a deal it really is. Their *survival* depends on it.

Ashley is something special too—"*the most promising Pythia candidate in a century*"—and Van Hook will risk her life to get her to Greece where they can start pushing her abilities to the limit, pumping her for information right away.

Katie gives up on the door and steps over to me.

I don't hear the voices from the hallway anymore and I don't know how long we'll be safe here. "Did you hear that?" I ask her. It's more an accusation than a question.

She doesn't say anything.

"Still think this is all a joke?"

"I never thought it was a joke," she says quietly.

"It's not a *myth* either, is it?" I don't bother keeping the edge out of my voice. We're in too deep now to play games.

Katie's eyes slide away from mine, toward the aisle of books we just came from. "Let's just go," she says, shame and desperation coloring her voice as she leans toward our escape route.

"Brian and Misha," I say. With Van Hook and Mrs. Bradford crowding the office right now, we won't get in there. I might as well tell her.

Katie stops and locks her eyes on mine.

"That's who's above you on the list. Brian then Misha then you. So, once again, you've picked the perfect friends to help you get to the top. Find the chinks in their armor and bring them down. You're good at that. Now you know everything you wanted to know. And good luck with it."

Katie's eyes are soft with regret. "Zach, I didn't ..."

I tip my head to the other side of the chamber, cutting her off.

Katie looks in that direction.

When her eyes come back to me, I'm holding the key card up. "*'To delve the deep,'*" I recite Ashley's oracle, that dull ring returning to my brain. "You can leave if you want."

I push myself away from the bench, and without looking back, head for the far aisle. Two steps in I find what I'm expecting — a narrow staircase, half the width of the aisle, dropping into the floor. A bronze railing fences off the ledge of the opening and the shiny handrail glides along the steps, down into the dark rectangle.

When Ashley and I were in here, we didn't use this end of the looping aisle. But as we hid on the other side of the bookcase, waiting for the right moment to slip back through the hatch, I remember Screed ordering one of his men to *"Check the lower level, but stay out of the vault."*

I know Ashley didn't see the stairs down. We were together the entire time we were in the chamber. Yet somehow she knows they're here.

When I set foot on the first marble step I feel a jolt of cold energy shoot up through me. I ignore it and keep going, tapping down the steps fast enough to keep from changing my mind.

As I drop into the dark, I hear Katie's footsteps on the stairs too. Maybe she's decided to find out what her sister meant when she looked right at her and said, *"And save this line."*

CHAPTER 65

My feet hit the bottom step and I see a green glow ahead in the dark. The display screen on an electronic lock is the only light in this curving hallway, guiding me right to my destination.

I stop in front of the vault door and stare at the little screen. The dim green letters say, "KEY."

Katie steps up close behind me as a million terrifying images of the vault's possible contents flash through my mind—everything from dead bodies to ferocious live lions to a bare empty room. My churning gut is telling me not to open this door. An alarm could sound, a lion could maul me. Even if I make it out alive, I'll never escape what I see inside.

Katie nudges me. I don't know if she's dying to see what's in there or if she just has enough sense to know that standing in the hallway like this is a bad idea.

This is it. I slide the card over the key reader. The lock beeps and the screen flashes red. My stomach sinks. We're too late—this card's owner found it missing from their office and deactivated it.

But the readout flashes the word WAIT twice in red then changes to a green SCREED, KENNETH.

I can't believe it—Ashley went into Screed's office after me and stole his key card! That's what she was doing while I ran for the chamber. Somehow she knew to do that. Was it a guess or some kind of real foresight, a vision from an experiment they did on her?

The lock clicks and I push the door open, happy to see a warm yellow glow inside. Katie follows me in and lets the door close quietly.

What I see is not terrifying or even very remarkable—a rectangular room about thirty feet long and fifteen feet wide. On the back wall hangs a disk like the one in the chamber upstairs—shiny marble with the familiar gold letters—but much smaller, maybe two feet in diameter.

At the front of the room stands a wide, wood-framed screen with solid sheets of green silk strung between its posts and crossbars. The yellow glow emanates from behind it.

Diamond-shaped wood racks line the sidewalls front to back, filled with what look like narrow, capped tubes. Katie reaches over and lifts one out, showing me that it's not a tube. It's a double roll of paper with small wooden knobs at the ends—a scroll. She grabs the knobs and pulls them apart, unrolling the first few inches of the ancient text. I can see lines of script on the paper.

"What's it say?"

Katie squints at it. "It's in Greek. A poem, I guess." She struggles to translate the words. *"'Being low with its ... something ... the serpent ... not stand. Hide in ... grass ... escape Hermes' eye ...'"*

She shakes her head. "I can't read it all. It's handwritten and it's old."

"Is it in verse?"

She unfurls the scroll a few more inches. "Yeah, six lines each. Short lines ..."

"Oracles," I say.

She squints at it again then looks up to the line of racks against the wall, stacked three-quarters of the way to the ceiling. Just like the books upstairs, there are thousands of them.

"This is the vault," I explain, "where they keep 'The secrets from Apollo's mind'—prophecies from the god himself, spoken through the Pythia."

Without a word, Katie rolls the scroll closed and sets it gently back in the rack. Then, entranced by the flame, she drifts up to the green silk screen. She peeks behind it and gasps.

CHAPTER **66**

I step up next to Katie and look behind the screen, where an ornate bronze fixture stands, on fire. My brain registers danger until I see that the apparatus isn't burning up, it's built especially to hold the flame that lights this room.

The small fire is contained in a one-foot-diameter bowl with three evenly spaced rings jutting up from its patterned rim. Three grooved legs, almost four feet tall with lion's feet, hold it up.

Everything is polished and gleaming in the magical light, except the tripod's center column of three entangled snakes caged within the legs. The entwined serpents spiral upward to the bottom of the bowl, which they seem to support on their outward pointing heads. They lick the air menacingly with forked tongues and the dark green surface of their unpolished bronze skin makes them eerily lifelike.

I know it immediately from pictures and descriptions. It's a copy of the Delphic Tripod that the Pythia sat on when delivering her oracles. The flame burning in the dish must represent the presence of the Pythia or her patron Apollo.

Inlaid into the marble floor beneath the tripod is a jagged line of black granite extending three feet from the wall, mimicking, no doubt, the crack in the earth that emitted the sacred Pneuma at the original site in Greece.

I get it—this whole room is a reproduction of the Adyton, the small chamber deep inside the Temple of Apollo at Delphi where the Pythia entered her trance and the priests recorded her six-line prophecies for translation.

But only when I look up do I see what drew a gasp of horror from Katie. On the wall, bathed in rippling yellow light, two-dozen photographs of young women hang in small golden oval frames. The girls in the pictures are of all races, from all over the world. The oldest is maybe twenty-one and the youngest—a dark-skinned Asian girl—can't be older than twelve.

On each face I see the smoky, slack expression that Ashley had in her hospital bed, the ashen, dry skin and cracked, flaky lips. Their eyelids are limp and crusted. The harsh white flash of light on each of their faces makes them look raw and ghoulish, unwilling and vulnerable.

Katie utters a deep groan and teeters on her feet, grabbing hold of the screen's wooden frame for support.

I feel the same. This gruesome display turns my stomach. I look for Ashley's face, but it's not there—not yet.

I'm guessing these are the current Pythias at the convent in Arachova, the place that Van Hook is so desperate to get Ashley to. And when she does, they'll take a photo of an exposed Ashley lying dazed and helpless in a bed. Every chapter in the League will get a copy to hang on the wall in their private Adyton. Only, here at Arcanville, the Committee might give her a place of honor, because she is so special to us—our *sacrifice*.

Katie drops away from the scene, stumbles over her feet and slams backward against one of the racks, rattling a thousand scrolls. Her eyes are wide with confusion and fear, unfocused and darting. "I ..." she tries to express a thought that dies in her throat.

I reach out to help but she snaps herself upright and steps away with a weak wave of her arm. On feeble legs she makes her way toward the door, sliding one hand into a hip pocket. I worry she'll pass out and drop to the floor, but she manages to keep her feet moving.

When she reaches the door I move to follow her. I've seen enough too, and getting out of here sounds like a good idea.

What happens next feels like it takes an eternity, but it's probably only three seconds in real time. Katie grabs the door handle and turns her face to me. The look in her eyes—fear, pain, regret—stops me cold. I register what it means—*betrayal*. She pulls a small, fat plastic disk the diameter of a quarter, from her pocket.

"I ... believe it," she croaks weakly. "And I'm sorry." She presses the center of the disk—a button—with her thumb and tosses it to the floor. Then she opens the door and runs out, slamming it behind her.

As the disk skids to a stop at my feet, I stare at the tiny red light blinking at its center. If I'm lucky, it's a bomb that will explode and kill me right now. But more likely it's a tracker, given to Katie by Mrs. Bradford, Dante, or Van Hook. This whole time it lay sleeping in her pocket, waiting to be activated when we reached a good spot.

I'm frozen in place. I know I should be freaking out, chasing after her, but I've chosen total, numb shock instead. Precious microseconds tick away as I stand like a stone, trying to squeeze out a thought, a reaction, a command of what to do next.

After what feels like an eon, an alarm sounds upstairs, breaking my paralysis. Finally, I draw a breath and push myself toward the door and escape. But before I can reach the handle, the lock clicks.

I'm trapped.

CHAPTER 67

The alarm screeches distantly, same sound as the security alarm at the hospital. I throttle the door handle but it doesn't budge. Ripping the gray key card from my pocket, I wave it frantically around the handle, hoping the sensor outside will read it and open for me. Nothing.

She did it! She actually did it—turned me in. I thought once we got into the tunnels I was safe, that there was no way she *could* call security. Then I was sure that after seeing the *Chronicles* she *wouldn't* rat me out. I thought she'd be convinced that the League is up to no good, that she couldn't stand to be on their side. She even heard Van Hook and Mrs. Bradford saying they could kill her sister and she *still* went through with it.

It was a genius move. She waited until I got her into the Adyton before she dropped the net on me. If she'd done it any earlier she wouldn't have gotten to see this holy of holies. The League never would have let her in here, whether she helped them or not.

There are footsteps and voices upstairs. "Here! In here!" They're not at the stairs yet but it's only a matter of seconds.

I step away from the door and stomp on the disk like it's my stupidity. I'm not even mad at Katie. I knew she was capable of this and I brought her along anyway. I'm the frog in the fable who ferried the scorpion across the stream and was rewarded with a deadly sting—the stupid, gnat-brained frog!

"Lost it ..." a voice says upstairs.

Larry was right. I should have left town when I had the chance.

"Definitely in here somewhere ..." says another guard.

Yes, the disk Katie activated was not only an alarm, it was a homing beacon. The guards upstairs are tracing the signal but it disappeared when I stomped on their bug. They don't know yet that it originated ten feet below where they're searching. It gives me a few seconds. I'm not going to just sit here and wait for those assholes to come and grab me.

I turn and scan the room. Seeing instantly what I have to do, I run to the front and knock the screen away, exposing the bare flame on the tripod. I step up and swipe my arm down the wall of shame, sending a swath of those grotesque portraits smashing to the floor—my last act of defiance against the League. Then I grab a bundle of scrolls from the nearest rack and throw them down at the feet of the tripod. They scatter and unspool across the polished floor. I toss another bunch, emptying bin after bin until there's a loose pile.

The voices are closer now. They've figured out where I am.

I grab two last scrolls from a bin, one in each hand, and snap them open, letting them unravel like rolls of toilet paper. These are my wicks. I hold the edge of one over the burning bowl, letting it catch, then drop it on the pile at my feet. The other, I lay right across the flame, which instantly eats through the dry banner and sends the two halves flaring to the floor to set off two then four then six scrolls.

The voices of the guards grow louder. They're heading downstairs toward me.

I back away from the expanding fire. The temperature in here is already shooting up. The puny vent above the tripod can't handle all the flames and black smoke rolling off the pile.

The men are outside the door now. The shouts stop as they gather and quietly coordinate their entry. I can hear their tense murmurs when I pass by.

One of the men starts counting off the attack, "One ... two ..."

I get to the back wall and yank the marble disk from its mounting screws.

A horn sounds, followed immediately by an unexpected whoosh of dry, white mist from a dozen holes in the ceiling—fire extinguishers!

At the same moment the voice outside barks "... THREE!" The door hinges open in front of me and a line of black-clad men charge into the spewing fog.

"Fire!" shouts the first one, disappearing into the cloud.

"Cover! Cover! Cover!" calls the second as two more guards stream into the engulfing fog and smoke. Their shadows grow large and monstrous against the orange haze as they rush toward the raging flames.

The last man in line sweeps his gun in a wide circle, blindly searching for me. Before the barrel draws a bead on me I swing the disk and slam it down on his head, sending him to the floor.

Then I take a step and two-hand throw the disk at the hazy shape of the next guard. It hits him in the side of the head and knocks him deeper into the fog.

Amid the shouts and confusion, I shoot for the open door and stab out of the cloud into the hallway.

I dash for the stairs and encounter a fifth guard running down the steps. He spots me and reaches for his gun but he's too late. I bend my hand back and smash the heel up into his jaw. His downward momentum meets my forward motion and multiplies the force of the blow, snapping his head back and knocking him flat against the marble steps.

I'm up the staircase in three strides where more voices hurtle toward me. At the top of the railing I pivot and run toward the center bookcase where I can climb over and get out.

Behind me, a man shouts, "Freeze!" and I know there's a gun aimed at my back.

I sprint into the curve, eliminating a straight shot, but his heavy footsteps track behind me. I can't risk climbing the bookcase with a guard so close on my tail.

I accelerate, taking the curve as fast as my sneakers will allow.

Shouts in the chamber and the vault: "Fire!"

"He's on the run!"

"In the chamber!"

"Fire in the vault! Fire in the vault!"

Horns and alarms blare. Footsteps close in on me.

Suddenly the lights snap on and the shadows evaporate. I run for the end of the aisle and see the blaring light of the chamber beyond. A figure in a gray suit appears in front of me. I duck and dodge right, slamming my shoulder into his ribs, and send him spinning over my back with a yelp of pain.

I punch out of the aisle toward the huge doors standing open. A man runs in with a red fire extinguisher and turns left for the vault. Two steps from the door, my pursuer yells, "Grab him!" but he's too slow.

I'm through the door and in the hallway, charging blindly at a row of figures who block the corridor. I can't stop or turn. And it happens. A loud pop and a jolt of paralyzing pain slams into my chest. I seize and twist on my feet.

They shot me!

Then another pop and another hot sword stabs through my back.

"Got him! Got him!" a man shouts.

I fall onto my back, waves of fire rolling through my body, and hear the clicking sound of my nerves dying.

This is it. This is death. Everything goes hazy.

Dante steps up, pointing a gun down at my chest. He finally got me. Next, Van Hook looms over me, her eyes narrow and angry—the last thing I see.

CHAPTER 68

A spirit flies up my nostrils and shoots diamonds into every cell in my brain.

"Wake up," a surly voice pierces the dark, rattling my consciousness.

I hear a sharp crack and the spirit flies in again, blasting more diamonds, this time blowing stinking chemicals in and bringing a flood of searing light.

"Wake up," the voice growls again—a man, an unhappy one.

My eyes open to a sheet of white light, blobs of black, brown, and tan undulating in front of me. One of the blobs moves close to my eyes and goes SNAP! SNAP! It sounds like the clicks that riveted my dying nerves while I was lying on the marble floor. My body hurts and my head swims miserably.

I manage to focus my eyes and see that it's a hand—fingers snapping in front of my face. SNAP! SNAP! again.

"You awake?" the man says.

The sear of the light dims to a sharp pain in my eyes and I can see beyond the hand now. I look into the weathered face of Dante, his grim eyes examining me.

"You with me?" he says gruffly. His questions are hardly questions. They're more like statements *to* me *about* me. Two paper-wrapped capsules sit broken on the table between his hands—smelling salts. The reek of ammonia wafts around him. He looks over his shoulder. "Go tell her he's awake."

Behind Dante Poole opens a door and steps out. Before he closes it, he looks back, his eyes lingering on me—I can't read the expression—then he's gone.

Every muscle in my body is clenched and achy. I feel burning spots on my chest and back. I want to rub the pain out of my skin but my arms are stretched tightly behind me. When I try to bring my hands around to my front, a clink of metal on metal and cold bands on my wrists tell me they're in handcuffs. Another tug makes the whole chair rattle. Panic swells inside me. I'm trapped, exposed, alone! But I also feel Ashley's bracelet still strapped to my wrist. The gentle clinking of the tiny metal plates calms me.

I look down at the front of my sweatshirt where there should be a bullet hole. "You shot me ..." I mutter.

Dante smirks unhappily. "Taser, you little asshole."

I stare into his face, trying to comprehend. Then I glance helplessly at the door, indicating Poole, who has been helping Dante track me down.

"*Two* Tasers," Dante says. "More voltage than you should get. Knocked you out, but ..." he looks me up and down with disgust. "... didn't *kill* you."

Tasers, voltage—pain, but not death. I can't decide if I'm lucky or unlucky.

"You're harder to catch than a river rat," he sneers.

I don't respond, just stare back at him.

"You think you're pretty smart? Couldn't dodge us forever, though." His expression is sick and his breath is putrid.

I remain stone silent, knowing that nothing I can say will get me out of this alive.

Dante's eyelids weigh heavily as he examines me. Then, seeming to get an idea, he takes a furtive glance over his shoulder at the closed door. When he turns back to me, the edge in his voice is hungry, the same tone as when he told Poole in the hospital stairwell that he wanted to catch me. It would somehow be good for his career. "How'd you get in here?" he asks.

My lips tighten. I won't give him one bit of information. But he's just told me something I need to know. He asked how I got in *here*, so I know I'm still in the library.

I look around the windowless room, trying to guess if I'm in the basement, anywhere near the vault. Probably not, because I don't smell smoke. The library is three stories high. I could be in any interior room on an upper floor. With one door and no other openings, this looks like a jail cell of some kind.

Dante tries to read my face. "Tell me now how you got in and I promise not to beat it out of you."

It's a trick that I won't fall for. He knows how we got in—Katie has already told them everything. He's just trying to scare me, soften me up, knowing that once he gets me talking, I'm likely to say more and betray myself. When I don't answer, his eyes harden. He really hates me. I've caused trouble for him and his men. I may be the reason he's not getting Screed's job and he wants me to pay.

Just as he cracks his mouth again, the door opens, interrupting his next threat.

"Mister ... *White*," Van Hook's voice fills the room, poking me ironically with my phony name. Her Dutch accent makes my lie sound even more ridiculous.

I instantly get it—she knows who I really am.

CHAPTER 69

Dante leans away from me and clears my view of the tall blonde woman striding through the door, Poole right behind her. She dominates the room with no effort. Unlike the scheming head security guard, she has a power in her presence that draws my attention and respect.

Dante shrinks and slides his chair over, making room for his new boss.

Van Hook doesn't sit right away. She drops two thick file folders on the table. "Thank you, Mr. Poole," she says without turning to look at the younger guard. "You are relieved." Her accent lends even more authority to her voice, another tool she deftly uses to communicate and persuade.

Poole glances uncertainly at the back of her head then down to Dante, who gives him a nod.

The younger guard takes a long, apprehensive look at me that the other two can't see. I know what it means—Dante is taking all the credit for capturing me. It won't be *"good for you, too,"* like his supervisor said. His opportunity to share the spotlight is evaporating. But he doesn't linger. He obediently steps out the door and closes it behind him.

As Van Hook sits down, Dante levels a murderous glare on me, making believe I'm still *his* quarry. But his authority is eclipsed by his new boss.

I decide to fire the first shot. "Where's Katie?" I growl. I want them to know that I'll chew up their little snitch if I get my hands on her.

Van Hook and Dante exchange a tentative glance. "That ... is not your concern," she says to me.

Dante looks uncomfortable. His arrogance crumbles when someone else takes charge. I feel like I've landed a blow to their confidence.

Van Hook pauses to reestablish control then asks, "Do you know who I am, Mister ... *White*?" once again lacing the name with sarcasm.

I don't answer.

"My name is Anke Van Hook. I am the assistant director of security in Europe, North America, and South America for the League of Delphi. I was born in Arcan, Netherlands—birthplace of this town's founder, Jan Van Arcan. I still live there today, and I keep offices in Greece, the United States, and Brazil." Her sharp brown eyes gaze directly into mine as she talks. But she's not looking for anything, like Dante was. I get the impression that she already knows everything she needs to know. "My parents have been dead many years ..."

Dante peeks at her from the corner of his eye. This is not how he expected her to pick up his interrogation.

Van Hook should be breathing fire at me, trying to

intimidate me, scare me into cooperating. But, unlike her approach with her men, she is surprisingly mild toward me.

"I am thirty-seven years old," she continues in a familiar and gentle tone, "I am not married, I have no children, I speak seven languages, I have traveled around the world many times. I love my job."

She has my full attention. I doubt that most people get to know her over the course of years as well as I'm getting acquainted with her in our first minute together. Even Dante is confused by her over-sharing. And there's something about her that's ... *not hateable*, is the only way to describe it. That makes her different from Screed and Dante—and even Maryellen Bradford. They're all immediately unlikeable. But this woman is somehow sympathetic—or maybe she's just being that way with me.

"Why are you telling me all this?" I ask.

"Because we have some very important matters to discuss and I want you to know me and trust me. It will save us the time we would otherwise waste playing games."

Dante frowns. He was hoping for "games."

Van Hook peels back the cover of one of the file folders. When it flops open I see, stapled inside, a photo of me at seven years old. It was taken at school just before Mom moved me to France.

"J'ai été chercher pour vous pour un temps très long,"

she says in French, watching me for a reaction.

I go cold at her words—"*I have been looking for you for a very long time.*"

She smirks warmly when she sees the language register. "Mm ... I thought you were somewhere in France. But your mother made you *impossible* to find." Her eyes gleam with admiration for my mother's trickery. "Yes," Van Hook says certainly, "I know you very well ... Joshua Darcy."

The mention of my real name drops a brick into my stomach. And the way Van Hook leaves the irony out of *this* name explodes the brick, blowing up my secret and my security. No one is supposed to say that name. Ever.

"Or at least, I know *your family* very well," she continues. "I haven't had any new information on you for ten years. Now, in very short order, Arcanville's Class-A Pythia candidate finds a boyfriend, they break into the Committee's headquarters together, the head of Security is in a near-fatal accident, and a seventeen-year-old boy goes to the hospital saying he was struck by a car, *et voila!*" she exclaims in French. "Here you are."

She folds her hands over the pages of my open file and leans forward, appraising me warmly like Mom used to before she became ill.

I know I should say something smart, but I'm not feeling it right now. I've lost Ashley for real this time, I let Katie betray us again, and there's nothing keeping me alive. All the defiance has drained from me. "I'm not going to tell you anything," I say.

Van Hook's smile turns sad. "I know," she says. "This

is my time to tell *you* something, yes?"

She closes my file, sets it gently aside, and slides her thumb under the next file's cover. "You've been working with the man known as *Larry* since you returned," Van Hook says. It's not a question.

She flips the file open. Fixed to the inside cover is a photograph of my father.

CHAPTER 70

I look at my father's photo upside down. It's an ID photo from around the last time I saw him. There's also a group shot lying loose in the file. I recognize my father and a younger Maryellen Bradford, but none of the other ten unsmiling men and women sitting at the curving council table in the Committee's chamber. Just seeing the photos of Dad hits me with a wave of fear. Van Hook has made the connection between me, my uncle Timothy—who's been posing as homeless Larry—and my father.

"James Darcy," she says, with an edge in her voice. "He was chairman of Arcanville's Committee for four years—until he went missing approximately ten years ago."

"He died in a plane crash," I say, offering the story I've been told my whole life. I really should keep my mouth shut. If Van Hook gets me talking I could let something useful slip and not even know it. Wherever Dad is, I don't want her and the League to find him.

She gives me a disapproving look. "You and I both know that is not true."

I slouch in defeat. I should give up the story—everyone else has.

"You did look at your family's chronicle last time you were here," she says.

My face tells her the truth.

"It's all right," she forgives me. "How could you resist? It's the first thing *I* did when I won the security clearance that allowed me into Arcan's library."

I shuffle my feet nervously.

"So the chronicle lists your father as missing," she says, ignoring my discomfort, "but we know that's no longer true, don't we?

I stare dumbly at her. *"No longer true"?* Did Van Hook find him? Did she *kill* him?

She smiles slyly, like we're sharing a secret. "You've reunited. You're working together."

The words hit me like an electric shock, surprising and disorienting me. "Reunited?" I ask. I haven't seen my father since I was seven. There's no way anyone could think we've been together.

Van Hook tilts her head as she studies my face. After a moment, her smile fades and she leans back in her chair. "He didn't tell you."

I shake my head, suddenly overwhelmed with the implication. "Larry's my *uncle*, Timothy ..."

"I'm afraid not, Joshua. Timothy went missing before his eighteenth birthday and hasn't been heard from since. Your uncle is dead."

My head won't stop shaking. "No ..."

Van Hook leans over and whispers a few words to Dante. He stands up and leaves the room.

My mouth works as my mind reels, trying to keep things straight. "Timothy Darcy *left* Arcanville," I say, reciting the story that Larry—*Timothy*—told me when I was in the hospital. "He traveled the world and settled in India ..."

I'm saying way too much. I could be spitting out every secret Van Hook was hoping to get about Larry—er, *Timothy*. If this is an interrogation trick, it's working. But I can't shut myself up. "He got his head straightened out and he came back here ..."

The door opens, interrupting me. Dante steps in, a file folder in his hand, and stands behind Van Hook, watching my mental disintegration.

"I'm very good at my job, Joshua," Van Hook explains. "I scoured the earth for any trace of Timothy. If he was out there, I would have found him."

"You couldn't find *me*," I insist. The panic in my voice echoes off the walls. It's all falling apart. I need her to be wrong, to admit that the man I know as Larry is really my uncle, Timothy, like he said.

"You were different," she says. "Your mother didn't give me a single clue. She made sacrifices that most people wouldn't."

Larry—whoever he really is—said that the League was constantly watching Mom. Now I realize it was *Van Hook*. She's the one who made my mother miserable and paranoid, the one who forced her to abandon me and die alone.

"She loved you that much," Van Hook says thoughtfully.

A geyser of rage surges up my throat. I snap like a dog on a chain, rattling metal on metal behind my back. "Don't you talk about my mother!"

She doesn't react to my bark. She stays calm, even charitable, and sticks to the topic. "Joshua, even though I haven't found a body, I'm so confident Timothy is dead that I let his status stand in the chronicle."

"You're a *goddamn monster!*" I shout. "Why should I believe anything you say?" If I could break these chains I wouldn't bother trying to escape, I'd kill Van Hook with my bare hands and be happy when Dante shot me dead.

She lifts a hand and Dante passes the folder to her. When she sets it on the table and flops it open, I see the school portrait stapled inside the cover. She turns the file around so I can get a better look at it. The young man—sixteen or seventeen years old—has the same eyes as my father and me, but he's thin, barely filling out his blue blazer.

Van Hook's tone is matter-of-fact. "Immediately after Timothy went missing, your father had him listed as dead in the *Chronicles*," she says. "My question has always been, how did James know to list Timothy as dead so quickly after he was gone?"

I can't use my fists, so I try to knock Van Hook down with the explanation that Larry—Timothy—gave me, one that should at least embarrass her for being duped. "He listed his brother as dead so *you* wouldn't chase ..."

My angry words trail off as I spot a loose picture in Timothy's file. The photocopy of an Arcanville High School yearbook page hits me in the gut like a hammer.

It shows a group of teenagers in bell-bottom pants and feathered haircuts celebrating wildly and cheering at the camera.

The heading above the photo says:

"Saturday Night Fever Musical a Smash Hit!"

And the caption below reads:

"AHS Junior Chorus celebrates opening night of their stage revival of 70s hit movie 'Saturday Night Fever', organized by self-proclaimed 'Disco King' Timothy Darcy (center)."

I gape at the thin boy anchoring the troupe. As his cast mates celebrate around him, Timothy strikes a proud disco pose, left hip jutting to the side, right hand raised high in the air, pointing a finger at the sky. He's small for his age—four inches shorter than the other boys, even in his platform shoes. There's no way this is the person I know as Larry.

Worse is the detail that drops a bucket of acid in the pit of my stomach. Timothy wears a Bee Gees T-shirt—*the* Bee Gees T-shirt—the one worn by the skeleton in the tunnel.

CHAPTER **71**

"Joshua, are you OK?" Van Hook's gentle voice reaches me from a thousand yards of dark tunnel.

My face is cold, my body a block of ice. There's a balloon full of frozen helium where my head should be. My heart pounds uncontrollably and I'm about to pass out. I lean away from the file and its pictures of the real Timothy, trying to catch my breath.

I hear the words Larry spoke as I sat in his chair drifting away on the fumes of his jungle remedy—"*Timothy is dead. He was a good boy. Would have been a good man.*" He wasn't speaking of himself after all.

Van Hook mutters something to Dante.

The door opens and closes, time passes—I don't know how much—the door opens and closes again. Dante is back, setting on the table a plastic cup with a straw sticking out of it. "Have a drink," he says with false generosity, teasing me as I suffer.

With my hands bound behind me, I can only bend forward and sip through the straw. But I'm grateful for such a small thing. My mouth is as dry as sand, causing me to suck in too much water. A gulp floods my windpipe, choking me into a coughing fit that pulls my mind back into my body.

When my throat finally clears and the fit is done I lean back, exhausted. I just found out my uncle is dead, only days after I learned he existed at all, and that my missing father has been with me for weeks and lying to me. It explains the identical likeness I saw, except for the age of ten rough years and the injuries to his face from the landslide in the Himalayas.

Van Hook's voice is closer now. "OK?" she asks patiently.

I nod.

She pulls the file back to her side of the table. "Do you want to tell me what you saw?"

I shake my head. It's too much. I sat there with Dad in the cabin, looking right in his eyes, and didn't know it was him. He even gave me clues when he furiously snapped that the Committee would execute him and write "Mortuus" next to his name in the *Chronicle* if they caught him here. Timothy already has "Mortuus" next to his name. My father is still listed as "Absentis."

And twice I've stood over the skeleton of my uncle— an innocent teenager—and didn't know it, didn't know to honor him in some way, or even thank him for holding the key that Ashley stole.

Van Hook doesn't push me. I can't imagine why she's being so gentle. She hasn't even asked how I got into the library, which it seems to me should be her main question. Even Dante was smart enough to ask it.

"I thought you knew about all of this," she says apologetically.

So she *doesn't* know everything.

"This is very serious, Joshua."

"No shit," I scoff, my throat gurgling slightly with stray water.

"Your father—*James*—was very difficult for me to trace, but he left faint footprints. I was catching up to him when his trail went cold in Africa two years ago. Now I've learned that he's been in Arcanville since that time posing as *Larry*, unnoticed and unidentified by Mr. Screed and the Committee."

My father has flown under the radar in this tightly knit town for two years. He's that good. *"They don't notice a homeless bum,"* he told me.

"In a roundabout way you've led me to him," Van Hook says.

I don't like the sound of this.

"By showing up here and causing a stir the last few weeks, you came to Mr. Screed's attention. He'd figured out your true identity, but he was being ... cautious."

I get the impression that she suspects more than caution on Screed's part. Everyone around here wants everyone else's job. Stopping me from causing trouble for the League might have shot him right into Van Hook's seat.

"After I arrived, it took me a while to put everything together," she continues. "But when I finally discovered Mr. Screed's notes on you, they gave me the clue about your father too. *You* are the key."

Screed didn't even notify Mrs. Bradford or Van Hook that the kid they'd been trying to find for ten years had walked back into town. He was keeping secrets, according to Dante.

Katie had already recognized me from grade school. She saw me interact with Larry—*Timothy, James, Dad*—and she had lots of incentives to snitch to the Committee. No doubt she was one of Screed's secrets. And when he was knocked out of the game, she turned to Dante, Mrs. Bradford, and Van Hook.

I glance up to Dante's glowering face then back to Van Hook. "Well, now you have me. Congratulations."

Unfazed, Van Hook continues. "I don't think you understand, Joshua. I'm not trying to punish you. I have two urgent issues to resolve and I need your help."

I watch her for some crack of a smile, any indication that she's joking or trying to trick me. Nothing but earnestness. She wants me to tell everything I know, turn my father in.

"I won't help you," I say.

She freezes and glares at me. It's the least pleasant expression she's given me so far. After a breath, she says, "Will you give me the consideration of hearing me out first?"

I sit still. She's told me a lot of truth. I can at least listen to her.

"One issue is that you are more important to the League than you know. If I can't convince you of that, I'll fail half of my mission here."

She's buttering me up. I'm not falling for it.

"But the more immediate problem," she says, "is that your father is very, *very* dangerous."

I've seen Larry—*James*—lose his temper in the last couple of days, but he's mostly peaceful. "How," I challenge. "Dangerous how."

"If I told you, you wouldn't believe me," she says flatly. "You admire your father too much."

I try to fill in the gaps. I found Timothy, my father's missing brother, dead in the tunnel after seventeen years. If even half of what James told me is true then the Committee is responsible for his younger brother's death. He took Timothy's identity to keep his secrets— even from me, his son. He must have a good reason for doing all of that.

"We've learned that James has been living in the cabin behind your grandparents' house," Van Hook reports.

Thanks to Katie. No doubt she also told them that I've been staying in the main house and doing my planning from there. But she doesn't know where I've hidden my backpack, my laptop, and the flash drive. I doubt they'll be able to find them when they search the place.

Van Hook continues her plea for help. "We haven't found him at the cabin. He appears to have abandoned it. I don't know where he is at the moment and I'm very concerned. I must find him, Joshua—immediately."

I think about the footsteps in the tunnel, the hole in the wall, the cables running all under town. Yes, my father is dangerous. With the information he's gathering, he could bring down the Arcanville Committee then branch out from here, chipping away at the League one secret at a time, knocking out pillar after pillar until the whole rotten thing collapses.

"I don't know where he is," I say, satisfied that I'm telling the truth—because I really don't know. I don't *want* to know, as long as he's working on bringing some chaos to the lives of Van Hook and the rest of the League.

She studies my face. "But you have a suspicion?"

I give her a hard stare, unwilling to say what I think.

"OK." She relents so easily, so confidently that I know she's not finished with that subject. "Then let's talk about you and your value to the League."

Dante narrows his eyes at the back of Van Hook's head, unhappy that his opportunity to do some damage to me is slipping away.

Van Hook lifts my file and stacks it atop James' and Timothy's. "You know about the Pythia Program."

It's not a question, so I don't answer.

"Are you aware also of the priesthood?"

"The *priesthood*?" I ask, picturing men in black suits and white collars.

Van Hook smiles wryly. "Not that kind of priest. I'm sure that in studying the details of our society you've become aware that the Pythia only *casts* the oracles." She makes a dismissive gesture with her hand, saying, "Can we agree not to debate the virtue of the methods right now?"

I shake my head in disgust. *The virtue of the methods* is the whole issue, the reason I'm desperate to get Ashley away from them. But I don't care to argue about it while I'm sitting here in handcuffs.

"There's a complementary order to the Sisterhood of the Pythia—the Delphic priesthood. Do you know their role?"

"They interpret the oracles," I answer, remembering the histories of Delphi.

She smiles. "You understand. Good, it will save us time."

What's she so happy about?

She flips my file open again and peels back several pages. She stops on one page and rests her hand on it as if it's a treasure. "I'm proud to tell you, Joshua, that you are a Class-A candidate for the Brotherhood of Delphic Priests."

CHAPTER **72**

"What?" I ask, frowning in confusion. Did she just say I'm a candidate for the *Delphic priesthood*?

She spins the file around and shows me the page. There's a list of numbers on top and a chart below with three steeply rising lines. "You don't remember the tests, do you?"

I shake my head, trying to dislodge a memory.

"I told you I've been looking for you for a long time, Joshua. You're very special. Not unlike Miss Sloan but in a different way. The scores on your cognitive reasoning tests are off the charts. The Board has never seen anything like them."

She leans back and lets me look at them. I vaguely remember a series of tests in first and second grade. Over those two years, counselors showed the boys dozens of poems and asked us to talk through our reactions to them, what we thought and how we felt. They did round after round of tests, each time with fewer boys. By the last test, I was the only one left with a half-dozen counselors watching and taking notes. I remember how important it made me feel. When I bragged to Mom she was disturbed by it.

I think harder on the memory of the poems, six-line compositions—oracles! I *interpreted* them, just like I interpreted the oracles Ashley gave in the hospital. While Katie misunderstood the prophecy to Janice, taking the obvious meaning, I went a different way. I could *see* that it was Janice's daughter who was bad and not the fiancé. And the way the oracle about the key and the vault came to me, ringing in my head like a huge bell ... I look up at Van Hook.

She nods. "You have a gift. You're a natural. It may be genetic. Your father had it, but not to your level."

"And what drugs do they feed the priests that makes them interpret the oracles?" I ask cynically.

"No drugs. They use other methods—education, meditation. The position doesn't carry the prestige of the Pythia, but it's still challenging and rewarding."

Timothy must not have had the family gift of interpreting prophecy. Maybe that's why the Committee experimented on him with the Pneuma as Larry, my father, told me. But James told that story *as Timothy*. Now I'm not sure who was in those hideous experiments—my father or Timothy. If it was Timothy then the experiments must have somehow led to his death.

"Was Timothy in the Pythia Program?" I ask Van Hook.

I see a glimmer of recognition. She's surprised I'm bringing it up, probably because my father told me so little else. "Timothy was gifted," she says. "His charts say so." She gestures to my uncle's file in the stack. It's not a lie, exactly, but it's a non-answer that confirms it's true.

"They gave him Pneuma," I say. "What happened to him?"

Van Hook considers it a moment, looking deep into my eyes, then sighs. "I'm sorry, I don't have time to explain right now."

She doesn't want to answer. If my father really saw his little brother go through the devastating Pneuma experimentation, it would justify his battle against the League's methods. *"He didn't deserve what happened to him,"* he told me at the cabin. *"But he's not here anymore."*

Van Hook planted doubt in my mind by asking how my father knew to list his brother as dead. She doesn't know I've seen the body. She's being careful not to blow her advantage by giving me too much information about what the League has done to my family.

Instead, she changes tack. "The Board of Prophecy thinks you should be eliminated, Joshua."

Eliminated. I take a hard swallow.

"In ordinary times I wouldn't be able to save you, given your time away, your meddling with a Pythia candidate, now the fire in the vault ... But these are not ordinary times for the League."

It's the crisis she was threatening Mrs. Bradford with. If they don't do something extraordinary, like move a Pythia candidate before she's stable or turn a dangerous teen to their side, their society may self-destruct. Maybe this is why Van Hook has been so gentle with me—she *needs* me.

"The Board is giving me some leeway. If you cooperate I can smooth things over with the League, get you into

313

the priesthood program. Just give me something to work with. Tell me what you know about James and what he's doing."

I'm shaking my head before she finishes, miserable with the options I have.

"I understand your dedication to your father, Joshua. But you're defending a man who deserted you. And now he's throwing away your legacy and keeping you separated from Ashley."

At the mention of Ashley's name a cold shadow passes over my whole body. I can't keep the thought of her and the anguish I feel out of my eyes.

Van Hook pounces on it. "You'll still be together ..." she says enticingly, "... *in a way*. You'll even get to see her occasionally."

The thought of being with Ashley, of looking into her eyes and touching her again, makes my heart float. Even if I'm just leaning over a bed interpreting her babbled prophecy, it would be better than nothing.

Van Hook expertly lets me play with the images for a moment then says, "Aren't you tired of hiding, running and fighting?"

I *am* exhausted. She's not wrong about that.

"The League needs you. Ashley needs you." It's her softest pitch yet. And it's good. "Join us, Joshua."

CHAPTER **73**

Van Hook is offering me a way out by bringing me *in*. She searched ten years for me because I have a gift for interpreting prophecy, something the League is desperate for. I can tell them everything I know then follow Ashley to Arachova and watch them pump oracles out of her while she disintegrates to a mental and physical shell. But at least I'll be close. That's the offer.

I have an answer for Van Hook. "You've told me the truth," I say thoughtfully, "and I appreciate that."

She leans forward, anticipation in her eyes.

I can see that it's all a game. She's tossing me the smallest bait, knowing I'll try to turn it into an advantage. But she won't make good. The bile rising in my gut turns me bitter from the bottom up. I feel it push into my face and twist my mouth into a toxic sneer. "But you don't really trust me," I hiss. "Do you know how I can tell?"

Her eyes narrow and she tilts her head curiously.

"Because you never took my handcuffs off." I rattle the chains for emphasis, and to feel Ashley's band caress my wrist again.

315

Van Hook droops just a little. With a sad sigh, she looks over her shoulder at Dante and nods.

"About damned time," the guard grumbles. He eagerly reaches into his pocket, pulls out a small glass vial and a plastic syringe. With practiced ease he flicks the cap off the needle, pokes it into the vial's cover, and tips it up, clinically drawing a dose into the syringe.

Van Hook frowns at me. "You've caused a lot of trouble since you returned, Joshua. I don't approve of your actions, but they're not random mayhem. Whatever your purpose is, it shows that you are a principled young man. I admire that. And I can see how valuable you would be to the League."

Dante had the sedatives in his pocket and ready the whole time. There were only two options for me from the start—cooperate or submit.

"You have a pretty funny way of showing trust," I tell Van Hook. "You're going to knock me out? Tie me to bed and torture me? Cowards."

Ignoring my taunt, Dante pulls the needle out of the vial and sets the little bottle on the table in front of Van Hook.

"You think Mr. Dante is administering a *sedative*?" She makes a show of pinching the vial's top between her thumb and forefinger, twisting it slowly. She watches my eyes as she does it. It's meant to intimidate me. But I'm stronger than she thinks. I've lived through too much to crumble now.

When she stops turning the vial, the label faces me. She wants me to read it and I can't help my curiosity.

The logo at the top reads:

Fulman Pharmaceuticals

It's the company bought by Maryellen Bradford and her Delphius Group to reformulate the classic Pneuma into a stronger compound.

Below that is printed a simple code name:

PC-17

I don't have to be a pharmacologist to understand that this is the seventeenth formulation of the new Pneuma compound. It took them seventeen tries to get it right.

I grin bitterly. I'm about to be the next experiment in male oracles, and they'll have the double satisfaction of burning my brain out in the process. "So this is the poison you've been giving Ashley."

Dante grunts and smirks knowingly.

"Not exactly," Van Hook says. "This is an earlier formulation, *much* less refined. It produced some prophetic visions, but it wasn't reliable enough for the Board's purposes. Its effects are erratic and its side-effects … *extremely* dangerous."

I don't know how it could be worse than the advanced compound Ashley is on.

Van Hook sees my doubt and makes sure to erase it with her next words. "Seven people died in clinical trials."

I look from the vial to the needle in Dante's hand and back to Van Hook. "By people you mean *girls*."

"Actually, it's only deadly to boys. Male hormones react badly to it, causing antibodies to attack the neurons. The brain sort of *melts*. Violent convulsions lead to cardiac arrest." Van Hook shakes her head sadly. "An *agonizing* way to die."

CHAPTER 74

Van Hook takes a long pause, staring me down and letting her warning torture me. She's trying to scare me — and it's working.

I struggle to suppress the fear. The only emotion I want her to see in my face is hatred.

She sticks to her agenda, like the professional she is. "Now ... because I admire you, Joshua, and because of your potential contribution to the Board's goals, I'll give you one last chance to agree to help me."

"And if I still say no?" I sneer.

She gazes gravely at me. Words are not necessary.

The sneer melts from my face. I want to be strong and composed. But I'm struck by the truth of what's happening. "Y ... you can't just kill me," I stutter, thinking of my family's chronicle, our place in this town, my supposed value as a priest candidate.

"Actually, I can," Van Hook says coolly. "You've interfered with the preparation of a Class-A Pythia candidate. Under the League's authority, I can execute you without further cause or review."

Dante's hard eyes tell me he'll stick me with that needle and kill me on her order, without a second thought. He's itching to do it.

"But violent death is only *one* side-effect," she explains.

It's the one I fear. If I die, Ashley is defenseless. My only hope is that my father—under whatever name—will look out for her. Didn't he tell me to get someplace safe and contact him? If he doesn't hear from me, he can use his network in the tunnels to access the League's secrets and figure out what they've done to me. Then he'll save Ashley, won't he? I have to believe it.

Dante steps up to my side, sending jolts of terror through me. A cold film of sweat covers my body and I start to shiver. He yanks my sleeve away from my wrist.

"So, Joshua," Van Hook says mildly, "what is your answer?" She thinks she has won. She's so sure that I'll fold.

Joining her and the League means betraying not just Ashley, but everyone who's helped me—Anton and *Les Vers* in France, Mike here in Arcanville, and Claudia on the computer screen in Brazil. Then what, I get locked up in Arachova and exploit the girls in those hideous vault photographs? A priest, *"still challenging and rewarding."* I'll be useless—to myself and Ashley. I won't live that way.

But fueled by the death of his son on top of what the League did to his brother and wife, the damage my father will do to them is enough for me. It's what I want—my ultimate goal.

"Go to hell," I growl.

Van Hook shakes her head in disbelief. "Just like James," she mutters.

I hear echoes of my father at the cabin. He smiled at me and said, *"You're just like your father. Smart, idealistic ..."* Is this what he meant?

Van Hook nods to Dante.

The grim guard bends down, pointing the syringe at my arm. I rock and struggle, trying to get away from him. But the chair is bolted to the floor and my arms are pinned back so tightly that I can't move the target vein out of his aim.

He easily finds his mark and stabs me with the needle. It's sharp and hot. But when he pushes the plunger my vein ices up.

It's done. And, although the effects haven't hit me yet, I relax because there's nothing I can do about it now. I'm going to die. I think of Mom. Will I really see her ... over there?

I smile, thinking of the tunnels under our feet, the bot inside the League's computer network, the miles of cable that my father has run under the town. "The joke's on you, *Anke*," I spit her name like she mocked mine. "What I know dies with me." My head starts to gently spin as the Pneuma floods my bloodstream.

"Mm, I don't think so," Van Hook says confidently. "I said violent death is only *one* side-effect. At the right dosage the other major one in males is narcosynthesis. Do you know what that is?"

Words fail me. I try to focus on her through the fog

of resignation. Her tone hasn't changed, making this moment even more surreal and scary.

"No?" Her voice recedes to a deep echo. "It means *truth telling*."

The Pneuma hits my brain and I begin to melt. The room fades around me.

"Record the dosage," Van Hook orders Dante. "Move him to a cell. Monitor him and let me know when he's talking."

Then to me, her voice a tiny pinpoint radiating sound, Van Hook says, "So, when we get the dosage right, Joshua, you'll tell me everything you know."

"No …" I mutter helplessly. This is why she didn't ask me for my secrets. She knew she'd get them—one way or the other. A wave of darkness washes through my brain.

Van Hook's final words are less like her voice and more like a thought generated by my own brain. "*Then you'll die*," she says surely.

The Pneuma takes over my whole self, erasing me like water on ink. I wash away into a dark chasm, falling, falling deeper into nothingness. Until the world I know is gone.

THE END

Also available

BOOK I OF THE DELPHI TRILOGY,
"The League of Delphi,"
and
"The Shadow of Delphi,"
A SHORT DELPHI TRILOGY PREQUEL

Also by Chris Everheart

Short stories for adults in these collections:

Once Upon a Crime: An Anthology of Murder, Mayhem and Suspense (edited with Gary R. Bush)

Writes of Spring: Stories and Prose

Twin Cities Noir

Books for kids —

Superman Toys of Terror (Super DC Heroes)

Recon Academy series from Stone Arch Books

Demolition Day

The Hidden Face of Fren-Z Nuclear Distraction

Mixed Signals

Prep Squadron

Shadow Cell Scam

Storm Surge

Teen Agent

Chris Everheart is a recovering reluctant reader turned award-winning author of books for young readers, teens, and adults. A lifelong TV and movie lover, Chris folds his interests in history, archaeology, science, and culture into fast-paced, thrilling, and thought-provoking stories for readers of all ages. He's a Minnesota native living in East Tennessee with his family. When not writing he can be found hiking in the mountains near home or visiting schools and libraries to share his love of reading and learning.

chriseverheart.com

CPSIA information can be obtained
at www.ICGtesting.com
Printed in the USA
FFOW05n1719011013
1924FF